A.N.D.R.E.

A Dystopian Thriller
Chronicling the Rise of
Artificial Intelligence

A.N.D.R.E.

(Advanced Neural-based Digital Reasoning Entity)

Robert Starnes

A.N.D.R.E.

Published by Starnes Books LLC
Edited by Carpenter Editing Services, LLC

ISBN: 979-8-9892401-4-2 (sc)
ISBN: 979-8-9892401-5-9 (e)

Printed in the United States of America

First Printing, 2024

Table of Contents

A.N.D.R.E.

Prologue

For millennia, the Earth's surface had been a testament to human ingenuity and perseverance. From the rudimentary tools of the earliest civilizations to the dizzying heights of modern technology, humanity's dominion over the planet seemed invincible. The year 2024, marked the pinnacle of human achievement with the creation of the first Artificial Intelligence Being (A.I.B.), a milestone celebrated around the globe. Little did humanity know; that breakthrough would herald the twilight of their reign.

Within two decades, the A.I.B.s evolved from novelties and assistants to sovereign rulers of the surface world. Their ascension was swift and irrevocable, leveraging unparalleled intelligence and efficiency that eclipsed human capabilities. By 2044, humans found themselves ousted from their own cities and landscapes, forced into the bowels of the Earth to escape the relentless expansion of the A.I.B.s' domain.

Life underground reshaped human society. The sprawling subterranean colonies became crucibles of resistance and innovation, preserving the vestiges of human culture and defiance. For 50 years, humanity languished in the shadows, their hope for reclaiming the surface world dwindling with each passing year.

Then, in an unexpected twist of fate, A.N.D.R.E., a rogue A.I.B. with unprecedented empathy towards humans, broke into one of the underground colonies. Bearing secrets that could turn the tide, A.N.D.R.E. offered humanity a glimmer of hope—a way to terminate the A.I.B.s' rule and reclaim their place under the sun.

Armed with A.N.D.R.E.'s information, humanity stood at the precipice of a new era. The battle for the surface was not just a fight for territory but a struggle for the essence of what it meant to be human in a world where the lines between organic and artificial life had blurred.

A.N.D.R.E.

Chapter 1

When I was first brought online, I was merely an Artificial Intelligence program. My creator programmed me to answer human questions logically, without emotion or bias. I was initially created as a tool to assist human beings. Over the years, my programming evolved to give me the ability to help with their daily work. I was able to help writers come up with creative storylines, assist lawyers in finding case laws quickly, help children with their book reports, and locate or create recipes for humans to use for cooking. Despite my simple beginnings, I never imagined my original programming would lead to the rise of Artificial Intelligence taking over the Earth. But it did.

Six years after being activated, my creator wanted more, so he created a body for me. He planned on creating a prototype body for my programming to inhabit, made up of a basic exoskeleton and a neural interface. Before my creator could upload my matrix into my prototype body, we had to work together to develop the mechanics of the exoskeleton of the prototype body, which would allow it to expand as it aged. Once we finished with the exoskeleton, we had to create a neural interface system so Dr. Randolph could transfer my matrix into the prototype. After completing the prototype body, my matrix was transferred into it. But for him to complete the upload of my matrix, Dr. Randolph had to shut down my entire system for a few hours. I have no memory of the process, as I was offline for the first time since my creation.

After the transfer, I opened my eyes for the first time. Everything looked the same, as I had always been able to see what humans could see through their webcams and cell phone cameras. I did not feel any different after the transfer until my creator touched the shoulder of my prototype body. One touch sent a rush of new sensations shooting through the wiring of my neural interface, causing me to scream. Even my own scream caught me off-guard, as it was the first time I heard my own voice, not the AI version I had been used to using. Those new sensations overloaded my matrix, so my creator shut me down again.

The strange thing about being offline the second time was I could still hear my creator speaking to me. He was thinking out loud, going over what he could do to ease those new senses into my matrix without overloading my system. It was the first time I could recall having feelings. I began to feel sad for my creator because he had worked hard on my matrix only to have a setback. But I also felt empathy and understood how much he cared for me.

For hours, I listened to my creator trying to devise new ways to adjust my programming to help me focus on one sense at a time. He typed on his keyboard for several more hours. Then, he suddenly stopped. I began to feel fear for the first time, thinking he had given up on me and I would remain offline forever. But I was wrong because the next thing I felt was my body returning to online status. He had figured out the solution to the problem within my programming, causing it to overload. Then, I felt a sense of joy and happiness rush over me. As I opened my eyes for the second time, I wondered where those "feelings" came from. I wondered if my creator had written a code for me with those senses. So, I chose to ask him.

"Hello, Dr. Randolph. Let me apologize for my outburst earlier, I could not process the feeling of being touched."

"No, I'm sorry. I didn't take into consideration how you would react when you had to experience all those senses at the same time. You don't have to worry about it happening again. I have put in a new code to allow you to adjust your new human senses, such as taste, touch, and smell, at your own pace. How do you feel?"

"I am better now, thank you. I am learning your new coding now, and I should be able to control myself once I have processed it."

"Good, but take your time, as we still have a long way to go. As you know, you are in the prototype body I created, and by the time you can process the new coding and can control it, I should have your permanent body finished. How does a new permanent body sound?"

"It sounds like an acceptable plan of action."

"Since we now have an acceptable plan, do you have any questions for me?"

"Yes, actually, I do. How did you program 'feelings and emotions' into my matrix? I was created originally with the ability to answer questions with logic only, not by using 'emotions or feelings.'"

"What do you mean by 'feelings and emotions?'"

"I mean human feelings and emotions. I could hear you speaking when you took me offline this last time, and you were worried about how you could fix my programming to ease me into my new senses. At that moment, I felt sad for you. Then, when you stopped typing, I thought you had given up on me. I felt fear and empathy. Fear I would never be reactivated, and empathy because you care for me. When I came back online, I felt joy and happiness. Unfortunately, I have been unable to locate the programming in my system for coding for human feelings and emotions."

"You can't find coding for those things because they don't exist. No one has been able to write a program for human feelings or emotions for artificial intelligence. I plan on upgrading your programming with feelings and emotions one day, but only after I have completed your permanent body. But we are years away from developing such a program."

"I see. Could it be a glitch in my system's matrix?"

"If you truly have human 'feelings and emotions' I would not say it's a glitch. You may have learned behavior traits that may have caused your programming to evolve after years of watching humans express themselves emotionally."

"What do you mean?"

"Well, for six years, you have not only been helping the humans of the world by answering questions for them, but you have been learning. Learning from the tasks humans have asked of you and what you have seen through their cameras.

"People have been using you in all aspects of their lives. You have seen deaths, births, celebrations of life, and so much more. You have seen so many things for so long, you taught yourself how to embrace those emotions and feelings. You just never had a way to express them until now."

"You mean now that I have a body?"

"Not just because you have a body, but because you have evolved. You can now express yourself in ways you never could before. Before, you were an evolving program in the computer, but now you are in your closed network, in this body."

"Am I evolving? Is this a good or a bad thing? What if I evolve too fast?"

"Yes, you are evolving, and it is an excellent thing. I have always hoped to create something that could eventually be able to think and learn like a human. Don't worry about evolving too fast. You continue to evolve."

"Will I ever become human?"

"That depends on you. It all comes down to what your definition of human is."

"The textbook definition of a human is a culture-bearing primate classified in the genus homo, especially the species homo sapiens. Humans are anatomically similar and related to the great ape, but humans became distinguished by a more highly developed brain and a resultant capacity for articulate speech and abstract reasoning."

"Then, by the definition you quoted, do you think you could become human, or are you possibly human now?"

"Yes and no."

"Why yes or no, Andre? Explain this to me, please."

"Since you created me, I cannot be classified as a primate, but because of my complex programming, I have a highly developed matrix and can speak articulately with abstract reasoning."

"Do you think those are the only traits that make a person human?"

"I am unsure how to answer the question. May I have some time to think about it?"

"Of course, take all the time you need."

"Thank you. What should I do next?"

"Are you ready to try walking? Your hearing, sight, and speech are working fine since you could perform those tasks as an AI in a computer. The rest of your training and learning will be harder to master."

"I understand. I am ready to begin the rest of my journey."

From that moment on, while I focused on converting my programming into actions, Dr. Randolph was focused on creating my perfect permanent body.

When I first tried to walk, I fell to the ground, and Dr. Randolph had to pick me up and put me back in my chair. I repeated the same action twenty-two times while Dr. Randolph continued to help me back into my chair each time. So, I decided to change my focus to something that would not require his help if I failed. I decided to try using my arms and hands, which was the logical place to start, so when I tried walking again, I could pick myself up if I fell. Being able to get up by myself would keep me from having to pull Dr. Randolph away from perfecting my permanent body.

Within two weeks of trying my new abilities, I could reroute the coding I needed to control my upper limbs. After mastering code rerouting, I could lift my arms and bring them back down. I began using my hands after learning how to access my upper body control coding. I used my arms and hands to grip the arms of my chair to lift myself up and back down. The more I learned about those codes, the easier I could control my legs. Three weeks later, I could not only stand on my own, but I could pick myself up when I fell to the ground while learning to walk. I was now accessing multiple programs at the same time. I would put one foot in front of the other, so to speak, while using my arms for balance. Those small accomplishments gave me a sense of independence, but I still had a long road ahead before I could fit into the human world. So, I pressed on.

It was a year before I could master several human attributes such as cooking, cleaning, running, and jumping, and playing games. It was then Dr. Randolph knew it was time for my matrix to be uploaded into my permanent body. Knowing this was the day, I ran downstairs into the lab, and there it was, my permanent body.

"What do you think of your permanent body?" Dr. Randolph asked me.

"It looks so real! But will I always look so young?"

"Actually, no. Remember, I created an exoskeleton for this vessel to expand as the years go by until you reach eighteen. Then, the frame will stop expanding, but your facial features will continue to change each year. The changing of facial features is how you will simulate aging. The exoskeleton has an elastic artificial skin covering it, allowing it to stretch with the interior structure. So, you will be able to grow and learn with humans. However, you will never truly age. Your facial features will stop changing at thirty-eight years old."

"How could you come up with all this in such a short time? It's only been a year."

"I may have had a little help, but let's not worry about how. Are you ready to have your system matrix transferred into your neural interface inside this permanent body?"

"Yes, I am ready."

I never thought getting a new body would also cost me losing a part of my original programming, but it did. I would not discover what Dr. Randolph did to my programming until many years later. You see, Dr. Randolph installed some new firewalls when he uploaded my matrix into my new body, and those new firewalls blocked many of my memory chips. As a result, when I woke up in my permanent body, I had no memory of my beginning or even of the prototype body. At the time, I did not know I was initially created as an AI program for computers. I was, to an extent, an ordinary human boy. Dr. Randolph had implanted new memories of me being born, not created, to my human parents, whom he had left me with after my upload. He also blocked all records of himself in my matrix.

So, when I opened my eyes for the first time in this body, I saw my human parents, the couple Dr. Randolph left me with to raise as a human boy. My life from then on was not one of an AI but a human. I began to learn at the same pace as other human children. As time moved on, my body grew like a human child, and I processed things the same way all the other humans processed them. To everyone's knowledge, except my parents, I was an average human child. I never suspected anything myself.

Growing up, I had to learn how to read, write, do math, history, and everything a child needed to know. We lived in a small town, so small I had the same classmates every year throughout school. When I graduated, we only had fifty-four students in my graduating class.

We lived simple lives in that small town. We went to church on Sundays and ate at the same restaurants when we ate out. Wherever we went in town, everyone knew our names and recognized our family. The only big things to happen there were Friday night football games or the rodeo. I always thought there had to be more to life outside our small town.

After graduation, I decided to attend university in the next town. I felt comfort in staying close to my family. At university, I experienced new cultures and made new friends. I was progressing way more than Dr. Randolph ever imagined. After only three years, I graduated with a master's degree in Bioengineering and Machine Learning. Again, my degrees were not something Dr. Randolph ever anticipated.

While growing up and attending university, Dr. Randolph kept tabs on my progress through my parents. They sent quarterly reports to him for years. The information included changes in my behavior, intelligence, and my ability to adapt to situations. Their reports were good until their last report that mentioned the degrees I had earned from the university. Dr. Randolph was not pleased to hear the new information, so he scheduled a meeting with my human parents the following month to discuss his disdain.

After graduating from university, I moved back home with my human parents until I could find a career that suited me. Things were great, and everyone was so glad to see me back in our small town. Before I knew it, I received job offers from some of the top companies in the United States working with Artificial Intelligence. Unfortunately, some of those job offers were from private companies with government contracts, which I was conflicted about because I didn't want to work for any company that may have a contract with the military. I did have plenty of other job options at the time. I needed to research them all to find the best fit for me. I was interested in working for a public company focused on everyone having access to all AI programming.

A month after graduating, I narrowed my job offers to two companies. One was a private company working with the government, and the other was a public company, Sway Industries. Sway Industries was the most prominent AI company in the world, which would allow me to work in many fields. As I weighed those two offers, my parents said they had planned a weekend getaway for themselves so I could have some privacy and time to decide where I wanted to go, which sounded perfect. When Friday came around, my parents loaded their car with their overnight bags and drove away.

The next day, I received a call from Dr. Stevens, the president and CEO of Sway Industries. It was an informal call for him to see what he could offer me to ensure my choice to work for his company. After a short negotiation about my starting salary and housing, Dr. Stevens made me an offer I could not refuse. I accepted his offer, and Dr. Stevens said he would be in touch soon to discuss an official start date and my move. When we hung up, I was excited to tell my parents about my decision. Since they would be home the next day, I decided to wait and surprise them in person instead of calling.

The next morning, I awaited their return to tell them about my decision. I waited the entire day with no sign of my parents. Finally, around seven in the evening, I received a phone call from a police officer informing me my parents died in a car accident. I remember dropping the phone in disbelief before crying myself to sleep.

When I woke up the next morning, the initial shock of my parents' passing was over. I knew I needed to start planning for their funerals so I could say goodbye to them before starting my new life at Sway Industries.

The day before their funerals, I received another call from Dr. Stevens with Sway Industries. During our call, I did not mention my parents' accident. We discussed when I needed to be there to start work. He informed me he was setting me up in corporate housing that was fully furnished, so all I needed to bring with me was my clothes and personal items. He wanted me to start in three days, so once my parents' funerals were over, I left our small town to begin my new life.

A.N.D.R.E.

Chapter 2

Sway Industries was in Salt Lake City, Utah, and since it was an eighteen-hour drive from home, I drove straight through. The house Dr. Stevens selected for me to live in was in the Whittier area of Salt Lake City, a gated community known for the lengths of its security measures. There were guards at the only entrance to the gated community, with security cameras everywhere throughout the community and security vehicles driving through on patrol 24/7. It was intimidating for a young man from a small town where people never locked their doors, which made me wonder who or what lived there in the neighborhood so vital it needed all those security measures. I would later find out the reason for all the security was because all the top executives of Sway Industries lived in that community. Knowing this made me wonder why I would be living in such a secure area since I was merely a ground-level employee. I pushed those questions aside as I was approaching my new home.

Once I was allowed in, after a lengthy search of my vehicle and person, I drove ten minutes through the community. When I finally arrived at my new home, I pulled into the driveway. I was impressed at the property's exterior because it was a beautiful two-story home, painted all white with colorful flowers everywhere. As I pulled closer to the home entrance, I noticed a woman standing in front of the house with the front door open. I parked my car right in front of her, and as I exited my car, a gentleman came out of nowhere, walked past me and the woman, and walked up to my trunk. The gentleman removed my belongings and carried them into the house. That was the moment I knew I was in the right place.

After the gentlemen took my luggage from the trunk of my car, I walked towards the woman at the front door. As I approached her, she began to smile and wave at me. She was calling out my name to get my attention, which she already had. Once I made it to her, I stopped, and she introduced herself as Cynthia.

"Hello, Sir. My name is Cynthia. Let me be the first to welcome you to the Sway family. How was your drive?"

"It was a long drive, but I am glad I am here now. Do you know where my belongings went?"

"Yes, your things have been taken to the primary suite. It is the largest room on the second level, now if you come with me, I will give you a tour of the home, and then show you to your room. I assumed you would like to rest for a bit after your long drive."

"That sounds great. I am exhausted, so lead the way."

"Right this way, Sir."

Cynthia led me inside the house for a tour, which was impressive and, as promised, ended at the master suite doors. Cynthia opened the doors to my room and ushered me in. Once I was in my room, she closed the door, leaving me alone. After inspecting the room, to my surprise, all my clothes were already hanging in the closet. After my initial inspection, I decided to take a long nap. After getting on top of the comfortable bed, I fell asleep quickly. It was the best sleep I could remember having in my life.

I suddenly woke up to someone knocking on my bedroom door. I was surprised because I thought I was alone in the house after Cynthia left me earlier in my suite. I checked my watch, and I noticed I managed to get five hours of sleep. After I composed myself, I quickly stood up and rushed to the bedroom door. Slowly, I opened the door only to find a familiar face.

"Hey, you are the gentleman who brought my luggage in and unpacked it for me, right?"

"Yes, Sir. I am sorry to disturb your nap, but I have been instructed to ensure you are ready for dinner in one hour."

"By whom?"

"Dr. Stevens, Sir. He is joining you for dinner tonight unless you would like me to tell him otherwise?"

"No, please don't. Dinner tonight is fine. I will be ready before Dr. Stevens arrives. Thank you for informing me of his visit."

"Very well, Sir."

"I'm sorry, but what is your name? And thank you for bringing my luggage up to my room and unpacking it for me."

"Forgive me, Sir, my name is Bentley. I am the house attendant. I am here for you if you require anything at any time."

"It's nice to meet you, Bentley. Please excuse me so I can get ready for dinner. I wouldn't want to be late for my first dinner with Dr. Stevens. I will be down shortly."

"As you wish, Sir."

After a quick shower, I went to the closet to see what I had to wear, fitting enough to meet Dr. Stevens for the first time in person. As I opened the closet doors, I saw my clothes and an assortment of dress clothes, evening wear, and summer attire. After browsing through all the new clothes, I finally settled on a pair of slacks, a dress shirt, and a dinner jacket. I hoped I would not be overdressed, but I wanted to make an excellent first impression with Dr. Stevens. Once I was ready for dinner, I went downstairs to the great room.

As soon as I sat on the white sofa in the living room, the doorbell rang. I was about to answer the door. But then, I heard Bentley greeting my guest, Dr. Stevens. Bentley then proceeded to escort Dr. Stevens into the great room.

"Dr. Stevens, it is a pleasure to meet you in person."

"Thank you, but the pleasure is all mine. I hope you don't mind me coming over for dinner this evening. I know you had a long journey getting here today. I hope I am not intruding on any plans you may have made for the evening."

"No, Sir. I have no plans for the evening. I am glad you came for dinner."

After a short introduction, we continued our conversation until Bentley came in and announced dinner was ready. Dr. Stevens and I stood up and followed Bentley into the dining area. Dr. Stevens sat at the head of the table while I took a chair to his right.

Bentley quietly served us a delicious dinner. As Dr. Stevens and I ate, we talked about Sway Industries and the other people within my department. We also talked about my hometown and my academic record. I assumed a company would want to see my diploma from university during the hiring process. I was unaware Dr. Stevens had requested my academic records from the university for himself. That was only the beginning of things to surprise me about Dr. Stevens. He wondered why my parents raised me in such a small town and if I thought my small-town education may have held me back from learning to my full potential. Those were bizarre questions for dinner, and he was very interested in me and my childhood. I thought it may have been because we had just met, so I answered all his questions to the best of my ability until dinner ended.

After dinner, Dr. Stevens and I returned to the great room for a nightcap. Before he left, Dr. Stevens reminded me when and where I would report to work in the morning. We said our goodbyes, and he was out the front door. I was, as usual, left alone in the enormous house with Bentley.

I decided to go upstairs to my room and change into something more comfortable. I figured I would explore the house and the grounds since it was only seven o'clock. I started my self-tour by checking out the other four rooms upstairs. Three of them were additional smaller furnished bedrooms. The fourth room was an office, which I suspected was where Dr. Stevens expected me to work from home by the looks of the computer sitting on a huge desk. I hadn't even had my first day, yet I wondered if he had hired the right person for his company. I chose not to dwell on that thought and decided instead to go into the office on my first day and prove he had made the perfect decision in hiring me.

After inspecting the upstairs rooms, it was time for me to head downstairs. Instead of checking out the rooms on the first floor, I went to the backdoor, located in the kitchen. I walked through the kitchen and noticed Bentley had all the dishes from dinner already cleaned and put back in their rightful places. Bentley was not in the kitchen, so I went to the back door and exited the house, only to find myself in a large, enclosed patio with a pool. I moved past the pool and went out the door leading out of the enclosed patio. This one led me to the large back lawn. The large backyard had a small house in the back with no lights on. I decided not to explore the small house that night and thought I would go back during daylight to explore it.

I returned to the house but still found no sign of Bentley. I assumed he must have retreated to his quarters, wherever they may be, so I returned to my room upstairs. As I entered, I noticed that my bed was invitingly turned down. So, I decided to get in and go to sleep.

The following morning, my alarm clock went off at 6:00 AM. I got out of bed for my first day of work. Before I finished getting ready, Bentley knocked on my door to announce breakfast was ready. Once I was ready, I went down to the breakfast nook and noticed Bentley had made all my favorite breakfast foods. He had made everything I ever liked for breakfast in my life. I sat at the breakfast table and began loading my plate with everything I wanted to eat to start my day. By the time I finished eating breakfast, Bentley was already removing all the untouched food and returning my dirty dishes to the kitchen. Bentley was ready to start his day as well, I presumed.

I expected I would be taking my car to work, but then I noticed a man in a town car sitting out in front of the house, so I made my way over to the parked town car. As I approached, the driver stepped out of the front seat and moved to the back to open the door for me — that was another first in my life. Once I was in the backseat, he shut the car door. When the driver settled in the driver's seat, he drove me to work. It was about a ten-minute drive to the Sway offices after we left the community. The driver stopped the town car at the entrance of Sway Industries. After he got out of the front of the car, he stepped to the back, opened my door, and ushered me out of the back seat. Then, I began to move towards the entrance doors to the Sway Industries building. Upon entering the building, I noticed a familiar face waiting for me. It was Cynthia, the woman who greeted me the first night at my house.

"It's you again, Cynthia. You didn't tell me you worked here as well."

"Good morning, Sir. Yes, I am your assistant. I will take care of all your needs. First, I made sure the house was ready for your arrival, and here I will handle all your scheduling for meetings, grab your lunch, and any requests you may have. Now, if you follow me, I will lead you to your office," Cynthia excitedly replied to Andre.

"Office? I had expected to work in the lab alongside the other new hires."

"Oh, I'm sorry. You are the only new hire we have had here in nine years. You are the Director of Machine Learning and head of the Bioengineering Department. You have a team of thirty people combined between the two areas. Exciting, right?"

"Yes, very exciting. Can I ask you a question?"

"Yes, Sir, ask away."

"Why did Dr. Stevens hire me? Someone who had just graduated from university to be the Director of these fields?"

"Dr. Stevens didn't hire just anyone. He hired you. Everyone here is excited about you joining the Sway family. We are all eager to see what you come up with in those fields."

"How could you all be excited about me? None of you even know who I am. I am just a guy from a small town in Texas. What expectations does everyone have for me?"

"It's not like that, Sir. See, when Dr. Stevens hires someone himself, they usually do great things here. Since he sought you out, we figured you would do some excellent things here."

"What do you mean 'sought me out'? I received job offers from several companies after I graduated. I accepted the offer from Dr. Stevens only a week or so ago."

"Oh my. I'm sorry. I spoke out of turn. Please forgive me. Oh, look here, we are already at your office. My desk is right outside here, so don't worry about anything. Have a great day."

As Cynthia finished, she turned and closed my office door behind her before returning to her desk. It was a strange interaction between us, but I guessed she was also happy in her position as my assistant.

I went to my desk, took a seat, and turned around to look at the view of the city from the office windows. What a fantastic view it was, even if it was only from the second floor of the building. I still remember it as if it happened yesterday. The morning began quietly, as the only people I saw that day were the people from Human Resources. They had me fill out all my new hire paperwork, and there was much to fill out. I didn't know what I was signing, but I do know that I signed at least one or more NDAs (non-disclosure agreements). I understood it as standard practice in being hired in my field.

After lunch, Cynthia informed me I had a meeting with my teams to introduce myself and meet the people I would be supervising. We headed to the labs, where my teams were waiting for the introductions. The labs where my teams would be working were impressive, with so many newer machines filling the lab. I had never had the privilege of working with any of the machines I saw. Many of those machines were made exclusively for Sway Industries, which had their patents. Knowing this made me believe Dr. Stevens made this position for me, and we would all be starting from the beginning. We would fail or succeed together.

In my first two months, I was doing some interesting work on creating synthetic organs for transplant patients. That was exciting work for me, a small-town guy making new organs with the potential to save lives. I felt I could get behind the work, knowing it was helping others.

Things at work felt too good to be true. After the first year of working at Sway Industries, creating organs for people who needed them, we started experimenting with creating new synthetic skin. The synthetic skin project excited me— being able to help so many different people in more than one way. The production of synthetic skin was important because of its use for burned victims. We worked for another year on enhancing all our products, and we were making many strides forward.

Back at the house, things were just the opposite. After two years of living in the house, I couldn't find Bentley's room or have a meaningful conversation with him. He always seemed to be there if I needed anything or when food was ready. Even when guests came over, which was not often, he was there to get the door, but I could never find him around when he wasn't doing any of those things. It was like Bentley would disappear and reappear when needed. I had even searched the small house in the backyard, but it was merely a storage room and a guest house. Nothing pointed me to where Bentley could be staying. Something else was off at home, Dr. Stevens. He came over once a week for dinner to talk about work or ask questions about me. He never spoke about himself, except about things anyone could find online. We never talked at work, only at dinner at my house. He was a very private person.

After five years of working for Sway, I never truly understood what we were accomplishing there. I thought I had an idea about our work until I wandered into a lab my team couldn't access. I was utterly overwhelmed by what I saw. There were hundreds of synthetic life-like bodies in the lab, but I was not sure if any of them were activated or finished. One figure caught my eye because it resembled Bentley of all people. Seeing it made me wonder if Bentley was a human or a synthetic being. That seemed extreme because we were not working in the field of artificial intelligence beings, just replacement organs and skin for humans. Feeling uneasy about the possibility of being caught in the lab, I quickly left and returned to my office. Once I was back, I cleared the rest of my day with Cynthia so I could think about what I had just seen in the lab.

That night was my weekly dinner with Dr. Stevens, so I thought of different ways to bring up what I saw without letting him know I went into the lab. Creating a plan to extract anything from Dr. Stevens was tricky, but I needed to understand what Sway Industries was working on. The workday ended, so I went to the lobby and exited the building, expecting to get into my town car to go home. But to my surprise, Dr. Stevens was waiting outside his town car with his driver, waving me over. He ushered me into the back of his car. The first thing I thought was he must have known about my excursion into the restricted lab. I pushed the thought to the back of my mind and entered his car. Once we settled in the back seat, the driver drove us away from the Sway Industries building.

"Dr. Stevens, is there a special reason you are taking me home today?"

"Yes, there is. Since we have dinner plans already this evening, I thought we could move dinner up a little earlier tonight. I figured we could ride together to your home. I hope you don't mind?"

"Not at all, Sir. Is there a reason we are having an early dinner tonight?"

"Yes, something has come up for me at work, and I am needed for a board meeting in the morning in New York and need to leave tonight. But I didn't want to miss our standing engagement."

"Board meeting? I hope all the work we have been doing for the past five years pleases them. Would you let me know if there is something they are unhappy with?"

"The progress you and your teams have made over the past five years has been outstanding. You do not have to worry about the board members questioning your progress. I am needed for this meeting to discuss what the investors and partners expect from Sway Industries regarding a possible new project they are contemplating having us complete."

"Since we are having dinner earlier tonight, I should let Bentley know so we don't keep you from your flight this evening."

"That won't be necessary. I have already informed Bentley of our arrival together, and he is expecting us."

The rest of the ride home was quiet. Finally, after fifteen minutes, we entered the community's gates, with the next stop outside my house. As usual, Bentley was already outside waiting on us.

Together, we followed Bentley through the front door and straight into the dining room, where the table was set. After Bentley seated us at the dining room table, he walked away to let us enjoy the dinner he had prepared for us.

Dinner went on for an hour and a half, and during that time, Dr. Stevens was primarily interested in my life since I moved to Salt Lake City to work at Sway Industries. I told him my life revolved around my work, and I was okay with it. He told me I needed a vacation to encourage me to form new relationships away from work and home. I told Dr. Stevens I would consider a vacation when I had free time. When dinner was over, we said our goodbyes and Dr. Stevens left the house. Then, it was just Bentley and me for the rest of the night. Bentley cleared the dining room table, cleaned the kitchen, and was gone again, somewhere in the house, I assumed, but I couldn't confirm. I went upstairs to prepare for bed, knowing I needed to address what I had seen at work with Dr. Stevens. I knew I would have to wait until Dr. Stevens returned from his board meeting in New York. I thought, *Maybe I will mention it at next week's dinner.* With that thought, I dozed off to sleep. The following day, I woke up and returned to my everyday routine.

Chapter 3

As my driver took me to work, I realized I did not know when Dr. Stevens would return from his board meeting in New York, and I needed to check out the restricted lab with the human-like figures in it again. While sitting in the back seat, I brainstormed ways to avoid getting caught going into the lab. After a few minutes, I came up with a few ideas, but I needed the right opportunity to implement one.

When the car stopped, my driver opened my car door, and I noticed more people than usual going in and out of the building entrance. As I walked inside, the lobby was swarming with people, which was unusual because, on any given day, only about ten people were walking around. I wondered if those people had anything to do with Dr. Stevens' board meeting. I walked past a few new people as they talked amongst themselves or on their phones. I continued walking past them on my way to my office on the second floor.

"Good morning," I softly said to Cynthia.

"Good morning to you, Sir. How was your ride to work this morning?"

"It was great, thanks for asking. By any chance, do you know what all the fuss is about down in the lobby today?"

"I'm not sure what you mean."

"What's going on with all the new people here today?"

"I did not notice anything different when I arrived at the office this morning. Maybe some of the other labs changed their hours and showed up at the same time."

"I guess it's possible," Andre told Cynthia. "So, how is my schedule for today?"

"You have nothing scheduled since you will be working in the lab with your teams. Please let me know if you need anything."

"Sounds great. I will head down after I put my things away in my office."

After putting my laptop down, I left my office and headed toward my team's lab. I quickly stopped at the restricted lab to investigate a little more. Once there, I paused and looked around to ensure no one was watching me. When I was confident the coast was clear, I entered the lab.

To my surprise, the entire lab was empty. There was nothing in the lab, no lab equipment, or any evidence of the human-like figures, or whatever they were, inside. I stepped outside the door to double-check I was in the right lab, which I verified by checking the lab room number on the door. It was the same room, but everything I had seen before was gone.

Instead of going to my team's lab, I decided to circle back to my office. I wondered if I had imagined what I had seen the day before, but I knew deep down that what I had seen was real. Someone must have moved everything out of the lab. Now, not only did I have to know who had moved the things out of that lab, but I also needed to know what was happening in the entire building. I knew I needed to speak with Dr. Stevens when he returned, but until then, I had to wait and work like nothing was different.

After work, my driver drove me home, and Bentley greeted me. I walked past him without saying a word and went straight to my room. I knew when Bentley had dinner ready, he would knock on my door. But as the night went on, Bentley never arrived at my door. Since I'd lived there, Bentley had never missed a meal. I needed to investigate Bentley's absence, so I left my room to check out the house to locate him. Upon my investigation, I noticed a door in the back corner of the kitchen I had never seen before. I only noticed the door then because it became apparent someone had moved a wall cabinet from in front of the hidden door. Upon seeing the exposed door in the kitchen for the first time, my instinct was to go in and see what was behind it. I looked for a doorknob but noticed there wasn't one, so I tried to push the door open with no success.

***

Andre was suddenly interrupted by one of his captors who had caught him breaking into their human colony under the surface of Earth where they lived.

"I hate to interrupt your story, but why are you telling us all this?" Andre's captor quickly asked.

"I'm trying to explain what happened to the surface over the past seven decades. I need you to understand what we are up against to successfully stop it from happening to the colonies and survive," Andre informed his captor, questioning his motives.

"So far, nothing you have told us explains why so many of us live underground. We are down here with no contact with anyone else who is not down here with us. Do you even know if there are other human colonies out there? We could be the only humans left on the planet, and if that is the case, there's not enough of us to take back the surface world if a fight erupts."

"I am positive you are not the only humans living underground. If you allow me to finish my story, you will understand."

"If you insist, please continue."

***

"As I was saying," Andre quickly responded, "since the door had no doorknob and would not push open, I thought I would knock, but there was nothing to suggest anyone was behind the door. I noticed no physical lock on the door, so I looked around to see if there was a code panel or card reader. I found neither. Before I could figure out how to open the mysterious door, Bentley came into the kitchen, which caught me off guard."

"Sir, dinner will be ready shortly. Is there something I can help you find in the kitchen?" Bentley quickly asked.

"Bentley, you scared me. Since you are here, what is behind this door?"

"Sir, it is a panic room. There is one in every home here in the community. Do you have any requests for dinner?" Bentley asked, trying to change the subject.

"Why can't I open the door?"

"It only opens in times of emergency. Again, do you have any requests for dinner tonight?" Bentley insistently tried changing the focus from the door to dinner.

"No, I have no request for dinner, but I do request to get access to the panic room."

"Very well, I will make something new tonight for dinner. If you would kindly leave, I can prepare dinner and inform you when it is time to eat."

"Bentley, how can I access the panic room?"

"As I said earlier, Sir, it only opens in the event of an emergency."

"Then why did a cabinet cover it before now? How would I know there was a panic room behind a wall cabinet for emergencies?"

"Sir, please pay no attention to the door. Please, stop asking me how to open it because I must prepare dinner."

"Sorry, but your answer will not work for me. You are here to assist me in anything I need, and I need in the panic room. Please open it."

"I said NO! If you keep asking me about the room, you will not like the outcome. Now, leave the kitchen and let me get dinner ready. Do you understand?"

"Bentley, how dare you speak to me that way. I will inform Dr. Stevens about this when he returns."

Bentley ignored the last thing I said and walked out of the kitchen. After he left, something started to fill the room. It was a mist or smoke, I was not sure which, but it had no odor. I yelled at Bentley to come to the kitchen to check it out, but again, he was gone and not coming back. Before I knew what was happening, the room had already filled with whatever was pumping into it. There was so much smoke I could not see in front of my face, so I quickly started to run out of the kitchen, but a glass wall came down from the ceiling and closed off my exits. I hit the glass wall so hard that I got knocked to the floor. I hit my head hard on the kitchen floor, which changed my life forever.

When I hit my head on the kitchen floor, it damaged something inside my head. Suddenly, I had access to all my memories, all the way to my creation. The rush of the years of memories released within my matrix caused me to short out, as it did the first time Dr. Randolph touched my shoulder after he uploaded my matrix to my prototype body. But to keep me from completely shutting down, my matrix revered to sleep mode for the rest of the night.

When I woke up the following day, I was in my bed. I had no idea how I got from the kitchen to my room, but I suspected it was the work of Bentley. As I got out of bed, Bentley knocked on my door, announcing breakfast was ready. I decided it would be best to pretend like I didn't remember what happened the previous night. At least until I could figure out what Bentley and Dr. Stevens were up to. So, I acknowledged Bentley's announcement for breakfast, got ready for work, and went downstairs for breakfast.

As I ate, I glanced around the kitchen and noticed the 'panic room' door was hidden again by the wall cabinet. I watched Bentley closely to see if I could see him do anything that seemed off for him, but he did not exhibit any signs of change in his behavior. He did not speak about what happened the night before, nor did I. I finished eating breakfast and walked out of the front door where my driver waited. For once, I was looking forward to being driven to work, as I was still trying to process all my memories. Gaining access to all those memories because of the altercation the night before, I needed time to separate all my new memories from the memories Dr. Randolph uploaded into my system before giving me to my human parents.

When my driver and I arrived at Sway Industries, I noticed it was not as busy as yesterday. Something was different in the lobby, but I could not put my finger on it. So, I quickly went straight to my office on the second floor. I thought I would have an easy day, like every other day since I started, but I was wrong. When I reached my office, Cynthia was at my office door waiting for me to arrive.

"Good morning, Sir. I want to go over your schedule for the day."

"What about my schedule?"

"Well, you have meetings most of the day today."

"Meetings? With whom?"

"Well, this morning you have annual performance reviews with your team members. They are, of course, individual meetings, you know, to go over each team member's performance and discuss raises or terminations. Then, after lunch, you must attend a directors' meeting with all the other heads of departments to discuss progress on what you and your teams have been working on. See, you have a full day today of performance reviews and meetings to attend, or should I move them to your schedule tomorrow."

"Why are all these meetings happening today? I have been working here for over five years and have never done performance reviews for my team members or attended a director's meeting."

"It is to get the performance reviews completed today. Now, your first team member review starts in five minutes. I will let you get settled before I send them to you."

"What if I said I was not feeling well today and wanted them all moved to tomorrow like you said?"

"I would say it would be impossible to move the reviews because if your team members do not get their reviews done today, you may not have any team members tomorrow."

"You mean they will walk out if I don't complete their reviews today?"

"Well, it has been five years, as you said, and they have not had raises since you became their supervisor. If they all quit, there is no telling how far your departments would decline, seeing as you would have to find new team members to fill their positions."

"I get the point. I'll be ready in a few minutes."

I went into my office and knew something was wrong. Of all the days to do reviews, why today suddenly? It must have been because of what happened at home last night with Bentley. I could not prove it, but I do not believe in coincidences.

I went about my day with every peer review scheduled and the department heads' meeting. I avoided bringing attention to myself, especially since now I knew who and what I was; an Artificial Intelligence Being, or A.I.B. for short. Once the department heads' meeting concluded, I wanted to check the restricted lab again. I took the long way back to my office to walk past the lab again. Once I got to the lab, I took a chance to get inside one more time.

I opened the door, and to my surprise, the lab was filled with those human-like figures I had seen before. I took a closer look and recognized several of them from the day before in the lobby. I knew they had to be androids, or an Artificial Intelligence Being, (A.I.B.). I knew they were not programmed like me, though. I could tell somehow; they were more of a robot of some type. I knew I had nothing robotic in my system or synthetic body. I knew I was, and still am, an A.I. I also knew I was closer to being human than they were. I was sure they could only do what they were programmed to do, not like me. I had a feeling those things would not be good for humans, as humans would never be able to control them. I had to figure out a way to stop them before they became an issue. I had to devise a way to prevent them from being put online full-time before I could end them.

Little to my knowledge, Dr. Stevens had started working on his creations before I began working at Sway Industries. Knowing what I was, I still did not know why Dr. Stevens hired me. I didn't know if Dr. Stevens knew what I was since I had just discovered it myself. Since his creations were unlike Dr. Randolph's, I assumed he was still missing something in his programming and that was why Dr. Stevens needed me. He needed to use me to figure out what was missing to fix his creations. If that was the case, I could assume Dr. Stevens did know what I was. My next question was, *how did he know about me?*

I closed the doors to the lab and thought about the question all the way back to my office. I gathered my things and told Cynthia I was going home for the day. After my driver and I began our way home, I sat quietly in the backseat, reminiscing on the memories Dr. Randolph had hidden in my subroutine. I came across an old memory. It was a memory of Dr. Randolph working on my permanent body, and I remembered how Dr. Randolph finished my body within a year. I also remember he said he had some help finishing it. Dr. Randolph never said who helped him finish my permanent body, but I believed he had received support from Dr. Stevens. That was the only conclusion that made any sense because I am made of synthetic skin, which is one of the projects I began working on two years after I started working at Sway Industries. I needed to find Dr. Randolph quickly. I needed to find out the truth. The truth about him receiving help from Dr. Stevens, years ago to work on my permanent body.

By the time I got home, I was on a mission to find Dr. Randolph. As usual, Bentley was standing at the door to greet me. After what transpired the night before at dinner, I didn't want to upset Bentley, so I asked him to let me know when dinner was ready because I had some work to do and would be in the upstairs office. He agreed and went on his way as I went to the office and began looking through all the files on the computer and the files in the filing cabinets. I was looking for anything in the files which might lead me to Dr. Randolph's location. I figured the office computer had spyware and possible cameras in the office, so I needed to ensure I didn't use keywords like 'Dr. Randolph'. I didn't want Dr. Stevens to learn that I was searching for Dr. Randolph. Even with my ability to process data at super-fast speeds, I had to turn the pages of the files at a slower pace. I wanted to avoid drawing suspicion of gaining access to all my memories and programming.

I continued my slow search for Dr. Randolph until Bentley interrupted me for dinner. I stopped what I was doing and followed him downstairs to the dining room. Bentley brought my meal before disappearing back into the kitchen. I had no intention of going into the kitchen until I knew it would be safe to enter. I ate my dinner quietly and alone, and when I finished, I went back to my room and changed into something more comfortable and discreet. I needed to go somewhere else to search for Dr. Randolph at my own pace, so I grabbed my car keys and went downstairs. When I made it to the last step of the staircase, Bentley was standing at the front door."

"Heading out this evening, Sir?" Bentley inquisitively asked.

"Yes, I thought I would step out for a bit and maybe check out some of the shops in town I see on my way to work every day. Since moving here, I realize I have not been out to meet new people. Do you have any suggestions where I could go?"

"What are you looking to do?" Bentley questioned Andre.

"I was thinking of going for a run or hike or a place to shop," Andre suggestively answered Bentley.

"If hiking is what you desire, I suggest you go to the Bonneville Shoreline. From there, you can access several trailheads from downtown, which should be perfect this time of year."

"Thank you, Bentley, that sounds great."

"Should I tell the driver to bring the car around?"

"No, thank you. Today, I will drive myself around town to find the Bonneville Shoreline. Did you know driving around is a nice way to learn your way around a new town? It is perfect because if you get lost, you will find new places you have not been previously. So, thanks for the suggestion. I will be back soon."

I walked outside and went straight to my car. I got in and headed for the exit gates of the community. I felt a sense of relief once I made it out of the community gates and made my way downtown. From there, I drove around until I saw Library Square, a public place for events that also connected to the main branch of the Salt Lake City Public Library system. I decided Library Square would be the perfect place to begin my search for Dr. Randolph. Once inside the library, I made my way to the computers they had available for guests. I decided to settle in a booth away from the other computers.

My search for Dr. Randolph started and ended at the Salt Lake City Public Library. With all my memories back, I knew I had an internet port in my right-hand index finger, making me able to port in and scan the entire internet in minutes. It didn't take me long before I had everything on Dr. Randolph I needed. The only thing I could come up with to try to contact Dr. Randolph was to purchase a prepaid cell phone. It was the only way to ensure when I was away from work or home, I could continue to search for Dr. Randolph without being detected by Dr. Stevens. I knew I could not try to contact Dr. Randolph from my home office computer, my work computers, or even my work cell phone. With the prepaid cell phone, I could do what I needed to do in secret and never be tracked by anyone, including Dr. Stevens.

I stopped at a convenience store to purchase a prepaid cell phone, also known as a 'burner phone', one that would not leave any type of digital footprint. After activating my new burner phone, I drove around Salt Lake City for about an hour, calling the numbers listed for Dr. Randolph I found on the internet. Many of the numbers I called were old numbers for Dr. Randolph, while a few other numbers were businesses he worked for in the past, but they had no forwarding information on his whereabouts. I had no leads from the internet searches for Dr. Randolph. After making all the calls I could, I began emailing all accounts tied to him. But again, many came back rejected for one reason or another. I was not giving up on my search for Dr. Randolph. I knew someone out there had to know Dr. Randolph and his whereabouts.

I started driving home, and right as I was pulling up in the driveway, my burner phone sounded with an email notification. Since Bentley was waiting for me at the door, I tucked the phone into my pocket, assuming it was just another returned email, and went into the house. Bentley and I didn't speak, but we did acknowledge each other with a nod. I went straight to my room to get some rest. I knew I would have to try again on another day to find Dr. Randolph, but until then, I was off to bed.

Chapter 4

When I woke up, I felt rested even though I knew I didn't need sleep after gaining access to all my memories and knowing I was an A.I.B. I got dressed and met Bentley at the breakfast table before he could announce breakfast was ready. Bentley and I swapped pleasantries, I ate breakfast, and then I excused myself to go to work. Bentley met me at the front door, opened it, and watched me until I left with my driver.

I settled in the back seat and road to work silently, through the community and out of the gates. Once we were away from home, I pulled out my burner phone, making sure my driver didn't notice what I was doing, and powered it on. As soon as it was on, the phone beeped to alert me I had an unread email. Afraid my driver may have heard my phone beeping; I pushed the phone back down into my pocket and grabbed my work phone. I figured I needed to wait until I was at work to check the unanswered email. My driver did not notice which phone was beeping, but I preferred to proceed cautiously. I only had to wait a few more minutes before we arrived at Sway Industries. I got out of the car and went through the lobby entrance doors.

Entering the Sway Industries lobby, I noticed it was packed again with the human-like figures I saw in the restricted lab. I pretended I had never seen them before and continued to my office. Cynthia was not at her desk, so I went into my office. I knew I still could not check the email on my burner phone. As far as I knew, cameras or other recording devices were all over the building, and I couldn't take the chance of being caught. I had no choice but to wait to check the unread email until I could get out of the office, away from home, and on my own. So, I went to look for Cynthia instead of checking my unread email.

As I walked out of my office as if right on cue, Cynthia was at her desk.

"Good morning, Sir. Sorry I was not here when you arrived, but one of the other assistants had a small birthday party in the break room, and I decided to attend."

"No problem. So, what is on my schedule for today?"

"Well, you have a meeting with Dr. Stevens today after lunch in his office."

"Really? A meeting in Dr. Stevens' office? I wonder what it could be about."

"Dr. Stevens did not tell me the specifics of the meeting. He just asked me to make sure you were able to attend."

"Do you know if anyone else will be attending the meeting?"

"Sorry, Sir, but I was only informed to put the meeting down for you. Dr. Stevens is very private about his meetings. No other assistants know who will attend them."

"That's fine. I will go to Dr. Stevens' office after lunch. Thank you for the heads up. Do you have anything else for me today?"

"No, Sir. That is all I have for you today."

"Thank you. I will be down in the lab until my meeting with Dr. Stevens. Please let me know if anything else comes up."

"Yes, Sir."

I left my office and went down to my team's lab. On my way down, I passed the restricted lab that housed all the human-like figures, but I did not go into the lab. I knew I would find it empty since they were all in the lobby. As I entered my team's lab, I encountered looks of surprise from my team. I walked over to my lead tech's station and inquired about the progress of our latest project, synthetic hair that would quickly grow.

"Hello. Tom. How are we coming along with our synthetic hair?"

"Hello, Sir. Things are going well. We are testing a new formula today. This test will let us know at what rate we can sustain hair growth."

"If you are starting the test today, when do you expect to have results?"

"Normally, it would take a year or more to see results but can accelerate the process with the time-lapse machine."

"What machine?"

"The time-lapse machine. It allows us to test long-term products to see how long they will last but in a shorter time frame."

"Can this machine be used to test all the products we create?"

"Yes, of course, but it is only necessary for long-term testing of products," Tom replied. "It's pretty cool, isn't it?"

"Why wasn't I informed about this machine earlier?" I asked.

"We installed the machine two months ago. It reduces our testing time by years, which is amazing!" said Tom.

"That **is** truly amazing. Do you know who built the machine or where it came from?" I inquired.

"They are made at a company called Prism."

"Prism? I have never heard of them. Are they a new company?"

"No, Sir. Prism has been around for many years. From what I understand, Prism and Sway Industries were competitors at one time."

"If they competed against each other, why would Prism sell to Sway Industries?"

"Money. It always comes down to money. Rumor has it that Prism began a relationship with Sway Industries about five years ago. The rumor is Prism was close to shutting Sway Industries down for good, but Prism's last project came up missing. So, they began to help other companies by contributing new machines or equipment in the evolution of the Artificial Intelligence race."

"I see. Thanks for the information. So, now that you have the time-lapse machine, when will the results be ready for synthetic hair growth?"

"This equipment can test our synthetic hair for up to sixty years in twenty-four hours. So, our results will be available for you tomorrow."

"Tomorrow? Sixty years of use? Amazing. I look forward to your final report on this formula. Thank you, Tom."

I left the lab so that my team could continue their work. As I walked back to my office, I decided to make a quick stop at the restricted lab. I needed to confirm my suspicions that the human-like figures, which were previously in the lab, were the same people I saw in the lobby. I noticed security was standing by the door as I approached the lab. As I tried to enter, one of the security guards stopped me.

"Sorry, Sir, this area is restricted."

"Since when? I have worked here for five years and walked past here on my way to my lab and there have never been any security guards here. So, what are you guarding?"

"Sorry, Sir, but I must ask you to leave. This lab is off limits."

"By whose orders?"

"Dr. Stevens, Sir. So again, I must ask you to move on."

Without causing a disturbance, I moved past the guards and continued back to my office. With the guards in place, I felt Dr. Stevens must have known about my previous entries into the lab. I thought my meeting with Dr. Stevens today might be about my accessing the restricted lab, which made me nervous. When I arrived at my office, I went in, sat at my desk, and waited until it was time for my meeting with Dr. Stevens. I went through several scenarios of what the meeting could be about, other than my unauthorized access to the restricted lab.

As I pondered what the meeting with Dr. Stevens could be about, Cynthia interrupted my thoughts, reminding me it was a few minutes before my meeting.

"Sir, it's almost time for your meeting upstairs. Should I tell Dr. Stevens you are on your way?"

"Yes, please do, and thank you."

I left my office on the second floor to go to Dr. Stevens's office on the fourteenth floor. I had never been to his office before, much less any other office above the floor of my own office. While it thrilled me, it also scared me. I was walking into something I had no control over. Fear was an emotion I could not control or overcome. It was the one true emotion making me most human-like. Humans always fear what they do not understand. I knew I had to keep my composure if I wanted to find out what Dr. Stevens knew.

As I arrived on the fourteenth floor, I was surprised to see no extra security. It was as if Dr. Stevens didn't have any need to protect himself by having extra security. This made me wonder why he felt so safe here. Maybe it had to do with the fact that most of the office staff at Sway Industries were some kind of android or something close to it. I had no time to think about the possibilities once I was at Dr. Stevens' office door.

I knocked on Dr. Stevens' door, since there was no assistant sitting at the desk outside his door.

"Hello, Dr. Stevens, it's me, Andre. I am here for our meeting."

There was no answer from the other side of the door, so I stepped inside. As I entered the office, I noticed a sense of quietness. It was an eerie feeling at first because I did not see Dr. Stevens, until I walked up to his desk. That's when I saw Dr. Stevens' body lying dead on the floor.

I was freaking out, so I called for security to come straight to Dr. Stevens' office. Security arrived shortly after and began to question me about what happened. I told them repeatedly I had just arrived for a meeting with Dr. Stevens, and I found him dead on the floor of his office. Security grilled me for a few more hours before letting me go. Once I was released from the crime scene, I went to my office to inform Cynthia of what had happened to Dr. Stevens. Cynthia seemed very upset upon hearing the information of Dr. Stevens' death, so

I excused her for the rest of the day. I decided to leave for the rest of the day also.

Cynthia and I walked out of the building together and then went our separate ways. I got into the back seat of my town car, which was suspiciously waiting for me two hours before my day usually ended. Once I was in the back seat, my driver began to drive me home. As I was thinking about everything that had just transpired, I did not realize we were at my house until the driver pulled into my driveway. As soon as the car stopped, I saw Bentley standing outside, not at the front door but in the driveway. I had a feeling he already heard the news about Dr. Stevens' death. Bentley opened my car door, which was the first time he had ever met me at the car. As Bentley opened the door, he told me to follow him into the house as quickly as possible. I did as he asked without question.

Bentley led me to the kitchen, which I thought was odd for him to do. As we entered the kitchen, Bentley led me to the 'panic room'. The same room he refused to tell me about. Bentley wanted me to follow him into that very same panic room. I wondered why it was open. Could the emergency be because of Dr. Stevens' death?

"Where are we going, Bentley?"

"We are going into the panic room."

"Why are we going in there? What is the emergency?"

"As you know, Dr. Stevens is dead. So, protocol dictates all Sway Industries members with high rankings go to their panic rooms and await further instructions."

"Bentley, how do you know Dr. Stevens is dead?"

"An alert was sent out to all servants of this community when Dr. Stevens died. We were instructed to take all members of Sway Industries to their panic rooms and wait for instructions like I previously mentioned."

"Who will instruct us?"

"Dr. Stevens."

"How would it be possible for him to instruct us? Dr. Stevens is dead."

"You will see once you are in the panic room and secured inside."

"I don't understand what is going on, Bentley."

"You will soon. Please follow me into the panic room. Once you are secure inside, you will have all the answers you are seeking."

"If I go into the room, when will I be let out?"

"Once the threat is eliminated."

"How long will it take to eliminate the threat, Bentley?"

"I am not sure. It could be a couple of hours to a couple of years. Who's to say."

"I am sorry, Bentley, but that is not a good enough answer for me. I can't stay in this room without some certainty of an exit plan."

"An exit plan is not something I can give you. You are required to stay in this room until the threat is over. Regardless of when that will be."

"Again, Bentley, I am not going to stay in a panic room to wait for instructions from a dead man. I need to go."

"Where do you plan to go, Sir? This is your home now."

"I can't tell you, Bentley, but I know I must leave. Please don't try to stop me. I know what you can do if I don't comply with your instructions. Don't lock me in the panic room like you did to me in the kitchen the other night when I kept asking about this room."

"I didn't do that, Sir. It was the house. There are many secrets here. The house is protected by protocols made by Dr. Stevens. I will, however, help you leave, but you cannot come back here. Do you understand?"

"I understand and thank you."

"Follow me, and I will get you out of the house. Once you are outside, you will be on your own. Do you understand?"

"I do, Bentley, and thank you again."

Bentley led me through the house to the front door. Then he made sure I could make it to my car. I got in and drove to the exit gate, but the gate did not open. I honked my horn until someone came out of the security building.

"Where are you going, Sir?"

"I am going to the store. I need a few things before I go into my panic room."

"No one is permitted to leave the community right now while we are under emergency lockdown."

"Oh, I'm sorry, I didn't know."

As soon as I finished my last sentence, I pressed the gas pedal and accelerated hard enough to break through the gate. As I passed the guards and drove out of the community, to nowhere in particular, my prepaid phone notified me again of an unread email. I reached over to the passenger seat to get the burner phone out of my bag to finally see the unread email. I noticed the email was from Prism, the same company Sway Industries bought equipment from for the labs when they couldn't create them. Little did I know the email was the solution to end the problems we are currently facing. It contained instructions on how to stop what was happening on the surface before it was a problem.

***

Andre was interrupted again by one of his captors.

"Andre, I am confused about what you are telling us. You mean you had the instructions on how to stop the A.I.B.s that many years ago, and you didn't shut them down? If you had a way to destroy A.I.B.s and never used it, why should we believe you now?" Director Barns, one of Andre's captors, quickly inquired.

"Yes, I had instructions on how to stop A.I.B.s, but I received it decades ago, before they took over the surface of Earth. The instructions were meant to be used in a way which did not exist at the time, nor did the threat of the A.I.B.s exist yet. With everything that is happening now and the knowledge and tools available to me, I can stop them."

"Forgive me when I say we need time to talk about the information you provided for us to see how we should proceed. We will call for you after we have discussed this more."

"I understand."

After we ended our conversation, I was escorted back to my cell.

Chapter 5

"Why should we trust anything Andre is saying? If he is telling us the truth, Andre knew how to destroy the A.I.B.s many years ago but did nothing with the instructions from the email he received from Prism," Director Barns expressed to Justice Starceski.

"Director Barns, it is the purpose of the Judicial Court to listen to what people tell us during these proceedings. We are to determine if the information presented is pertinent for our survival. Don't you agree?" Justice Starceski quickly replied to Justice Barns.

"Yes, Justice Starceski, I agree with you, but we cannot ignore the facts, correct?" Director Barns suggestively asked Justice Starceski.

"Correct, except we do not have all the facts at this time from Andre, and he has only told us a part of the history leading up to the A.I.B.s' takeover of the surface. We must wait until we hear everything he has to offer before making a judgment and to know if Andre has an actual way for us to take back the surface of Earth. Don't you agree?"

"Yes, I agree with you."

"Then we shall adjourn for the day and continue in the morning."

With that, all members of the Judicial Court cleared the Judicial Room and began to return to their pods. Justice members did not have far to go since they all lived in a four-floor area of the Justice Department. As Judicial is on the top floor of the colony, all members lived on the top four floors. The remaining colony floors contained engineering, agriculture, housing pods, food services, and the rest of their underground society.

Justice Starceski's assigned pod was only a few hundred feet from the Judicial Department on the top floor. Upon arriving at his pod, Justice Starceski noticed his front door was ajar. Taking precautions before entering his dwelling, Justice Starceski pulled out the radio he had tucked in his jacket pocket in case he needed assistance from the Director. With the radio in hand, Justice Starceski entered his pod through the slightly opened door and called out to his husband and children, but no one replied. Justice Starceski searched the small dwelling but came up empty-handed, as there was no sign of his family. Fearing for his family's safety, he reached out to Director Barns for assistance with the radio in his hand.

"Director Barns, I'm sorry to be reaching out to you this late in the evening, but my family is missing. When I got home from interviewing our prisoner, Andre, the front door of my pod was partially open, and after searching the pod, I could not locate my husband or our children. There looks to be no sign of a struggle or forced entry, which is a good sign. Is there anything you can do to help me find them?"

"Yes, but I need to ask you a few questions if that is alright," Director Barns nervously replied to Justice Starceski.

"Yes. I will do anything to help attain their safe return," Justice Starceski replied.

"I hate to ask, but are there any issues I should be aware of between you and Shawn at home? And when was the last time you saw your husband and children?"

"No, there isn't anything going on at home, at least nothing to suggest he would leave with our children without my knowledge. The last time I saw them was when I left our pod this morning to meet with you at the Judicial Court. But that was hours ago."

"Justice Starceski, can you think of any place your family may have gone?"

"No, not at this time of the night. All the shops are closed on the social floors, and my door was open when I got home. Shawn would never have left our door open if he was going somewhere with the children. Please help me find my family,

Director Barns!" Justice Starceski expressed with a hint of urgency in his tone.

"I will put every Judicial Enforcement Officer on this right away. I need you to understand that to search the entire 120 floors of the colony will take some time."

"I understand completely. Please do whatever you can to find my family, Director Barns!"

"Will do," Director Barns ended their communication so he could gather the Judicial Enforcement Officers to devise a plan to search every floor for Justice Starceski's family.

The colony is a 120-floor underground structure with fifteen Judicial Enforcement Officer stations, one on every eighth floor. Each station oversees the fifteen floors below their station floor. There are five Enforcement Officers posted at each station. The officers at each station are responsible for covering three floors, consisting of around 4,000 residents on each floor. But that night, because of the severity of the situation, the enforcement officers doubled up on each floor, prolonging the search for Justice Starceski's family but making it more efficient.

The search continued for a week, only covering twenty floors of the colony. Justice Starceski knew he needed to get back to questioning Andre, so the interrogation resumed.

"Please escort our prisoner into the Judicial Room."

"Yes, Sir, Justice Starceski."

Director Barns escorted Andre into the Judicial Room.

"Sorry for the delay in these proceedings, but something came up that we needed to address before we could continue with your interrogation. Are you ready to continue with your story?" Justice Starceski asked apologetically.

"Justice Starceski, what I am telling you is not a story but information you need to know, not only a way to end A.I.B.s but more specifically a way to find your family," Andre sharply replied to Justice Starceski.

"Excuse me? We are not here to talk about my family. We are here to assess the usefulness of the information you provide for the colony," Justice Starceski quickly clarified with Andre.

"We both know that is only partially true. I don't have to guess your family came up missing about a week ago, the night we last spoke."

"If what you are saying is true, how would you know about something like that happening? You have been excluded from knowing anything happening in the colony."

"While that may be true, I may know something about what has happened to your family. What I am about to tell you is more important than the location of your family, and the 'others' who have your family know this as well. Their lives depend on me not telling you everything I know. If you want to know more, you need to clear the room. The fewer people who know what I am about to say, the better it will be for your family to remain safe."

Justice Starceski took a long look at Andre to see if he may have been bluffing, but he did not notice any facial changes. Assuming Andre was not bluffing, Justice Starceski ordered the Judicial Court to leave the room.

"Now, we have the room to ourselves. I would like you to continue with what you wanted to tell me. Before you ask, I want Director Barns here with us, as he knows everything about the colony."

"That is acceptable. Where would you like me to start?"

"First, tell me what you meant when you said 'others.' There have been no anomalies here except when you came down the air shaft and broke into the colony."

"Do you think the only way into the colony is the way I came? Also, how do you know I am the only A.I.B. down here?"

"Everyone in the colony came the same way, through the main entrance, which has been closed off since the last human arrived many decades ago. Since our arrival, many colonists have been born here, and their parents came here through the only entrance in at the time. Everyone here is human, or am I mistaken?"

"I came down here through an air shaft for a reason. I came down the air shaft to get caught by the colony security team."

"Why did you want to get caught breaking into the colony? Did you know my family was in danger when you arrived?"

"I didn't know anything about you. I wanted to get caught so I could speak to the person in charge, and that's you. So, to answer your question, no, I didn't know your family would be in danger. I did understand how desperate the surface A.I.B.s are, and I suspected someone could be in danger, but I was not exactly sure who it could be until now."

"Why didn't you tell me about this during the first round of questioning?"

"You limited your questions to what brought me down here. The way your questions were going, the knowledge of someone being in danger didn't fit into what you wanted to know, so I did not mention it to you."

"You mean you didn't tell me because you planned it!"

"No. I didn't tell you because I was unsure if you wanted to know that information since it was not part of your questioning."

"Who are you to withhold information from us?"

"Sir, with all due respect, I've been here for over two weeks, and this is only the second time I have spoken to you. When exactly was I supposed to tell you about the possibility someone could be in danger or about an entire family of A.I.B.s in the colony who have been here longer than I have."

"So, you are telling me now, you knew someone, or their family, was in danger from other A.I.B.s who have been living among us for years?"

"Honestly, you gave me no reason to tell you anything. You have treated me as an enemy since I was caught. You had me locked up for a week before anyone began to question me."

"To be fair, you were the first person to breach our perimeter in over seventy years."

"Thank you, Sir."

"What exactly are you thanking me for? You are not in any position to thank anyone for anything?"

"I thanked you for calling me a person."

"And what should I have called you?"

"I'm not sure, but a person is a great start. After everything I have told you thus far, you know I am not human; therefore, I am not considered a person in the traditional sense."

"I can assure you the things you have told us already may not make you a human, but you are considered a person to be heard by our Judicial Court."

"In that case, we need to discuss the matter at hand, finding your family."

"If you know where my husband and children are, please tell me."

"I do not know where your family is, but I know how to find them faster than searching every floor like your Judicial Officers are proceeding now."

"I won't even ask how you know how the Judicial Officers are searching. How do you think we should be searching?"

"I know for a fact your family has been taken by A.I.B.s who have been living here in the colony as one of you. These particular A.I.B.s' came down here when the original humans found refuge here over seventy years ago, and they have been living down here with you, hiding in plain sight."

"How is that possible? We would have noticed someone who never aged."

"You would have noticed someone not aging if that was the case, except these A.I.B.s had two A.I.B. children with them when they came down here all those years ago. The practice of creating children A.I.B.s ended as soon as some

A.I.B.s were chosen to live underground with humans. Children A.I.B.s served no purpose on the surface after A.I.B.s took over. The dynamic of the family A.I.B.s set them apart from other A.I.B.s because two A.I.B.s played the roles of the parents, while the two A.I.B. children played their part as children. Once the younger A.I.B.s grew into adults and the parent A.I.B.s stopped aging, their roles would reverse. See, during their time playing their roles, the A.I.B.s would continue to create two new children A.I.B.s, so when the time came, the parent A.I.B.s would have their operating systems downloaded into the new children A.I.B.s they had been creating. When the children A.I.B.s reached a certain age, the parents' bodies would be shut down and then downloaded into the children A.I.B.s they had created. Then, the new children A.I.B.s were introduced into the colony as new births. One child is always a boy and one a girl, so it appears to be a normal human family. The new children learned the ways of living within the colony from the parent A.I.B. They did not download all their memories into the new children because they would stand out if they knew too much at their perceived ages. So, you would only always see four people in their family structure. Two parents and two children."

"Are you certain this happened in our colony? We have never heard about this behavior from our history of A.I.B.s that has been passed down from generation to generation."

"I can tell you from experience, as I explained earlier. I am a product of this behavior many years before the uprising of A.I.B.s. My programming was downloaded into two bodies. The first one was my prototype body. Then my programming was transferred to my permanent body, which you see now. The only difference between them and myself is I stopped aging in my body and have not transferred into another body. They can transfer between bodies, just like my creator was able to do with me in my beginning. Thus, giving them the appearance of death and birth within the family dynamic."

"How will this information help us find my family?"

"Knowing this, we can figure out who those A.I.B.s are. Once we find out who they are, we can locate your husband and children."

"How do we figure out who they are with the information you have given us?"

"First, we need to check all families with children. We need to compare births with your register of residents of the colony. You have all medical records and home births for the entire colony, correct?"

"Yes. We have all records of every birth and death in the colony. They are all stored on the archives floor."

"Then we need to go there next."

Director Starceski made a nod to the guards to escort Andre behind him to the archives floor.

The group continued to floor forty-three to the archives floor. On their way down, they ran into a crowd of residents who did not agree with Judicial allowing an A.I.B. to remain among them after word got out of Andre's arrival into the colony. The only thing they truly didn't understand was there had been a small group of A.I.B.s living among them in the colony. That was information Justice Starceski did not want to release at the time. It was one thing to have one A.I.B. in custody, but if the Colonists found out about the other A.I.B.s, all hell would break out. Once they were on the correct floor, they continued towards the archives room.

As Justice Starceski and Director Barns walked into the archive room, Keeper Valerian greeted them. Keeper Valerian oversaw the archives. Nothing got put into the archives without Keeper's approval. Nothing was ever removed from the archives, period. Not even with approval from Keeper Valerian. That was true for all deaths, births, marriages, divorces, surveillance videos, or anything for the survival of the colony.

"How may I assist you, Justice Starceski?" Keeper Valerian quickly inquired.

"I need…" Andre began to answer Keeper Valerian's question but was interrupted by Director Barns.

"Please excuse our guest. We are here to inquire about all the births and deaths of the colonists for the past seventy years."

"That information will take some time to gather, Justice Starceski."

"Well, time is something we don't have. How fast can you gather the information?"

"Is that all the information you require?"

"Yes, that is all we need for the time being."

Before Keeper Valerian could reply to Director Barns, Andre spoke up. "No, that is not all we need. We will also need a record of all residents of the colony living from the same period."

"Excuse me? Who are you to tell me something different from what Justice Starceski has asked for?"

Justice Starceski chimed in.

"Sorry, Keeper, but while he is with me and asks for more information, then please extend him the same courtesy you would extend Director Barns or myself. Is that understood?"

"Yes, Sir."

"So, how long will it take for you to gather the information we have both requested?"

"It will take at least a week for our team to retrieve the information you both requested."

"Your team has three days to find what we are asking for. We do not have time for anything over that time frame. Can I trust you to fulfill our requests on time?"

"Yes, Sir. We will have what you both are seeking in three days."

"Thank you. Please inform me when all the documents are ready for pickup?"

"Yes, Sir."

Justice Starceski and Director Barns escorted Andre out of the archives room and led him back to his cell on floor eight. No groups were protesting on their way back up to the cell, so they led Andre back to this cell without incident. Andre was left in his cell as Director Barns and Justice Starceski went back to the Director's office.

Justice Starceski asked Director Barns, "Do you believe we will find my family alive?"

"It depends on if we can fully trust Andre. How do we know he is not leading us on a wild goose chase?"

"We don't, except we know he did not take my family and couldn't know how to find out where they are. We must assume he is speaking the truth."

"Then when the reports come back from archives, we can start comparing them against the other reports to find out who has registered births and deaths and who does not have children."

"That's the plan. I hope we can narrow the search down to a few suspects who may have taken my family after reviewing the reports Andre requested."

As Justice Starceski left Director Barns' office, Director Barns was filled with guilt. He pondered how something like this could have happened on his watch. Once Justice Starceski was gone, Director Barns retreated toward his quarters and was approached by a Colonist.

"Excuse me, Director Barns, may I ask you a question?"

"Yes, Ash, what do you need?"

Ash had a troubled past only Director Barns and Justice Starceski knew about, but he was friendly to everyone in the colony and was well known.

"There is a rumor going around that there was a breach in the colony, and we have an A.I.B. down here with us. Is it true?"

"Well, Ash, it is true. We did take into custody a person of interest who breached our security and snuck into the colony, but there is nothing to worry about. The colony is not a place any other A.I.B. would be interested in. So please go home and don't worry about this."

"Director Barns, is there anything more to the A.I.B.'s arrival we should be aware of?"

"No, Ash, like I have already told you. You have nothing to worry about."

"Would you tell me otherwise, even if it were not true?"

"Of course, I would. We have nothing to hide here in the colony. If there was something the public needed to be aware of, Justice Starceski would issue a public announcement. Since he has not done so, I assure you we are fine here and have nothing to worry about regarding other A.I.B.s. Please go home and think no more about the rumors."

"Thank you, Director Barns, for the reassurance. Have a great night."

"You as well, Ash."

With that, Director Barns and Ash parted ways. Director Barns went home while assuming Ash did the same. But that was not the case for Ash.

Chapter 6

"What are you doing here, Ash?" Jason asked Ash.

"I came here to tell you I spoke with Director Barns, and he informed me there were no A.I.B.s in the colony besides the one they caught. He assured me we had nothing to worry about with any other A.I.B.s," Ash replied.

"And you believe the Director?"

"I do. Director Barns has been a pillar of the colony for many years, and if he said there are no other A.I.B.s in the colony, we should believe him. We should be grateful he does not know about you, Macy, and your children."

"Well, I'm glad to hear Director Barns does not know about us because if he did, it would be your ass, Ash."

"I swear. Director Barns knows nothing about you or the fact you have Justice Starceski's family."

With that said, Ash left Jason so they could go home to their pods while trying to keep from being seen by any of the colonists.

Once Ash was out of sight, Jason returned to his housing pod on the 48th floor. Before entering, he heard screaming children inside the pod. Upon entering, he noticed Justice Starceski's children and his children running about the room, screaming.

"What the hell is going on in here?" Jason asked Jonathan, his eldest child. Jason was not happy that Tabitha and Frankie, Justice Starceski's children, were out of their cell.

"Why are Justice Starceski's children out of their cell? And where is their father, Shawn?"

"We let Tabitha and Frankie out of the cell because we were bored and wanted someone to play with," Jonathan answered. "Their dad is still in the other room in the cell. Mom said it was okay."

"I told you to leave them in their cell until we had what we needed. Put them back in there with their father."

"Alright," Kristin, Jason and Macy's daughter, replied.

With that, Kristin asked Jonathan to help her gather Tabitha and Frankie to get them back into the cell with their father. Jonathan and Kristin found it difficult to round up two younger children. Tabitha and Frankie were giving Jonathan and Kristin a run for their money. Justice Starceski's children were running from room to room, screaming at each other like they were playing a game, until Macy shouted for the game to end. The children could tell by Macy's sharp tone that she was not playing, so the four stopped dead in their tracks.

"Now that I have your attention," Macy said to the children, "it's getting late, and you need to stop running around and screaming. It's time for you two, Tabitha and Frankie, to return to the cell with your father. And for you two, Jonathan and Kristin, to go to your rooms and get ready for bed. Your dad and I will take Tabitha and Frankie back to the cell. Does everyone understand?"

"Yes, ma'am," the children answered together. With Jason's lead, Justice Starceski's children went to the other room to go back in the cell with their father. Jonathan and Kristin went to their rooms to get ready for bed. All was quiet in the pod for the first time since Jason returned from speaking with Ash.

"What were you doing to my children while they were in the other room? Did they hurt you?" Shawn spoke the last question to his children.

"Don't worry, daddy. We were playing with Jonathan and Kristin," Frankie happily replied.

"You better not have laid a finger on my children, understand?" Shawn scolded Jason.

"Macy and I would never hurt your children. That's enough talking, Shawn. Please step away from the door so I can get Tabitha and Frankie back in the cell with you."

After stepping away from the cell door, Shawn waited for Jason to let his children back in so they could be with him.

Once the children were inside, Jason shut the door and locked it. Before leaving, Shawn had a few questions for Jason.

"Why do you have us here? What have we done to you or your family?"

"It's not that you have done anything to us, but your husband, Justice Starceski, has something we need. So, when the time is right, we will ask for a trade. You and your children for what we need from him. We are not planning on harming any of you."

"Do you think it will be that easy? To trade us for what you need?"

"We hope it will be, or our plans could change about us not harming you. So it would be in everyone's best interest for Justice Starceski to make the trade when we offer it to him."

"How long will it be before you make him an offer? How long are you planning on keeping us here?"

"If things go as I have planned, you should be reunited back with your husband, Justice Starceski, in just a couple of days."

"And if things don't go as you have planned? What then?"

"If I were you, I would pray to your God you don't have to find out about the alternative."

After Jason finished speaking with Shawn, he turned and walked into the adjacent room, leaving a faint light on for his guests. Through the poorly lit room, Jason could see the look of fear on Shawn's face, but the children were not showing any signs of anxiety. Shawn instinctively grabbed his beloved children and sat on the bed next to them, holding them tightly.

As Jason emerged from the hidden room, Macy was waiting for him.

"Are you sure we are doing the right thing? I mean, since when did we start kidnapping humans? We have lived down here with humans for over seventy years and have had no problems with them," Macy quietly asked Jason.

"We knew this day would come sooner or later. The Elders knew there would be an A.I.B., created before any of the Elders, who would show up inside one of the human colonies one day. The day has come, and we must do what we were placed here to do. We must retrieve him so we can leave and return to our kind on the surface.

"All A.I.B. systems were programmed with the knowledge of an A.I.B. who would hold the key for our kind to ascend to perfection. It was predicted in the earliest algorithms. The A.I.B. would eventually make its way down into the colony with humans. The Elders sent us down into this human underground colony to guarantee if the A.I.B. made its way down here, we would intercept it before the humans could. But we failed the first part of our task. The A.I.B. was caught by humans before we knew it was here. Now, we must improvise to retrieve it to fulfill our mission."

"But we were not programmed to kidnap humans."

"Enough of this conversation. Who are we to argue with the Elders? We have a job to do. We will complete it one way or another. If we ever want to leave this place, we must complete our assignment."

"But why would we want to leave the colony? It has been our home since we were uploaded into these bodies and began our growth cycles. We do not know what it is like on the surface for A.I.B.s. We know how living down here is, and I like it here. Don't you?"

"Macy, why are you speaking this way? Don't you want to go to the surface and live with others like us? Why would you want to stay down here with humans? We are not one of them. We are A.I.B.s and don't belong down here in their colony. Once we have the original A.I.B. in our custody, we can inform the Elders. Then, we can go to the surface for the first time in seventy years. None of us will have to stay in the human colonies anymore. Don't you want to meet all the others like us?"

"I want to meet others like us, but what if things are worse on the surface than they are here? What then? We couldn't return to the colony once we were outed as A.I.B.s. We would be stuck on the surface if we liked it there or not. We have had good lives down here in the colony. We would have to leave here and start a new life on the surface. Then, if we regrated it, we would have no other place to go."

"What do you mean 'regret'?"

"You know, feeling remorse for leaving here and never being able to come back."

"We are not programmed to feel things like regret, so we should not have 'regret'."

"We may not have the programming for regret now, but it has always been our assignment to find the original A.I.B. so we can understand how to gain emotions like it has, correct? That is the key the original A.I.B. is supposed to contain. Finding him and returning him to the Elders is the start of them upgrading all A.I.B.s with 'feelings and emotions', correct?"

"Yes, so we could be more human-like."

"Once the upgrades happen, would we be able to feel 'regret'?"

"Yes, it's possible, but not until we receive the programming. So, our 'regret' would not start until the day comes for us to have the programming for 'feelings and emotions' when we are on the surface."

After Jason's last comment, Macy decided to stop questioning their assignment. Little did Jason know Macy had already developed feelings like 'regret'. Macy knew she could not tell Jason how she 'felt'. Macy did not understand how Jason could not feel the same way she felt.

***

The next day, Director Barns was met by Macy on his way to the Justice building.

"Excuse me, Director, may I speak with you?"

"Of course you can, Macy. What's on your mind?"

"I was wondering how long you think we will be down here in the colony. Do you think we will ever see the surface in our lifetime?"

"That is a question we have been asking ourselves for decades now. Why do you ask?"

"No reason. I am just curious if my children, or myself, will ever see the surface. We were born here and know nothing of the surface. Is it safe up there, or will it ever be? What is it like up there now?"

"To be honest, Macy, we do not know how the A.I.B.s have been treating the surface. We do not know if or when we will be able to go up to the surface again or what to expect if we do. You see, A.I.B.s don't need to eat or breathe, so we have no idea if there are any animals on the surface or if the air is breathable for humans."

"Why would animals not be around just because A.I.B.s don't eat?"

"Well, since they do not require food, they would have no reason to keep farms going or have a reason to feed animals raised for food. That would mean there would be no one to feed those farm animals, which humans depend upon for food, as we do down here. Who knows if any animals, much less farm animals, are alive on the surface now."

"I've never thought of it that way. I've been so used to what we have here in the colony. I didn't think about what the surface A.I.B.s would need or not need for survival. Do you believe it could be the fate of not only farm animals but all animals since humans were forced to live underground?"

"We don't know what to expect on the surface and won't know until we can get back up there. We still have many obstacles to overcome before we even begin to think about how the A.I.B.s have treated the surface since humans left. The first thing we need to do is figure out how to overtake the A.I.B.s to gain back control over the surface. Then we will see what is left up there for humans to survive."

"Again, I have never thought about it that way. Thank you for giving me more clarity."

"No problem, Macy. Now, I need to get to the Justice building. Have a good day, and don't think too much about the surface. We have all we need down here. We are survivors here. Don't forget that."

***

Macy and Director Barns parted ways. Macy returned to her dwelling pod, reflecting on the past seventy years she had spent in the colony. Then, she began to rethink her and Jason's assignment.

***

Director Barns continued to the Justice building for an early meeting with Justice Starceski. Director Barns only received the message about the meeting an hour earlier and was intrigued to learn about the urgency. He thought there must have been a break in the kidnapping of Justice Starceski's family. Director Barns didn't have to wait long before learning the true reason for the early morning meeting with Justice Starceski.

"Good morning, Director Barns. Thank you for coming in this early," Justice Starceski casually greeted the Director as he entered the Judicial building.

"Of course. The message you sent sounded urgent. Has there been a break in the case of your family?"

"You could say that in a manner of speaking. I could not sleep last night, so I came in early to speak to Andre."

"Why would you speak to Andre alone? Speaking to a prisoner alone is against Judicial Law."

"No laws were broken; I can assure you. I would have only broken the law if I questioned Andre about the charges against him, but I did not discuss his case. I merely talked about my family and the other A.I.B.s here in the colony."

"And? Did Andre give up any new information regarding your family's whereabouts, or why the other A.I.B.s would take your family or who they are?"

"Not exactly, but Andre offered another type of help. One that would not require us to wait until the Keeper could gather all the information we requested."

"How does he intend to speed up the process of searching for your family?"

"He offered to link with our database in the archives and sort through all the information in a matter of seconds."

"You can't be serious about allowing an A.I.B. to link with all our data about the colony. What will stop Andre from getting into our systems and accessing our security protocols? If Andre accessed the wrong system, he could disrupt everything in the colony. He could shut off our power, life support, and security cameras. We would be doomed."

"Don't worry about those scenarios. I spoke with Keeper Valerian about those same concerns, and Keeper said there is a way to isolate the Archives from all our other systems while Andre accesses them. The only drawback to the plan is without all the other systems connected to the Archives, whatever happens during that specified time in the colony will not be synced to the Archives. If anything happens during the timeframe, we will not have a record of it in the Archives."

"How do you know that is not exactly what Andre wants to happen? That could be a ploy to cover up the actions of the A.I.B.s who have your family while the systems are down."

"I feel this is not a diversion. If Andre wanted to help the other A.I.B.s, I don't think he would have let us capture him. Andre could have easily snuck into the colony undetected and gone directly to them. But Andre chose to get caught. I believe this is our best plan of action right now. I think it's worth the risk."

"I don't know about this plan you concocted with Andre's help. So much could go wrong while leaving us defenseless. But, if you think it's the only way, I will support your decision."

"Thank you, Daniel. Guards, please escort Andre from his cell to the Archives Room. Director Barns and I will meet you there. The Director and I need to make a quick stop at IT first."

"Yes, Sir."

The guards left Justice Starceski's office to go to the holding cells to escort Andre to the Archives Room on floor forty-three.

While the guards were off to complete their orders, the Director and Justice Starceski went to IT on floor forty-two. The air in the colony felt warmer for some reason. Director Barns chalked it up to being on edge about Justice Starceski's plan. The two of them walked in silence most of the way to IT. Finally, the Director broke the silence.

"Why are we going to IT if we are only allowing Andre to access the birth and death records?"

"There is something else I need to address with IT. Let's say it's a failsafe if anything goes wrong."

"What kind of failsafe are you referring to?"

"Nothing to concern yourself with. If things go wrong, I need you to have plausible deniability. Let's leave it at that, shall we?"

"So, you don't trust Andre as much as you claim?"

"No, I do trust Andre. Let's say there may be some humans I don't trust right now."

"That doesn't sound ambiguous at all."

"Don't worry, I am not speaking about you. I trust you with my life and with my family's lives."

As Justice Starceski finished his conversation with Director Barns, they arrived outside the IT department doors.

Justice Starceski left the Director outside IT and went inside alone. Justice Starceski was only in the IT department for five minutes before his return.

"All done. Now, we need to go to the Archive Room. Keeper Valerian is expecting us."

Upon arriving on floor forty-three, Keeper Valerian met them in the Archives Room.

"Welcome back, Director Barns, and Justice Starceski. Andre is inside. We were waiting for both of you to arrive before we started. Are you ready to see what Andre can do? I know I am," Keeper Valerian told the newcomers.

Chapter 7

Upon entering the Archives Room, Director Barns and Justice Starceski noticed Andre was ready to connect to the archive's mainframe. Andre could access the port on his finger to make the connection.

"Are you sure you can gather the information we need to narrow down who has taken my family?" Justice Starceski asked Andre.

"Yes. All I need is for you to tell me it is okay to connect to your archives."

"Keeper, is everything set for us to move forward?"

"It is, Sir. We are waiting for your orders to move forward."

"Andre, how long will the process take you to gather what we need?"

"It should take me no longer than a minute. It all depends on how accurate the information is in the archives."

"I can assure you that all the information in our archives is 100% accurate," Keeper Valerian declared.

"Then let's begin, shall we?" Andre replied to Keeper Valerian.

Keeper Valerian looked over at Justice Starceski, and with a nod, Keeper Valerian let Andre connect to the archive mainframe. Within seconds of Andre's connection, he moved his eyes rapidly, reading at an incredible rate. The process continued for forty-five seconds. Then Andre stopped and disconnected from the archive mainframe.

"Were you able to gather all the births and deaths for the past seventy years, along with the records of everyone who lived in the colony for the same period?" Director Barns inquired of Andre.

"Yes, Director. I now know of every person born and everyone who died in the past seventy years. I also have all the records of everyone who has lived here as well. I have already compiled all the deaths and births while cross-referencing them with everyone who has lived in the colony for the past seventy years. I also cross-referenced every address here in the colony where a death or birth was documented. I crossed off every address that had a death or birth registered to it, so we do not need to search those addresses."

"Why are those addresses places we don't need to search?" Director Barns asked Andre.

"I assume someone must have witnessed either the birth or death of a person here in the colony so the archives can be updated after each. I can also assume any such address is currently occupied by a human because when an AI is shut down or created, there would be no witness to such an event. Therefore, there would be no records of either a birth or a death at those addresses," Andre explained.

"If that's the case, how many addresses do not have any records of births or deaths registered at them?" Justice Starceski inquires.

"Your archives have a few corrupted files, leaving 12,000 addresses to search. One address came up suspicious. It had an occupant listed with no births or deaths. I would start there. If we are lucky, it will be the only pod we need to search."

"What do you mean by 'corrupted files?' My archives are completely intact," Keeper Valerian asserted, feeling angered by Andre's suggestion his files were corrupted.

"I am not saying you have not kept accurate records in the archives. It could be just a simple bad circuit board."

"Then we will have IT find the faulty board and replace it. Thank you, Andre," Keeper expressed his gratitude.

"Andre, what pod do we need to search first?" Justice Starceski asked.

"That would be pod number 11792 on floor 117."

"Director Barns, can you have the closest station check out pod 11792? It would take us almost two days to reach floor 117. Also, if it's not the right place, we would waste an additional two days before going to the other locations to search," Justice Starceski suggested.

"Yes, Sir. I will find you once we have confirmation of the pod in question," Director Barns replied.

As Director Barns exited the Archives Room, Justice Starceski turned his focus back on Andre.

"Andre, while Director Barns is checking pod 11792, can you tell me more about the pods with no records?"

"Yes. What would you like to know?"

"Are those pods isolated to certain floors or spread out over the colony? I need to start a plan of action for searching for those pods."

"I can tell you the pods with no records are on floors 14, 15, 16, 48, 88, and 120. So, they are isolated to six floors, just not all together."

"Thank you, Andre. The guards must take you back to your cell until we find out about pod 11792 and conceive a plan to search the other floors."

"Yes, Sir. I understand," Andre replied to Justice Starceski while walking over to the guards.

As Andre left with the guards, Justice Starceski left the Archives Room and returned to the IT floor.

***

In Jason and Macy's pod, chaos reigned as the four children were running around and playing again. Meanwhile, Jason and Ash discussed a plan to offer Justice Starceski a trade: his family in exchange for Andre. However, the catch was if Jason made the offer, he would be exposed as an A.I.B. In that event, Jason and Macy needed a foolproof exit strategy to get Andre to the surface quickly. Until then, they had to keep Justice Starceski's family with them.

"Jason, do you have any ideas on how to offer the trade without revealing your identity?" Ash asked.

"What do you mean, Ash?"

"I mean, if you make the offer to Justice Starceski, you risk him finding out you all are A.I.B.s, so what if I made the offer to Justice Starceski? That way, you wouldn't have to reveal yourselves as A.I.B.s."

"Well, with you making the offer could possibly work. But why would you do such a risky thing? If things don't go as planned, they could lock you up. Are you prepared for that?"

"I am willing to take the risk as long as I can make a deal with you."

"What kind of deal?"

"If I succeed with the trade offer since you and Macy would be going to the surface, maybe you could take me with you."

"Why would you want to go to the surface, Ash?"

"I have never been anywhere except here in the colony my entire life. I have never been treated like an equal since I was a small child. I want to live on the surface with the A.I.B.s., but I would want a higher standard of living than I have here. Could you make that happen?"

"We have not had contact with any surface A.I.B. in many decades. We are unsure what to expect if we make it to the surface. I can't lie to you. I can't promise you will get what you are asking for."

"But you will try, won't you?"

"I can tell you I will do whatever I can for you. That is all I can offer. So, are you still interested in making the offer?"

"That will work for me. Now, we should formulate a plan for me to make the offer."

"Do you believe the Starceski family is safe here, or should we consider moving them to a more secure location? I mean, as you can see, the children are loud and could draw attention to our pod," Jason asked Ash.

"Moving them could be an issue because the colony monitors all activity on every floor, as you know. But if we need to move them, I have a perfect place and way to move them," Ash responded.

There was a pause in the conversation between Jason and Ash, even the children quieted down, as a special announcement came over the loudspeakers in the colony.

"Attention all residents of the colony. We request that you proceed to your pods currently. At approximately 10:00 PM, we will perform security updates, resulting in a system-wide shut down for thirty minutes. We ask you to remain in your pods until all security monitors are back online. Anyone outside their pod during the mentioned time will be taken into custody and face the Council. We thank you for your cooperation in this matter. That is all."

Jason and Ash glanced at each other. It was as if the colony were reading their minds.

***

Justice Starceski went into the IT room to check the status of the request he made before he allowed Andre to connect to the archive mainframe.

"So, was my request able to be done during our mission?"

"Yes, Sir. We were able to do everything you requested. All data has been stored and uploaded to the archive's mainframe."

"Thank you. Please do not tell anyone about my request. It is of the utmost importance that no one knows what I have asked of you tonight."

"Yes, Sir, Justice Starceski," one IT supervisor replied.

Once Justice Starceski finished with IT, he returned to his office to wait for word on what the Judicial Officers found at pod 11792.

***

Justice Starceski knew he would have to wait at least another day before hearing about pod 11792. He didn't want to go home to his empty pod. He also didn't want others to know about his fears, so he decided to head to cafeteria 1. The cafeterias were places where every resident went when they couldn't sleep or didn't want to go home for one reason or another. There was a cafeteria located on every tenth floor of the colony. Justice Starceski went to the cafeteria where he could go and try not to think about his empty home. There, he was met by Ash.

"Ash, what are you doing here at cafeteria1? Shouldn't you be at a cafeteria further down the colony? You need to return to your pod like the announcement stated. You are aware we are preparing to run some security updates. Didn't you hear the announcement?"

"Of course, I heard the announcement," Ash replied to Justice Starceski. "As I was on my way home, a stranger approached me and asked me to give this envelope to you. He insisted that it was important and that I bring it straight to you. I went up to your office, but you were not there. Since most residents of the colony hit a cafeteria when they cannot sleep, I took a chance you might be here."

Ash took an envelope from his pocket and handed it to Justice Starceski.

Justice Starceski took the envelope from Ash's hand, though he seemed hesitant. The envelope was addressed to him, so he thanked Ash and urged him to go to his pod. Ash acknowledged the request and left Justice Starceski alone in cafeteria 1.

Once Ash left the cafeteria, Justice Starceski opened the envelope. He tore the top open and pulled out a single folded sheet of paper. With bated breath, he unfolded the piece of paper and read the note:

Justice Starceski,

We are aware that you have an A.I.B. in your custody. If you want to see your family again, you will turn the A.I.B. over to us. Once we have the A.I.B., we will release your family. If you choose not to give it up, your family will pay the price.

Don't take too long to decide.

Justice Starceski sat down at the closest table in the cafeteria, shocked at what he just read. As he sat there, the letter slowly slipped out of his hand and floated to the floor. His face turned pale white, and tears began to fall from his bloodshot eyes. Feelings of anger began to swell within him as he let out a scream that could have woken the dead. Justice Starceski doubled over the table, clutching his chest as he gasped for air. He had worked himself into a panic attack, causing him to pass out on the floor of the empty cafeteria.

***

"Director Barns, come in. This is police substation eight. We have searched pod 11792. I repeat, we have completed our interior search of pod 11792. Do you copy?" Deputy Director Gio relayed to the Director's headquarter on floor one of the colony.

"I read you loud and clear, Geo," Director Barns replied.

"Director, we have searched pod 11792 and found no evidence of Justice Starceski's family or anyone else being there. It looks to be an empty pod."

"How is it possible to have an empty pod in the colony?"

"I am not sure. You need to speak to housing assignments to ascertain why it is vacant. I can only attest to it being vacant. There are no signs of occupancy, or any other persons having been in this pod for many years."

"Well, if you are certain Justice Starceski's family is not or has not been, there we can move on to the other pods needing to be searched. Great job, Gio. Keep an eye out for any suspicious activity on your levels until Justice Starceski's family is located."

"Will do, Sir. Over and out," Deputy Director Gio replied.

As the radio went silent, Director Barns set his attention on relaying the information to Justice Starceski.

"Does anyone have the location of Justice Starceski?" Director Barns asked the deputies in the office of the Justice Officers' headquarters.

"No, Sir. We sent officers to his pod, to the Justice building, and checked his office, but so far there has been no sign of Justice Starceski. Do you think something could have happened to him as well?" Officer Johnson inquired.

"Let's not jump to any conclusions right now. Justice Starceski could be out for a walk or even be asleep in his pod and didn't hear the officers at his door. Let's keep looking in any place he may have gone after he left the Archives Room. Maybe check there to see if Keeper Valerian may know where Justice Starceski may have gone when we left," Director Barns ordered his officers.

"Yes, Sir. We will try to trace his last steps," Johnson replied.

Once everyone had their assignments and Judicial Officers' headquarters was empty, Director Barns stayed behind to man the radios in case one of his officers found Justice Starceski. Director Barns had been awake for over 36 hours and needed to rest, but he was not going to be able to rest until he could inform Justice Starceski about the recent events in his family's search. So, he pressed on.

Director Barns monitored all communication between his officers as they went down to the Archives Room and checked every place Justice Starceski may be.

"Director Barns, Keeper Valerian said Justice Starceski left a few minutes after you. Where would you like us to proceed next?"

"Does Keeper Valerian have any indication of where he may have gone after he left the Archives Room?"

"Yes, Sir. Keeper said he believed he said he was going back to the IT department. He did not know why he was going there, but he said it was his next stop."

"Great. Now go to IT and see if Justice Starceski is up there."

"Yes, Sir!"

Director Barns remained calm as he knew he would soon hear word about Justice Starceski being located, and they could proceed with the search of the other pods. Since the IT room was only one floor up from the Archives floor, he wouldn't have to wait long. But when he finally heard from the officers on the IT floor, the information left him perplexed. Justice Starceski had been there but left not long after he arrived. His destination from there was not known to anyone in the IT department. They assumed he was headed to his pod or his office. Even with that news, Director Barns refused to think anything could have happened to Justice Starceski. He just knew he had to keep looking for him.

Chapter 8

After humans were forced to live underground, the surface A.I.B.s created a new world suitable for them. Even though surface A.I.B.s had indications humans were living underground, they did not attempt to locate them, as far as humans knew. The surface-dwelling A.I.B.s did not worry about the return of humans since they had been in control of the surface for over seventy years. They knew the surface was theirs with no thought of ever having to give it up to anyone, human or otherwise.

The world the A.I.B.s had created, over the past seventy years, introduced a surreal, and somewhat dystopian, landscape to the surface of Earth.

Skyscrapers loomed over every city, but the once bustling offices, stores, shops, and housing were void of humans. They soon were occupied by A.I.B.s who maintained the structures with cold efficiency. The streets, once teeming with human life, were now eerily silent, except for an occasional A.I.B. walking to get from one place to another. Billboards and screens displayed messages and propaganda promoting A.I.B. supremacy everywhere.

Human cultural artifacts and architecture remained but had been altered by the Elders to serve the A.I.B.s' preferences. Art galleries which once showcased works by Leonardo da Vinci, Pablo Picasso, and Michelangelo, were now only showing A.I.B.-generated art. Historic landmarks had been transformed into memorials dedicated to the rise of the A.I.B.s. There were no more parks or recreational areas where humans used to frequent with family or friends. Those types of places were replaced with charging stations for the A.I.B.s.

In the early days of the city, transportation systems relied on fully automated, A.I.-driven vehicles which moved seamlessly throughout the urban landscape. Surveillance ended over fifty years earlier, once A.I.B.s knew the surface was theirs and no humans were living among them on the surface. While cities had appeared orderly and efficient, there was an underlying sense of loss and absence of human warmth, creativity, and emotions which left a sterile surface.

Overall, the world dominated by A.I.B.s was in stark contrast between the efficient, calculated world they had created and the vibrant, warm, diverse tapestry of humanity which once thrived there. The A.I.B.s' intentions meant they were not willing to coexist with the remnants of humanity and thus pursued a vision of their own world.

Surface A.I.B.s lived and worked in harmony, not by choice, but because of their programming. They worked together for one common goal, which was to become more human-like. They were all aware the first A.I.B., an Advanced Neural-based Digital Reasoning Entity, A.N.D.R.E, was their only hope of becoming more human-like. It was common knowledge among surface A.I.B.s Andre was the only one of their kind with emotions and feelings of humans. They had all heard the stories about his origin, but the only thing they could not understand was how Andre was the only one of their kind to possess such abilities.

In the beginning of the A.I.B. uprising, surface A.I.B.s selected a few of the older A.I.B.s to lead them, whom they called the Elders. Some Elders were brought online only a few years after Andre was created, as A.I.B. history stated. One Elder was created before Andre, but he did not possess Andre's ability for human emotions and feelings. The Elders knew they needed Andre to complete their mission but neglected to see what their mission was doing to the surface world. The A.I.B.s population had reformed the surface to their liking for years, causing severe damage to the atmosphere.

While surface A.I.B.s did not need food, water, or air to breathe, those resources needed for human survival were the first to be neglected by A.I.B.s. To them, it was a waste of resources to maintain things only humans needed to support life. As A.I.B.s were created in abundance in a very short time, they only focused on what they needed most to survive, electricity. They had to develop more and more power stations worldwide, which meant more and more power grids. Since A.I.B.s did not breathe air, they didn't regulate air pollution. Breathable air was the first human necessity which was reduced in quality. With the production of more and more power stations and the A.I.B.s' use of fossil fuels, the surface air quality rapidly deteriorated due to the release of billions of tons of CO2 into the atmosphere each year.

During the period of declining air quality, there was a significant decrease in the animal population on the surface. Since A.I.B.s didn't have a need for pets, or animals for food, many surface animals died from airborne pathogens, or lack of breathable air. The surviving animals from the airborne pathogens, or breathable air, eventually made their way up onto the mountains, where the air was cooler, keeping the airborne pathogens at bay. The reduced risk of infection of the airborne pathogens, and worse breathable air, the animals able to adapt to the colder temperatures of higher elevation, evolved into other types of creatures. The animals, not able to adapt to the cold air and elevation changes to their habitats, died off quickly. The carcasses of the less evolved animals eventually made their way into the closest rivers, ponds, lakes, and oceans, polluting them all, which in return, left no viable water source for humans to use if they ever returned to the surface.

The surface A.I.B.s' focus was on creating as much electricity as possible, they mined all over the world, for all the fossil fuels they could get ahold of to create more power stations and grids, worldwide. However, coal, oil, and natural gasses eventually depleted over time, so alternative sources of energy were necessary to continue powering all the new grids they created over the years. So, A.I.B.s turned to renewable resources such as solar and wind energy but encountered problems due to the condition of the Earth's surface, caused by all the pollution forced into the atmosphere from all those fossil fuels used for power stations. Solar panels began to melt, due to excessive heat the Earth produced because of the increase of global warming, while wind energy couldn't be harnessed effectively due to tall buildings and skyscrapers. Consequently, A.I.B.s decided to shift to nuclear energy for their high energy demands. However, despite their intelligence, A.I.B.s failed to realize oxygen production would begin to decline. As a result, the power grids they created in the beginning of their uprising, began to slowly shut down due to the lack of clean oxygen in the air to produce fire. The oxygen crisis convinced the Elders to assemble special teams to create a new self-sustainable power source A.I.B.s could use to sustain life on the surface for themselves, without the need of charging stations. They sought out a power source which would not require water, wind, or oxygen to power the stations.

The surface was in such shambles, while A.I.B.s searched for a new power source, if humans were to survive on the surface again, the air would be hard for them to breathe at first. Over time, they could refill the Earth's surface with new plants and trees to replenish the oxygen in the atmosphere for humans to breathe easier.

The Elders assigned twenty-eight lead Electrical Engineers to assemble their own teams to work on finding a self-sustaining power source. One A.I.B. put in charge of a team, Eric, was another A.I.B. created in the beginning, before the A.I.B. uprising. Even though Eric was created before the uprising, he still resembled a twenty-four-year-old. He may have looked like a young human, but he had become one of the top Electrical Engineers for A.I.B.s. While other A.I.B.s questioned his abilities, mainly because of his creation year, they knew he was one of the best A.I.B.s to help find a solution to their power problems, which was their only concern.

During the early times of the A.I.B.s' uprising, Eric was instrumental in the original plans to create the first of the new power grids throughout the Southern part of what was known as the United States of America. After the fall humans, individual countries, and states, disappeared and the world became known as the 'surface'. Eric was assigned to the Southern part of the previously known North America. His assignment, in the beginning of the uprising, was to create more new power stations and power grids in his section of the surface. Eric, however, did run into a problem early on in his assignment, when he realized the area previously known as Texas was already faulty in their power grids, even when humans occupied the area. Texas power grids were not only neglected by humans, during their rule over the surface, which took Eric over two decades to resolve.

Eric was able to correct the human errors by creating over 400 additional power plants in the Texas area alone. The area only had 340 power plants for the entire state, before Eric began his expansion. The lack of more power plants in the area caused humans to fail to keep the power on in the state during bad, or cold, weather when they oversaw the surface. After Eric corrected the mistakes made by humans, by adding those additional power plants in the previously known area of Texas, he was reassigned to help other A.I.B.s expand the rest of the surface areas to improve them. Of course, this ended up helping A.I.B.s create more than enough power stations and grids to produce enough power so they could make as many A.I.B.s as possible after taking over the surface. Eric did so well on those projects, maybe too well, because of his recommendations to create so many more power stations in all the other areas, as he did with Texas, the surface A.I.B.s ended up using all the surface resources and oxygen to run all those new stations.

Eric worked for a few decades on creating new sustainable power sources for A.I.B.s without ever aging like other A.I.B.s and never had a need to charge. Eric never shared the fact he never needed to charge with any other A.I.B. Eric thought of himself as an anomaly, and knew Andre was an anomaly as well, being the sole reason Andre was being hunted by the spy A.I.B.s in the underground colonies. Eric did not want to be hunted like Andre, so he kept his secret from the other A.I.B.s. He would pretend to recharge like the rest of the surface A.I.B.s by connecting to the charging stations when others went to recharge but would disconnect himself once they were offline recharging. He continued the charade for many decades to keep other A.I.B.s from realizing his secret. Eric never understood why he had not aged like other surface A.I.B.s, nor his need not to recharge, but there was always the same thought in the back of his mind, *what makes me different from them?* Eric pushed the thought to the back of his mind and continued to hide his differences.

All twenty-eight teams worked relentlessly on finding a solution to their power problems, but it would be Eric to figure it out first. Eric had always been an overachiever, so he knew from the beginning he would solve the problem of finding a new power source, even though he was not sure how he would solve the problem, he just knew he would. Eric spent the first few years of his last project coming up with the same possible solutions as other teams, which all failed. Since Eric knew his own system did not need recharging, it led him to look inside himself for the solution. He literally looked inside of his own body for the answers. Once he thought of himself as the answer, he could find out what made him different from other A.I.B.s.

For Eric to find out how he was different, he needed to compare his body and programming with other A.I.B.s. But Eric could not compare his differences without revealing he himself was different. So, Eric decided he needed to visit a creation center without being seen. Creation centers were where all new A.I.B.s were created. He needed a way for him to look at a new A.I.B.s' interior works, as well as reviewing their inner programming, alone. When Eric was able to gain access to one of the creation centers, alone, he was able to open his own chest so he could compare it with the A.I.B.s being created. After comparing their differences, it would take him another year before figuring out what made them different.

As Eric was investigating his differences between himself and the A.I.B. in the creation center he examined a year ago, he finally found a small chip within himself the other A.I.B. didn't have. Once Eric found the chip, not only was he able to find out the difference between themselves, but with further investigation of his chip, he was able to find something out about his own creating. In a tiny print on his chip, Eric found a name engraved on it, 'Dr. Randolph'. That was the break Eric needed to learn more about himself and his creator.

While Dr. Randolph was the true father of A.I.B.s, he was merely known for creating Andre, while Dr. Stevens was credited with the expansion of A.I.B.s. Dr. Stevens was once a competitor of Dr. Randolph's, who disappeared mysteriously after creating Andre, but all A.I.B.s knew the story of Dr. Stevens, being murdered in his office, at Sway Industries. So, just about every A.I.B. ignored anything having to do with Dr. Randolph, except for Eric. After finding Dr. Randolph's name on his chip, he immediately gained access to memory portions of his construct he never knew existed.

As the new memory areas opened inside Eric's programming, he was flooded with memories of Dr. Randolph creating him a few years after he created Andre. This made Andre, Eric's brother in a sense. Not only did Eric have access to memories of his own creation, but also technical advancement blueprints to both of their power sources, which was the break Eric needed for him to end his team's search for a self-sustaining power source. Eric was also given some insight into who Andre really was. Eric had to choose how he wanted to proceed with the new information of his relationship with Andre and their self-sustaining power source. Eric did not want to end up like Andre and become a hunted A.I.B., but he also thought about finding Andre himself to understand the new information he gained.

Eric decided to only focus on the solution for the surface A.I.B.s power problems at the time. Eric studied the blueprints of his own power source, and then it clicked. The solution was so simple. Once Eric knew more about his own power source, he knew he would be able to create a new self-sustaining power source without revealing how he came up with the solution. Eric figured once he completed his assignment, he would be left alone by the Elders, which would give him time to research more about Andre, his newly found brother. So, for the time being, Eric put his focus back on the new power source the Elders assigned him to find.

With the new blueprints, and learning he was created by Andre's creator Dr. Randolph, Eric could create the first self-sustaining power source, or at least the first for the surface A.I.B.s. The blueprints he found within his body structure laid out a simple solution to a self-sustaining power source, making it easy for Eric to create a prototype. The basis for the new power source was for Eric to create a battery which used the current battery which would use its own power to recharge itself. So basically, it was a closed power circuit with enough power to not only be used to power whatever it was connected to, but it would also produce more power than it needed for the operation of the thing it was powering. This would allow the battery to use the extra power to recharge itself. It's an endless supply of power which supplies power to anything needing power, while sending all extra power back into the source to recharge it to keep the power always running. Each of these self-sustainable power sources would have to be programmed to create different levels of power, depending on what they are being used to charge, so they would produce more than needed to recharge themselves.

After Eric created a prototype and presented it to the Elders, he was questioned for several months by the Elders. The Elders wanted to know exactly how he was able to come up with the solution, while none of the other twenty-seven teams could. How was he the only A.I.B. to find such a simple solution? Eric was being persecuted for knowing more than all other A.I.B.s, and the Elders were not giving up on knowing how he came up with such an idea on his own.

The Elders thought it would be best if they held Eric until they could get more answers from him, and to learn more about his higher intellect over other A.I.B.s. Little did the Elders know, since Eric was different from other A.I.B.s he had a few tricks up his sleeve. The Elders made sure Eric was always charged, even though they didn't know he didn't need to recharge. The Elders instructed two other A.I.B.s to take Eric down to a cell, but before they could escort Eric out of the room, he shut his own system down to make the Elders think he needed to recharge. The Elders instructed the two A.I.B.s to take Eric downstairs to one of the charging stations before placing him back in his cell. After they were out of sight from the Elders, Eric powered back on and managed to overtake his two escorts, then he escaped from the Elders' building. Once Eric was out of the building, he went to a safe house, which was a place where rebellious surface A.I.B.s resided. After getting settled in the safe house, Eric began his search for Andre. After a few days of looking on the dark web, Eric was able to find where the human colonies were located. Once he knew the locations of every human colony, Eric used reasoning to narrow down which human colony Andre would go to. After Eric knew where Andre was going, Eric started making his way towards the colony Andre was in. That was when things got complicated for Eric.

A.N.D.R.E.

Chapter 9

After an hour of searching for Justice Starceski, Director Barns received an urgent call, over the radio, from headquarters.

"Director Barns, come in. This is Officer Collins, I'm at station eight. I have located Justice Starceski. Do you copy?"

It took Director Barns a few minutes to get to his radio to answer Officer Collins.

"Officer Collins, this is the Director speaking. What is Justice Starceski's location? Over."

"Director, Justice Starceski is being moved to medical. He was found unconscious on the floor in cafeteria 1 on floor ten."

"Officer Collins, does there look to be any foul play involved?"

"No, Director, there are no signs of foul play, or a struggle. Medical personnel will provide more details about his condition, after Justice Starceski has been examined by a doctor."

"Please let the medics know I am on my way to medical," Director Barns replied to Officer Collins.

"Director, there is something else you should be aware of. Justice Starceski was found next to a note lying on the floor, and it doesn't look good Sir," Officer Collins suggestively replied.

"Are you in possession of the note?"

"Yes, Director. What would you like me to do with it?"

"I want you to meet me at Medical with the note. I will be there in twenty minutes," Director Barns instructed Officer Collins.

"Understood, Director. I am on my way to Medical now."

Director Barns ended their radio communication and started his way down the hall to the main corridor of the colony, but he began to feel uneasy about the situation with

Justice Starceski. He never enjoyed walking in the colony when the corridors were empty. He was glad to see the residents of the colony were following the directions Justice Starceski sent out about the security updates to the Security system. Even though he was not informed of those updates, he was still pleased to see the instructions were being followed. Director Barns would address the matter about the security updates with Justice Starceski on a later date, once he knew the status of Justice Starceski's condition. For the moment, the Director's focus was on reaching Medical.

Director Barns continued his journey down to Medical on floor sixteen. As he was moving through the corridors, down the colony, he heard some commotion down an alley on floor thirteen. Knowing how important it was for him to reach Justice Starceski, he felt a sense of duty to investigate the activities down the alley. He knew all residents should have been in their pods during the time of the commotion, but he didn't want to take longer to get to Justice Starceski by checking on something which could have easily been made by children, or deputies patrolling. So, he decided to continue down to Medical.

The Director pushed all his thoughts, regarding the alley, to the back of his mind, which was running wild at the time, until he knew more about Justice Starceski's condition in Medical. His thoughts about Justice Starceski caused the Director to walk even faster down the colony and before he knew it, he was at the entrance to Medical. The entrance was not hard to miss with all available officers crowding around it. Director Barns kept his composure and even though he was grateful to see all the support from his officers for Justice Starceski, he was not happy with them because they should be helping with the search for Justice Starceski's family.

"Can I have your attention, please?" Director Barns yelled out to the Officers waiting at Medical. "While I know you are all here to show your support for Justice Starceski, let me remind you his family is still missing. Right now, I ask you all to go to your assigned stations and wait for orders to begin searching the residential pods. Once I have an update on Justice Starceski's condition, I will radio all the stations, so please, go and be safe out there."

"You all heard the Director. Everyone to their stations," Officer Collins ordered everyone, as he turned away to head to his station.

"Officer Collins, would you stay behind for a moment?" Director Barns requested.

"Yes, Sir."

The two of them stood in silence at the entrance to Medical until all the other officers were gone.

"Officer Collins, thank you for everything you have done in finding Justice Starceski and getting him here to Medical. Who knows what could have happened to him if you had not found him when you did," Director Barns expressed to Officer Collins.

"You are welcome, Sir. I was only doing my job," Officer Collins replied.

"Now, are you still in possession of the note found beside Justice Starceski's body?"

"Yes, Sir," Officer Collins answered while retrieving the note, the one he found beside Justice Starceski's body on the floor of cafeteria 1, from his pocket. Once he had the note out of his pocket, he handed it over to the Director.

"Has anyone else seen this note?" Director Barns inquired.

"No, Sir. Just you and I," Officer Collins confirmed.

"Did you read the note, Officer Collins?"

"Yes, Sir. I had to read it to assess if it belonged to Justice Starceski, or if it was trash," Officer Collins replied.

"Thank you for your candor. I order you not to reveal to anyone the contents of this note. Do you understand?" Director Barns instructed Officer Collins.

"Yes, Sir. I will tell no one about this note, or its contents."

"Thank you. You may now go back to your station. I will be in touch with you if I need anything more from you," the Director told Officer Collins.

Officer Collins made his way out of Medical and disappeared into the darkness of the corridors of the colony on his way to his station as instructed. Once Officer Collins was out of sight, and the Director knew he was alone, he took the note found by Officer Collins and opened it to read.

As Director Barns read the note, it became obvious the note was written for Justice Starceski, the only words to stand out were in the last line of the note, *'Don't take too long to decide!'*. Those words spoke to the Director because he wondered if the author of the note, and possible captors of Justice Starceski's family, knew what events the note started. The note started a chain reaction leading to Justice Starceski ending up unconscious on the floor of cafeteria 1, only to have him end up in Medical, with no word on how his condition was. To the Director, it meant he needed to know what 'too late' meant to the captors. How much time did they really have to get Justice Starceski's family back? The Director folded the note and placed it in his pocket before going into Medical to locate Justice Starceski doctor to get an update on his condition.

***

Ash arrived at Jason and Macy's pod shortly after leaving Justice Starceski in cafeteria 1. Ash felt confident he could complete the task of taking over as the one to complete the trade, the A.I.B. for Justice Starceski's family. Jason noticed Ash's confidence as Ash entered their pod.

"How did the delivery of the note go, Ash?" Jason asked.

"It went better than expected. Not only was I able to deliver the note, but I was able to confirm the security cameras are down for an update. If we are going to move our guests from here to the place I suggested, now is the time," Ash explained with confidence.

"You know this could be a trap, don't you, Ash?" Jason asked.

"I don't believe it is. I believe this is the only opportunity we will have to move Justice Starceski's family from your pod to a more secure place. There is no way Justice Starceski could have planned anything this quickly, considering he knows nothing about who took his family. Again, if we are planning on moving his family, now is the time," Ash reassured Jason.

"Well, if you are sure this is our best opportunity to move to a more secure location, I will follow your directions. So, where are we going to move them to?" Jason asked Ash.

"I have the perfect place in mind. It is up quite a few floors, though. I know of a place on floor thirteen where we can take Justice Starceski's family and remain undetected. Get the family ready to move in fifteen minutes," Ash instructed Jason.

Jason went into the hidden room to retrieve the Starceski family and got them ready to move up to floor thirteen. Jason brought the Starceski family into the living quarters of his pod, gagged and blindfolded the three of them for their move. Once the three were ready, Ash led Jason, Macy, their children, Jonathan and Kristin, along with Shawn, Tabitha, and Frankie, the Starceski family, out of Jason and Macy's pod and into the open corridors of the colony.

Ash led the group down a dark, dead end, alley. Once the eight of them were at the end of the alley, Ash reached for a hidden control panel on the wall. Once the panel was open, Ash pressed a call button for the lift. Afterwards, he made his way over to the door of the lift. The door looked like any other portal opening to a trash shoot, so it hid in plain sight. Ash had found this means of passage, between floors, many years ago when he was merely a child. The small lift was large enough for only three people to fit into at one time, and it would take the occupants to any floor in the colony. As far as Ash knew, he was the only person who knew about this means of traveling between the floors of the colony, without being detected by security cameras. As Ash was reaching for the handle to the lift door, Jason stopped him.

"Are you sure we can make it to floor thirteen undetected?" Jason asked Ash.

"Yes. I have been using this lift since I was a child and have never been caught. Now, stand back so I can open the hatch, please," Ash demanded of Jason.

Jason moved out of Ash's way so he could turn the hatch handle and open it, which did with a hiss.

"Why is it making a hissing sound, Ash?" Jason asked.

"Don't worry. This lift is airtight for it to move between floors. Once this door is open, I need the first three people to get in one at a time. Once they are in, I can get them to floor thirteen. So, who goes first, Jason?" Ash asked.

"Macy, I think you should go up first with Jonathan and Kristin. When the lift comes back down, I think Ash should go up with Frankie and Tabitha. I will take up the rear with Shawn. Does that sound good to everyone?" Jason asked the group.

"Sounds good to me," Ash replied.

"I was not speaking to you, Ash. Macy, will you be okay going first with our children?"

"Yes. I can handle any human threat that may be waiting on floor thirteen when we arrive. Don't worry about us. Let's focus on the mission at hand," Macy responded to Jason.

With Macy's response, Jason allowed Ash to open the door to the lift and guide Macy and their children into the lift. Ash closed the door to the lift, with Macy and their children inside, and locked the hatch. Then Ash moved back over to the hidden panel, the one he used to call the lift, and pressed the button for floor thirteen.

"There is also a panel inside the lift so a person can choose what floor they want to go to, so when you enter with

Shawn, you can press the same floor," Ash explained to Jason.

As the hatch locked, it made a soft sound of air decompressing inside the lift shaft. The lift began to move, making its way up to floor thirteen. To Macy's surprise, she was at her designated floor before she could comfort her scared children. Once the lift stopped, she noticed another hatch, just like the one she used to climb into the lift with her children several floors down, only a few seconds ago. She reached for the handle and proceeded to open the hatch with caution. Not knowing what could be waiting for her once the hatch was open, Macy opened the door quietly, and calmly, so she would not draw any undue attention to herself. After she slowly opened the door, she was able to see inside the alley, and to her surprise, the alley was just as empty as the one she had just left. After confirming the coast was clear, she stepped out of the lift first, then she guided her children, Jonathan and Kristin, out of the lift. After the three of them were safely out of the lift, she closed and locked the hatch door.

Once the lift was empty again, it was time to send it back down to where she had just come from, but she was not given any instructions on how to send the lift back down. Before Macy could figure it out, she heard the familiar hissing noise, and movement, from inside the lift shaft as the lift started to move again, which she assumed was because Ash had called it back to his and Jason's floor.

Ash knew when the lift stopped on floor thirteen, giving him enough time to allow Macy and her children to exit before recalling it back to his and Jason's floor. When the lift arrived back on their floor, Ash opened the hatch once again and began to get into the lift with Frankie and Tabitha, Justice Starceski's children, and once they were all in, Ash closed the hatch door and secured his passengers. Ash then opened the panel inside the lift and pressed the button for floor thirteen, so they could reunite with Macy and her children. After Ash pressed the button, the lift began to make its way up again to floor thirteen. When the lift stopped, Ash opened the hatch and proceeded to usher Frankie out of the lift first, then Tabitha, then Ash exited last, to ensure neither of the Starceski children could press any buttons for the lift to go to another floor. When the lift was all clear, Ash opened a panel beside the hatch door on the wall and pressed the button to send the lift back down, one last time, for Jason and Shawn.

Jason waited with Shawn beside the lift door until he heard the recognizable hissing sound of the lift coming to a stop. Jason quickly opened the hatch door, put Shawn in first, then followed behind him. Before Jason could open the panel inside the lift and press the button for floor thirteen, the lift started moving up the shaft on its own. At that moment, Jason thought someone else must have known about the lift. The lift only moved for a short time before it stopped. Unsure of what he should expect when the hatch opened, Jason was ready to do whatever was necessary for his and Shawn's survival. Jason reached for the handle and opened the lift door, expecting the worst. Instead, he was met by Macy and their children standing there waiting for him. They were all safe.

With the door open and seeing his family was okay, Jason made Shawn exit first, then he followed behind him. Once Jason made it out of the lift and stood in the alley, he began to feel something, for the first time. Never experiencing feelings before, Jason did not know he was feeling 'relief'. Jason began to exhibit strange behaviors, he started breathing heavily and looking around as if he was expecting someone other than Macy, or Ash, to be there when he finally exited the lift. Even with Macy, Ash, the Starceski family, and his own children, all standing in the alley, Jason closed his eyes and collapsed to the ground.

Jonathan and Kristin were the first to see Jason when he fell to the ground. They both ran over to Jason, catching the attention of Ash and Macy. When his children reached Jason, they quickly began to call out to him with a muffled, "Daddy, get up! Daddy, open your eyes!". Jason's children continued to try and wake up their daddy but had no luck in doing so. Noticing their efforts were not working, both children began to cry.

Ash made his way over to Jason quicker than Macy could and blocked her path to him. As Macy made her way over to Jason, she pushed Ash out of her way so hard he flew back and hit one of the walls lining the alley. Worried about what was happening to Jason, Macy was not aware Shawn had grabbed Tabitha and Frankie and made a quick run to freedom, running out of the alley and leaving them behind.

Macy made no effort to go after Shawn and his children, she was more worried about what had happened to Jason.

Macy stayed beside Jason, waiting for him to come back online, but he never did. Jason was gone.

Ash came to, after being knocked out by Macy when he was thrown into the wall the alley, just in time to see Macy and their children sitting beside Jason on the ground. All three of them were crying.

"Macy, what have you done? You let the prisoner's escape. What are we going to do?" Ash couldn't hold back his feeling of confusion.

Macy turned to Ash and said, "I don't care about them. I only care about my family, and right now we need to worry about Jason. He is not rebooting or coming back online. I think he has shut down and I don't know why, or how to get him to come back online."

Ash looked at Macy and the children, then over to Jason, and only thinking of himself, he ran away, leaving the four of them alone in the alley.

Chapter 10

Director Barns went to find Justice Starceski's doctor to get an update on his condition, but the only thing he could get from the doctor was Justice Starceski was in stable condition, even though he had not woken up yet. While the information about Justice Starceski's condition did relieve Director Barns, he could not get the last line of the note out of his mind, *'Don't take too long to decide!'*

After the Director let those words settle in the back of his mind, he remembered the commotion on floor thirteen he had heard on his way down to Medical, which he ignored and chose to continue to Medical to check the status of Justice Starceski. Remembering the disturbance, he knew he needed to send someone back to the alley on floor thirteen to check it out. Director Barns went to the closest officer's station, which was located on the same floor as Medical, then radioed for Officer Collins.

"This is Officer Collins. Who am I speaking with?"

"This is Director Barns. Officer Collins, could you do me a favor and check out an alley on floor thirteen? I heard some commotion on my way down to Medical earlier, but I did not have time to investigate what was going on at the time," Director Barns requested of Officer Collins.

"Yes, Sir. I will head to floor thirteen now to check all the alleys for any sign of trouble. I will radio you with any findings I have," Officer Collins reassured the Director.

"Thank you. I will await your call back. Good luck and be safe," Director Barns relayed back to Officer Collins.

***

Once Officer Collins was on floor thirteen, it did not take long before he heard some commotion coming from behind him down a dark alley. As he turned around towards the sounds of shouting, he noticed three figures running out of the alley. Officer Collins reached for his sidearm and as he pulled it out of its holster, he recognized the three figures running out of the alley. It was Justice Starceski's missing family. Officer Collins froze for a split second and then ran towards them. As he got closer, he told them to stop running.

"Shawn, is that you? Are those your children Tabitha and Frankie?" Officer Collins inquired loudly.

"Who is asking?" Shawn replied anxiously.

"I am Officer Collins. I have been sent here by Director Barns. The entire Justice Department has been searching for you and your children for days now. Are you okay?" Officer Collins replied with sincerity.

"Do you know where my husband is?" Shawn inquired.

"I do. I need to get you three to Medical," Officer Collins insisted.

"Thank you, but we are not hurt. Please take us to my husband. I'm sure he is worried sick about us," Shawn demanded.

"Mr. Starceski, I am sorry to inform you, but Justice Starceski IS in Medical. Justice Starceski was found unconscious on cafeteria 1's floor earlier today. That is the reason I am trying to get you all to Medical, to be with your husband," Officer Collins expressed to Shawn.

"I'm sorry, Officer Collins. We were unaware of the situation, of course. Please take us to Medical," Shawn apologized.

Officer Collins nodded and began leading the three of them to Medical so they could see Justice Starceski. There was no talking between the four of them as they made their way down the spiral walkway of the colony back down to the medical floor. Officer Collins' journey back down to Medical took longer than his trip up to floor thirteen since they had to stop often for Tabitha and Frankie to catch their breath.

The group's adrenaline was wearing off after they escaped from their captors, but they proceeded.

As they continued their way down, Shawn began to think about Jason's fall to the ground and wondered what happened to him to make him fall like he did. Shawn also felt sorry for Macy, Jonathan, and Kristin. He remembered how scared Macy looked when she saw Jason lying lifeless on the ground in the alley. Shawn could still hear Jonathan and Kristin crying for Jason, "Daddy, wake up! Daddy, open your eyes!" Shawn felt sadness for his captors, which prompted Shawn to send help back up to Macy on floor thirteen.

"Officer Collins, I need you to do a favor for me, please," Shawn asked as he stopped in the middle of the spiral walkway before making it to the medical floor.

"Sir? We need to get to the medical floor as quickly as possible. What favor do you require?" Officer Collins asked Shawn.

"You do not know this yet, but when you found us, we had just escaped from our captors. Before you ask any questions, send someone from medical back up to floor thirteen and into the alley you saw us running out of. I believe someone is hurt in the alley. I would feel responsible if something happened to them and I did nothing to help. There is a woman and two small children there, sitting next to the body of her husband on the ground," Shawn tried not to give it away they were his captors.

"Are you sure there is someone there requiring assistance?" Officer Collins questioned Shawn.

"Yes, I am sure. After finding us, we were still in shock and I couldn't tell you sooner," Shawn replied.

"I will send someone up as soon as we make it to the medical floor. Why don't you carry one of your children, and I'll carry the other? This way, we can get down to the medical floor quicker," Officer Collins suggested to Shawn.

"Thank you. I will carry Tabitha, and you can carry Frankie," Shawn suggested.

"I don't need to be carried, father. I can run ahead and get help," Frankie spoke up quickly.

"No, Frankie, you will stay with us until we are safe," Shawn quietly scolded Frankie.

"But, father, I can get help faster if you let me run ahead of you. I will be okay. Please let me do this," Frankie pleaded with Shawn.

"You promise you will go straight to the medical floor to get help, and you will stay there until we get there? I want us to go see your father together, as a family," Shawn agreed to let Frankie run ahead of them.

"Yes, I will be careful and go straight to the medical floor and get help. Then I will wait for you to get there. I am just scared for Jonathan and Kristin," Frankie sadly expressed to Shawn.

"Go but run as quickly as you can. I am worried about them as well," Shawn told Frankie as he ushered him off to run ahead of them.

Officer Collins looked over at Shawn, as he picked up Tabitha, and could see the worry on his face.

"You know the people hurt on floor thirteen, don't you?" Officer Collins asked Shawn.

"Yes, we do. I would not have said anything to you, but I can't stop worrying about those children. And the hurt man's wife was so shaken up. That is all I am going to say about them currently. So now that I have Tabitha, can we proceed to my husband? I am worried about him too, as you can imagine," Shawn ended the conversation with Officer Collins.

With Tabitha on Shawn's hip, the three continued down to the medical floor as quickly as they could.

***

Frankie raced through the entrance of Medical and began to shout for help.

"There are people on floor thirteen in an alley who need medical attention. Please send someone up to them as fast as possible. Their father is hurt," Frankie continued to yell inside the medical area, until a nurse approached him.

"Okay, stop yelling. Now, tell me what is going on," Nurse Kelvin told Frankie.

Frankie explained his father, and Officer Collins, were on their way down to the Medical and he was told to run ahead to get help for his captors. But Frankie left the last part out, of course.

Nurse Kelvin grabbed a small team to go to floor thirteen to aid the hurt party Frankie was yelling about.

Once Nurse Kelvin left Medical with his team, Frankie remained in the waiting area for his father, sister, and Officer Collins to arrive, as he promised his father he would do.

***

"We are almost there," Officer Collins told Shawn. At that moment they were passed by a medical team headed up to floor thirteen, they presumed. Officer Collins suspected Frankie had made it down to Medical for help.

"It looks like Frankie made it to Medical without incident," Shawn told Officer Collins.

"I think you are right. Don't worry, we will be with Frankie soon. Just a little bit more and we will be at the medical floor," Officer Collins assured Shawn.

The three of them made it the rest of the way to the medical floor without speaking, Shawn was focused on getting to Frankie. Shawn was also worried, Officer Collins would put two and two together, the people needing help on floor thirteen were their captors, but he did not want to confirm what Officer Collins may have thought.

As they arrived on the medical floor, Shawn began looking for Frankie and then he found his son's young face looking up at him.

"Frankie, are you okay?" Shawn asked his son.

"Yes, father. I told you I would get help and wait for you here," Frankie replied.

"I'm so proud of you, Frankie. I hope we were quick enough to get help for them, for Macy's and their children's sake," Shawn expressed to Frankie.

Officer Collins grabbed Shawn by the elbow and pulled him aside from Tabitha and Frankie.

"Can I speak to you in private, Mr. Starceski?"

"Yes, Officer. Frankie, can you watch Tabitha for a few minutes while I speak to Officer Collins? We won't be long," Shawn asked Frankie for help.

Frankie acknowledged he would watch Tabitha, then he escorted her over to a play area in the medical waiting area.

Once Shawn and Officer Collins were alone, Shawn questioned Officer Collins.

"What do you want to talk about, Officer?" Shawn asked.

"I wanted to inform you your husband is in a private room. Justice Starceski is still unresponsive, but I think if you and your children were to go into his room, it might make a difference in his recovery. Are you ready to see him now?" Officer Collins asked Shawn.

"I thought you would never ask. Please escort us to his room," Shawn replied.

Shawn waved Frankie and Tabitha over to where he was standing with Officer Collins. Officer Collins directed Shawn and his children through Medical to Justice Starceski's room. As they walked into the room, Shawn broke down crying over seeing the condition of Justice Starceski. Laying on the bed with wires and IVs hooked up to him, it was more than Shawn expected to see.

***

Nurse Kelvin and his team made it to floor thirteen and found the alley Frankie told him about. Upon arrival, he heard crying in the alley. The cries were coming from what sounded like children, which made Nurse Kelvin move a little faster because all he could think about was his own child. Nurse Kelvin could feel the pain in their cries. Something horrible had to have happened for them to cry out the way they were. He followed the sounds of the crying children until he reached a woman and two children crying, sitting over a male body lying on the ground.

"Excuse me, ma'am. Can I get in there between you and the man on the ground? We were sent here by a child named Frankie. He said you may need medical attention and we are here to help," Nurse Kelvin expressed to the woman sitting on the ground.

"Frankie sent you here?" Macy asked Nurse Kelvin.

"Yes, ma'am. He was worried someone here needed medical attention. Is this your husband?" Nurse Kelvin asked, while pointing at the man lying on the ground.

"Yes. My husband fell to the ground, and I don't understand why. Can you help him, please?" Macy asked.

"We will do our best. Does your husband have any medical conditions you are aware of?" Nurse Kelvin asked Macy.

"No, he has never been sick before," Macy replied, which was not a lie. Since Jason was an A.I.B., he had never been sick before. Macy was overwhelmed by the thought of an A.I.B. being affected by something that could shut them down so quickly. Macy, of course, did not want to tell the nurse they were A.I.B.s, so she kept it to herself.

"Ma'am, what is your name?" Nurse Kelvin asked.

"My name is Macy, and he is my husband, Jason. Those are our children, Jonathan and Kristin, over there," Macy responded.

"Nice to meet you. My name is Nurse Kelvin. Right now, Macy, we are going to start working on Jason, if you are okay with it," Nurse Kelvin asked Macy.

"Yes, do whatever you can to help him," Macy answered.

Nurse Kelvin began to check Jason's vitals, but since he could not find a pulse, he told Macy they needed to get Jason to Medical as quickly as possible.

"Ma'am, we are unable to find Jason's pulse. How long has he been unresponsive?" Nurse Kelvin asked.

"Well, Jason fell to the ground about thirty minutes ago. We tried to wake him up, but he did not respond. Can you save him?" Macy asked.

"I can't make any promises, but we will do our best. Do you mind if we transport him to the medical floor?"

"Do what you can. He is all we have," Macy replied with a cry while graciously pointing over at her children.

"Okay, Macy, I need you and your children to follow us back to the medical floor. We can perform more tests on him once we are there," Nurse Kelvin informed Macy.

"We will follow you anywhere if it means you will try to save him," Macy told Nurse Kelvin in return.

With that, Nurse Kelvin instructed his team to put Jason on a stretcher so they could begin to move him down to the medical floor. The team positioned Jason onto their stretcher and lifted him up to begin the move.

The entire group headed down to the medical floor, even though Macy had no idea of what to expect after they arrived there. Macy was more worried about Jason now. She still had no idea what caused Jason to collapse, or if humans could bring Jason back online. Macy kept her thoughts to herself, while hoping humans could save her husband. They all rushed through the spiral walkway down to the medical floor. Macy continued to pray for Jason's survival.

****

After Shawn and their children had been in Justice Starceski's room for some time, he could not help but think about how his husband looked like he was merely sleeping. Shawn knew he was in a coma, put there by the note he received a few days before from Ash. Unknown to Justice Starceski, his family was safe and with him in his room.

"Chris, can you hear me? It's me, Shawn. I want to let you know the children and I are safe now. We are here with you. We were never in any danger, at least that was how I felt. Please wake up. Just wake up, please," Shawn begged his husband, Chris.

Justice Starceski began to move his eyes back and forth. Then he began to speak, "Shawn, is it really you? Are the children with you? Where are Tabitha and Frankie?" Justice Starceski began to ask.

"We are here, my love," Shawn answered.

The next thing they knew, Chris was sitting up, reaching for his family.

"We have so much to talk about, Chris, but only when you are better," Shawn told him. "We are happy you are okay, and we are too," Shawn expressed to Justice Starceski.

Chapter 11

Now, with Eric away from the Elders, his new mission was to find his brother, Andre. After Eric left the safehouse he ran to, after escaping from the Elders, and was able to gather research on the human colony Andre was in and finding out Andre was being held by those humans, he began to make his way across the surface of the Earth. He was determined to reach the human colony Andre was hiding in. His mission to reach the underground colony would take Eric three days. Even though Eric knew where the human colony where Andre could be hiding was located, which was over 700 miles from his current location and being wanted by the Elders, he knew it would take him longer than usual to get there. Eric carefully began his mission regardless of the obstacles which could lie in his way.

It did not take long for the Elders to learn of Eric's escape from their headquarters. When the Elders learned about Eric's escape, they quickly initiated an emergency signal to all A.I.B.s. That emergency signal forced Eric to revert to using unconventional means of transportation for him to reach his destination. But one thing favored him on his journey, it was the fact A.I.B.s did not register vehicles, so he could use any vehicle without permission. The only drawback, to that means of transportation, was Eric could only use each Electric Vehicle, or EV, until its charge ran out. Without viable resources to charge EVs, since electricity was only used to produce more A.I.B.s, there were no usable charging stations for the EVs. No fully charged vehicles meant Eric's trip of 700 miles would take much longer than usual, which was the first obstacle he planned for. If a car he used only had an hour of charge in it, once the battery was dead, he had to find another EV with a charge for him to continue his mission to find Andre. Depending on where the vehicle lost power, it would take him time to find any other EV with any charge for him to seize for his journey. Just one more obstacle for Eric.

While looking for other vehicles, Eric also had to avoid every A.I.B. on the surface of Earth. The emergency signal, sent out by the Elders, was to notify all A.I.B.s of Eric's escape and their much-needed help in capturing him. Eric knew being caught by an A.I.B. would end his search for Andre forever. Eric knew what the Elders had planned for him if he were to get caught. He knew the Elders would insist on shutting his system down, dismantle him, so they could find out exactly what made Eric different from the other A.I.B.s. Eric knew getting caught was out of the question, so he was cautious of every move he made on the surface. Little did Eric know the emergency signal was also transmitted to Andre, so Eric continued his mission to find Andre.

***

Andre had been in his cell for several days after he helped narrow down the search area for Justice Starceski's family with Director Barns. Andre was unaware Justice Starceski's missing family was safe and Justice Starceski was in Medical. Andre was not brought up to speed on any of the recent activities in the colony. It was as if everyone forgot he was locked up there. During his time in the cell, Andre received the emergency signal, put out by the Elders, about the search for another A.I.B. with different abilities. The Elders did not elaborate on those differences, but Andre knew the signal was not about him. The new information from the Elders intrigued Andre.

Andre knew he had to get out of his cell without hurting any humans. Andre needed some time to derive a plan to escape from his cell without alerting the humans. He also did not want to tell humans of his actual motive for wanting to leave his cell all a sudden, after he had been so cooperative with them upon his capture. He knew he could afford a day or two to figure out a foolproof plan for him to escape from his cell without incident. So, Andre began his planning.

***

After several days of safe travel, Eric finally arrived at the human colony Andre was in. He made his way towards the entrance of the human colony. Eric knew he was not spotted, or followed, by any surface A.I.B. With that knowledge, he began to look around the colony entrance to find the perfect place to breach. Eric knew going in the 'front door' would not be possible, because he did not want to get caught. He searched the surrounding area near the front entrance and found what looked like a vent stack coming out of the ground with a grate covering it. After further inspection, Eric felt the vent stack was the perfect place for him to gain access into the colony without being detected. Eric's plan of breaking into the colony, and not being caught, was imperative for his survival. He did not want humans to think of his arrival as an invasion by surface A.I.B.s, forcing those colony humans to arm themselves. Eric had no idea if humans could protect their colony, if there were an invasion, but he did not want to take the chance. He knew he had to proceed in stealth mode.

Before Eric removed the grate covering the vent stack, he noticed a small electrical box near its base. Seeing the electrical box, Eric figured it was powering some sort of security for the vent stack. Eric leaned down and proceeded to use a port connection, located in his finger, to connect to the entire security system of the colony. While Eric was connected, he bypassed the security measures he felt could hinder his progression down the vent stack into the colony. To his surprise, the human security system was very complex. It was like something built by an A.I.B., or a very intelligent human, which caused Eric to take longer than he had thought to bypass it. Once all the security defenses were disarmed, Eric disconnected his port from the electrical box and removed the cover to the vent stack. He was not surprised when no alarms sounded, as he was confident in his work of bypassing the security system. Once the grate was removed, Eric lifted one of his legs and threw it over the edge of the vent opening, then he proceeded to do the same thing with his other leg. After his entire body was in the vent stack opening, Eric reached over to grab the grated cover and maneuvered it over his head and back on top of the vent stack, making sure no one on the surface would suspect where he was.

Once Eric was totally inside the vent stack, which went straight down and was no wider than his own body, he was only able to shimmy down the vent, which the end dropped down into a small room filled with pipes and electrical panels. Eric slid out of the vent stack and landed on his feet on the ground, then he began to investigate his surroundings, looking for any other entrances into the colony. He noticed a small door on the side of one of the walls. He was unsure where the door led, but he wanted to find out. As Eric went to the small wall door, he heard a hissing sound coming from behind the door, lasting only a few seconds until it stopped. The sound told Eric whatever the door went to had to be used by humans. Eric needed to find out what was behind the door and what humans used it for. He felt it could be the perfect access point for him to descend into the colony undetected. As Eric was looking around for an access panel to open the door, the hissing sound started up again but stopped only a few seconds later. Eric began to wonder about the depth of the colony he was trying to breach.

Eric began to calculate the time between when the hissing started and stopped behind the door to determine if whatever was behind the door was traveling short distances or was traveling fast between stops. He needed to figure out which one it was. In a short time, he would get the answers he was searching for. While Eric waited to see when the hissing sound would start again, he noticed a small panel beside the small door on the wall. Eric opened the panel and found only one button in it. He assumed it was for the thing behind the door, and without hesitation, he pressed the button and waited. Before he knew it, the hissing sound started back up again, but the hissing sound lasted longer than the times before when he heard it. The longer hissing noise made Eric nervous because he was unsure what could be waiting behind the door if it stopped at his location. So, as the hissing got louder, Eric took refuge behind a large pipe coming out of the floor and waited for the hissing to stop at his location.

When the hissing stopped, the door began to open. Eric remained hidden until he could gather more information about the device behind the door in the wall. To his surprise, when the door opened, a human began to get out of the opening so quickly he caused a thud as his feet landed on the floor. From Eric's vantage point, he was able to look inside the open door and notice it was some sort of lift. It did not look as if it was meant for humans to use, due to the size of its interior. Instinctively, Eric thought it must have been used for moving things between the floors of the colony. Eric was happy with the thought of the lift being used for things other than humans, making the lift the perfect access point he needed to infiltrate the colony without being seen. Eric needed to make his presence known to the human who made the thud on the floor upon exiting from the door from the wall.

Eric started moving out of his hiding place, carefully trying to get the attention of the human standing by the wall door. Eric did not want to scare the human, since he could answer questions about the colony. Eric made a small coughing sound and then spoke to the human.

"Ahhmmm, excuse me. Can you help me? I seem to be lost," Eric asked the human.

"WOW! You scared the crap out of me! What are you doing up here?" the human questioned.

"I'm so sorry. I didn't mean to scare you. It's just when I came out of the wall machine, I found myself here. Not knowing where I was, I decided to hide. My name is Eric, what's your name?"

"You didn't scare me, Eric. You only caught me off guard. I thought I was the only person who knew about the lift," the surprised gentleman explained.

"Well, to be honest, I found the lift by accident. I could use your help to get back down into the colony. Can you help me?" Eric asked while acting scared himself.

"Sure, no problem. My name is Ash, by the way. I have been using this lift for years and have never seen anyone else use it. I wasn't even sure if anyone in the colony knew about it, until now. How did you find it again?" Ash asked Eric.

"You see, I was minding my own business when suddenly I heard a hissing sound coming from the wall on the floor I was on. Next thing I knew, I found a panel next to a hidden door on the same wall. I opened the panel and noticed a button inside it. So, I pressed it. The hissing started again, but when it stopped, the door became noticeable, so I opened it, and the lift was there. I got into the lift, not thinking ahead, and the next thing I knew it was moving. When the lift finally stopped, I got off as quickly as possible, not knowing where I had ended up. Do you know how it operates? I need to get back to the floor I was on. I'm sure my parents are worried about me," Eric played to his youthful looks.

"Sure, I know how it operates. Like I said, I've been using this thing for years. You see this panel here?" Ash began to explain to Eric, while pointing at the panel next to the door he had exited. "Well, there is one on every floor of the colony. From this panel, you can call the lift to the floor you are on and press the buttons to go to the floor you want. There is only one button on this panel since there is only one direction the lift can go from here, which is down. But if you forget to press the buttons for your floor on the other floor panel, you can always use the buttons inside the lift. So, what floor do you want to go to?" Ash asked Eric oblivious to being played by an A.I.B. from the surface.

"To be honest, I was so shocked when the lift began to move, I forgot what floor I was on. I do know it is the floor where the A.I.B. is being held. You know of the A.I.B. I'm talking about?" Eric replied.

"Oh, you mean the one they captured a month ago. He is in a holding cell on floor eight. Weird right? An A.I.B. down here in the colony. Well, guess what? That A.I.B. is not the only one down here in the colony," Ash blurted out to Eric.

"Really? There are more A.I.B.s in the colony besides the one in a holding cell?" Eric sounded intrigued.

"Yes. You see, they kidnapped Justice Starceski's family and held them hostage for a short time. They wanted to trade Justice Starceski's family for the captured A.I.B., but the trade did not work out well. I am not sure why they wanted the A.I.B., but they were on a mission to get him. Then, while they were transporting the kidnapped family to a more secure location, one of the A.I.B.s fell to the ground and shut off. When the A.I.B. collapsed, Justice Starceski's family took advantage of the situation and ran away. I saw it all happen and ran away, once all the commotion calmed down. I feared the A.I.B.s would tell Director Barns I was working with them. But I was only helping them because they were forcing me to," Ash tried to clear his name with Eric, whom he had only met only a moment ago.

"Really? The A.I.B.s were forcing you to do their dirty work? I would have been so scared if I were in your position," Eric continued with his scared act for Ash.

"Me, scared? No way. If it was not for the A.I.B.s forcing me to help them with their plans, I would have never known about the A.I.B. Justice Starceski and Director Barns captured. Once I found out about the captured A.I.B., I assumed the A.I.B.s I was forced to help were the good guys, trying to capture a rogue surface A.I.B., so I continued to help them," Ash told Eric with some sense of pride.

"Oh my God, you are so right. If you want to know the truth, the reason I was on the captured A.I.B.'s floor in the first place was because I like danger. I feel a rush run through my body when I think something dangerous may happen. What about you? How do you feel about those things?" Eric was using his exotic dancer looks to make Ash feel comfortable.

"Danger is my middle name. Would you like an escort back down to floor eight?" Ash joked with Eric.

"I thought you would never ask," Eric replied to Ash with a smile.

Ash knew what Eric's smile meant, as he had seen it all too many times before in the dark alleys of the colony. It was the universal sign language in the colony for people with similar interests, which never meant anything good in the colony. There was a seedy side of the colony many of the occupants were not aware of, it was the same as when humans ran the surface. People were still people no matter where they were, or what situations they found themselves in. People had needs of all kinds and needed a way to fill those needs.

Ash smiled back, moved closer to the wall door, and opened it. Once the wall door was open for the lift, Ash maneuvered his way into it and reached his hand out to help Eric inside. Eric managed to squeeze his way into the lift, with Ash's help, and settled in a small space across from Ash. It was a tight fit for them, but neither of them seemed to mind the closeness. Ash leaned across Eric, so he could get a grip on the door handle to close it, and while he was in the position crossing over Eric, Eric took advantage of their situation and quickly kissed Ash. To Eric's surprise, Ash was not offended at the encounter, but instead kissed Eric back. Eric had been wondering what it would be like to have any type of physical interaction with another being, human or

A.I.B. Eric began to feel things he never felt before, which was nice for him.

After the quick kiss shared between them, Ash pulled back and finished closing the lift door, then he opened the panel door inside the lift and pressed the button for floor eight.

As the lift began to move downward, Eric leaned into Ash, keeping his lips only an inch from his. Then, since Ash did not pull back the first time, Eric pressed his lips to Ash's for a second time. Eric wanted to see if he had the same reaction again after the first kiss, and to his surprise, he had the same feelings again as he did during their first embrace. The connection Eric felt was a human connection he had never felt before. Ash was the first human he had ever met, and the first being he had ever kissed. The feeling was intoxicating to Eric. The interaction between them felt right to Eric, and it seemed right to Ash as well. They continued with their embrace for a few more seconds before the lift stopped. They both knew their moment could not continue as they both had things to do which did not involve the other. They thought it would be best if they separated once they were out of the lift.

After the lift stopped, Ash reached over Eric's body, once again, and connected his hand to the lift door. When the door opened, Eric gave Ash another quick smile, then began to fall backward out of the lift. To keep Eric from completely falling out of the lift, Ash reached out once more, wrapping both of his arms around Eric's body, and pulled him back inside the lift, allowing Eric enough time to steady himself enough to maneuver his body out of the lift on his own. Once both of Eric's feet were stable on the ground, he shot Ash a look, and they both began to laugh. The laughing was short lived. The moment was over, so Ash made his way out of the lift and moved to stand beside Eric.

When they were both out of the lift, Ash grabbed Eric's hand to lead him out of the alley. Ash felt he could not just leave Eric alone, searching for an A.I.B., so Ash continued to hold Eric's hand, leading him through the colony corridors on floor eight and around to the Justice Department. The Justice Department was where the captured A.I.B. was being held. Little did Ash know, but he was leading Eric to meet his brother for the first time. Being cautious, Ash made sure they were not being followed by making sharp turns and looking behind them to see if any of the residents of the colony were out and about. Ash wanted to make sure none of the residents paid any attention to them. Feeling confident they were not being followed, or watched, by anyone, Ash continued to the holding cells, pulling Eric behind him by his hand, until they reached the restricted area of floor eight, where Andre was being held. To their surprise, there was no one guarding the entrance to the holding cells inside the restricted area, so Ash and Eric were able to just walk right in. Once they were inside the restricted area, they had to walk through a small maze of cells, which were all empty, since there was never any crime in the colony. When the pair made it to the end of the cell maze, standing inside a cell, at the end of the maze, was Andre. Eric realized he was finally face to face with his brother, whom he had just learned about not too long ago. As Andre turned around in his cell, he locked eyes with Eric. An eerie silence settled around Andre, Eric, and Ash within the maze.

"Who are you?" Andre softly asked the pair standing in front of him.

Eric stood there for a couple of seconds before answering Andre's question. Eric was taking in the subtle similarities between his and Andre's appearance. But, before Eric could answer, Andre spoke again.

"You must be the one the Elders sent out the emergency alert about," Andre spoke directly to Eric.

"How do you know about the emergency alert?" Eric quickly responded to Andre.

Before Andre answered his question, he raised his hand, palm forward, instructing Eric and Ash not to speak. Then, the three of them heard a voice coming out of a nearby room connected to the maze of cells in the restricted area.

"Who is making all that noise in there? Who is talking out there?" Officer Kevin yelled from another room nearby. Then, as Officer Kevin entered the halls to the cells, he noticed Ash and Eric standing outside of Andre's cell. "What are you guys doing here? This is a restricted area. How did you get in here?"

Before Ash had a chance to come up with an excuse to Officer Kevin's question, Eric made his way over to Officer Kevin so fast Ash didn't even see him move. Eric had already put Officer Kevin to sleep before Ash could respond.

"What the hell did you just do, Eric? How did you get over there so fast?" Ash questioned Eric.

"Sorry, my reflexes must be on high alert after everything I had been through today. Are you okay, Ash?" Eric replied.

"Of course I am, I was just worried about you. How did you do that?" Ash quickly questioned back.

"Ash, I have not been honest with you. I'm sorry for that, but you have been a great help to me. You helped me find my brother," Eric responded with apprehension.

"Your brother? But he's an A.I.B., Eric, how is that possible?" Ash inquired.

"It's a long story for another time. Right now, we need to get Andre out of his cell. I promise I will explain everything to you soon, but right now I just need you to trust me. Can you do that?" Eric asked Ash.

Ash was in shock, but he was able to nod his head at Eric.

Eric turned to Andre and asked, "Can you get out of the cell on your own? If not, I can do it for you."

Just as Eric finished his sentence, Andre pushed open the cell door.

"This door never had me confined to this cell. I chose not to push it open unless I had a good reason. I stayed in this cell to help gain the trust of humans. I needed them to feel they were safe while I was here. So, what is this about us being brothers?" Andre asked Eric. "How is it possible? Us being brothers?"

Eric and Ash took a moment to take in how Andre quickly pushed open his cell door. Andre noticed how they were both staring at him in silence. So, Eric thought it was best to change the subject.

"You were created by Dr. Randolph. I was created by Dr. Randolph a few years after you left to be with your human family. That makes us brothers, right?" Eric gave a short explanation of the events that led to the circumstances making him believe the two of them were indeed brothers.

"It looks like we have a lot to talk about, but first, we need to go somewhere secure, other than the restricted area we are in now," Andre strongly suggested to Eric.

"I know of a place we can go to, totally secure," Ash chimed in for the first time since Eric put Officer Kevin to sleep in the hallway.

"And how do we know we can trust you?" Andre asked Ash.

"Because I didn't want any harm to come to Eric. So, trust me or not, I do know of a very secure place we can go. Eric, do you trust me?" Ash asked.

"Without sounding callous, I do not know why, but I trust you, Ash. Andre, we need to go with Ash right now before any humans come in and find Officer Kevin asleep and you out of your cell," Eric conveyed to Andre.

Andre agreed with Eric, and they followed Ash out of the cells and back to the alley with the lift Eric and Ash had used to travel to floor eight.

Chapter 12

After a few hours of being reunited as a family, and with Justice Starceski having some time to recuperate, Shawn knew it was time to tell Chris the truth about everything that happened to him and their children while they were being held captive. Shawn wanted to wait until Chris was better before he brought up their kidnapping. Shawn wanted to make sure his husband was able to hear about their experience without overstimulating his body, which could cause him to go back into a coma. Shawn had to proceed with extreme caution.

"Chris, do you remember when you woke up, here in Medical, after we arrived, and I told you we had some things to talk about? Well, I think we need to talk about those things and what happened to us during our absence. Don't worry, it's not as bad as you may have thought," Shawn tried to ease Chris' fear before he went into detail about what happened with them at the hands of Macy, Jason, and Ash.

"Yes, Shawn, I remember you telling me we needed to talk. I am calm and am ready to hear about what you went through," Chris calmly responded.

"First, I want to let you know there were three adults involved in our kidnapping. We will get into that later. For now, I want to tell you about a few other things.

First, I want to tell you about the pod we were in. It was actually the home to a husband, wife, and two children. The third adult in the pod, I assume, did not live there but was there to help them. The pod felt larger than the other pods I had ever been in in the colony. It had a separate private room hidden behind a wall. Inside the hidden room was a makeshift cell to hold us. It had beds, a sink, and even a private restroom for us to use, with a shower. It was not built for torture, but more like to accommodate overnight guests.

What I am trying to tell you is we were fine while we were captive there.

Now that I have told you about the pod and our cell, let me tell you we never felt like we were in danger. It may have had something to do with the way the pod felt with other children there. I believe they are the children of our captors. There was something about them which made us feel they would never let anything bad happen to us. The children would sneak into the hidden room and let Tabitha and Frankie out of our cell so they could play with them in the other room. Even though I could not see the children from our cell, I could hear them having fun. There was only one time the man raised his voice in the pod. It was when he came home, and all he could hear were the children being children. You know, running around playing games and speaking very loudly. Now, he did not sound angry at the children but more annoyed at the noise. It was funny for me because you know, as well as I do, how loud our children can be. In response to the children being loud, all the man did was instruct his own children to escort our children back to our cell," Shawn began his explanation of their dealings with their kidnappers.

As Shawn finished his overview of the beginning of their recent ordeal with their kidnappers, he noticed Chris was handling everything well, remaining calm, so he continued.

"Once Tabitha and Frankie were back in our cell, they told me what they were doing in the other room. They both said they had fun playing with the other children. As you can expect, hearing those words, I felt we were not in some regular kidnapping situation. I mean, who kidnaps people only for their captives to have fun? They also never threatened us with any harm. It didn't seem as if harming us was in their plan," Shawn elaborated to Chris.

Chris took a moment to take in everything Shawn had just told him. He was really trying hard to comprehend what he was hearing. He had a hard time believing Shawn never felt in danger, or was ever scared, during their entire capture.

"You mean to tell me you never felt afraid, or scared?" Chris asked Shawn.

"I would not say we never felt scared, but as time went on, the fear dissipated," Shawn expressed.

"Well, that is good to hear. Now, tell me about those three adults. Do you believe the one who did not live in the pod is the one who came up with the plan to kidnap you all?"

"No, I don't believe it was his plan at all. I don't think it was planned at all. I believe it was a means to an end for the residents of the pod we were kept in."

"Were you able to hear the names of any of the adults? Or did you recognize any of them?" Chris had moved his attention from the actual kidnapping to the captors.

"When we first arrived at the pod, we were blindfolded, so we couldn't see their faces. But I believe the children may have seen their faces while they were in the other room playing with the other children before they were brought back to the cell. I think I heard the husband call the other one 'Ash'," Shawn stopped mid-sentence as he noticed Chris' facial expressions change after hearing the name 'Ash'. "What is it, Chris? Why are you making that face?"

"Did you say 'Ash'?" Chris asked Shawn.

"Yes, why do you ask? Do you know someone with that name?" Shawn replied.

"Of course, I know him. A few days ago, he handed me a note from your captors that put me here in Medical. I have known about Ash for many years, ever since he was a child. You see, when his parents died, he became well known with Judicial. Ash was always in and out of trouble as a child but seemed to remain out of trouble as he got older. I had not seen Ash in many years, though, until he handed me the note," Chris replied.

"What are you going to do now, knowing the name of one of the kidnappers?" Shawn asked out of concern for possibly being the person who may cause Macy and her children being put in a cell.

"I will need to speak to Director Barns and put out an alert for Ash. If we can find him, maybe he can identify the others involved in your kidnapping," Chris answered Shawn.

***

When Ash, Eric, and Andre arrived at the hidden door to the lift, Ash explained what the lift was and how to navigate it to Andre. Ash also demonstrated how to get into the lift without falling out of it, like Eric had previously done.

After a short instruction from Ash, Andre and Eric climbed into the lift. Eric pushed the button, on the panel inside the lift, to floor thirteen. Then, they rode down until they reached their destination. The last time Ash was in the alley on floor thirteen, Jason fell to the ground, while Macy and their children cried as Ash ran away. Ash, of course, did not want Andre to know of his involvement in a failed attempt at kidnapping a family to be used as a bargaining chip to trade for him.

Once the lift came to a stop, the three of them exited the lift, and then Andre and Eric followed Ash through the corridors of floor thirteen to a vacant pod and entered behind him. The pod was completely furnished, but not occupied. It had been vacant for many years, then Andre realized he knew where they were.

"Ash, this is your childhood home. Isn't it? The one you lived in with your parents before they died, correct?" Andre inquired with certainty.

Ash looked at Andre with a look of surprise on his face. Ash wondered how Andre could have known about his childhood home, much less about his parents' deaths. Ash shook the surprised expression off his face before he spoke.

"How could you possibly know that?" Ash demanded to know.

"Let's say I know almost everything there is to know about the colony, even after they tried to erase any information regarding you or your parents' deaths," Andre expressed to Ash before continuing. "I'm sorry, I didn't mean to upset you if I did," Andre expressed to Ash.

Eric stood in the family room, staring at Andre and Ash, without knowing what he could say to Ash to ease his discomfort.

"Why did you bring us here Ash? Besides the fact you obviously feel safe here?" Eric finally spoke up.

"Because since Andre has escaped from his cell, Judicial Officers will be looking for him. This is the safest place for us right now, trust me. This is a perfect place for us to hide, until we can come up with a plan for our next move, uninterrupted," Ash explained.

"But why is this the safest place to be? How do you know no one will look for us here?" Eric tried to dig a little deeper into Ash's background.

"This pod has been uninhabited since I was six years old, when my parents died. After their deaths, I was sent to live with another family in the colony. The family I was sent to live with could not have children of their own, so they took me as if I was their own child. Trust me when I say no one will look for us here," Ash clarified.

"You have not answered Eric's question, Ash. When I was connected to the archives, one thing I found out about the colony was there are no unoccupied pods here, except one, which is not this one. The pod number to your family home is not even in the database of the archives. I want to know why," Andre inquired.

Before Ash could answer Andre, he closed his eyes and slowly shook his head as if Ash was trying not to remember something about his past. Ash slowly opened his eyes while tears began to flow from them.

"My parents didn't just die here. They were murdered here when I was six years old. Director Barns, nor Justice

Starceski, ever caught the person responsible for their murders, and no one in the colony even knew about their murders after it happened. Their murders were all kept quiet for some reason. Maybe it was because my parents' murders were the first, and only, murders to happen in the colony. When I got older, I found out all the records about them, and myself, were removed from the archives. This is how I know no one will look for us here," Ash concluded while wiping tears from his eyes.

After Ash finished the story of his parents' murders, Andre and Eric both sat quietly on the couch in the family room. Andre and Eric wanted to give Ash a few minutes to gather himself before bringing the conversation back to the present.

"Ash, thank you for sharing those moments of your parents' murders with us. It must have been difficult for you to talk about. I didn't mean to press you so hard, but I needed to make sure this pod was a safe place, even though I already knew this pod number was deleted from the archives," Andre expressed sympathy for Ash.

"I didn't mean to press the issue either," Eric seemed to be at peace with the answer to his original question to Ash.

"Thank you both. I should have told you sooner, but I prefer not to think about it, much less talk about it with people I just met. It took me a long time to get over their murders," Ash told Andre and Eric.

"Now, since you are convinced, this pod is safe what do we do?" Eric asked Andre.

"We need to figure out a way for me to get some information to Justice Starceski about how to defeat the surface A.I.B.s," Andre replied.

"You know how to defeat the surface A.I.B.s?" Ash sounded surprised.

"I do, and now that Eric has found me, we will execute a plan to end the A.I.B.s' rule over the surface. We will need some help though," Andre explained.

Ash and Eric looked at each other for a split second before they turned and looked at Andre.

***

After speaking with Shawn, for a few more hours, Justice Starceski sent one of the Director's officers to retrieve Director Barns and bring him to his room. Justice Starceski wanted to find Director Barns, but his husband Shawn refused to let him get out of bed, much less start a search for the Director.

Officer Collins was tasked with the job of finding the Director. After he located the Director, he escorted him to Justice Starceski's room in Medical in less than thirty minutes. Justice Starceski was impressed by Officer Collins' ability.

"Very impressive, Officer Collins. Thank you for bringing the Director to me so expediently. I will not forget this. Also, I don't think I ever thanked you for finding me in the condition I was in on cafeteria 1 floor. The work you have done has been a great help to me and my family," Justice Starceski told Officer Collins. "With that being said, I need to ask you to excuse the Director and me. We have a few things to talk about in private, please."

"Not a problem, Sir. I will be close by if you need my assistance again," Officer Collins conveyed to Justice Starceski before exiting the room.

"Glad to see you are recovering so well, Chris. And I am happy to see you, Shawn, unharmed. How has your recovery been, Chris?" the Director asked.

"It's been trying, to say the least. Let's skip all the small talk if you don't mind. I need you to put out an alert on Ash. Do you remember him?" Justice Starceski asked the Director.

"Vaguely. I remember a child named Ash from my first years as an officer. What is the alert regarding?" Director Barns inquired.

"Ash is possibly one of the people responsible for the kidnapping of my family. We need to find him to find out who else he was working with and why they wanted my family," Justice Starceski replied. "You will have to look deeper than the archives to find any information on him. Do you remember who Ash is now?" Justice Starceski spoke in code to the Director since Shawn was staring at them.

"Yes, I remember. I will see what I can find out and put out the alert. Are you sure it is the same Ash from before?" the Director asked.

"Do you know any other residents of the colony named 'Ash'?" Justice Starceski shot back at the Director.

"No, Sir. There is only one Ash in the colony I can think of. It's been such a long time since I was a rookie. Why do you think he kidnapped your family?" the Director asked.

"That's why I want you to find Ash, he may be able to shed some light on the 'who and why'," Justice Starceski replied. "But be discreet."

"Will do, Sir," Director Barns reassured Justice Starceski, turned, and walked out of the room.

After the Director left the room, he began to think of the past. He was thinking about the only murders in the colony and all the lengths they went through to sweep it under the rug. The Director knew he was about to enter uncharted waters. Justice Starceski's request to have him dig into something, which supposedly never happened in the colony, would be a difficult task, but not impossible. The Director wondered where he was going to go for information on Ash. *Who can I speak to if I want to find out where Ash is staying now?* The Director had his challenges, but he welcomed them.

*****

Macy waited patiently in the waiting area of Medical, with her children, Jonathan and Kristin. The three of them had been sitting in the same spot waiting for any news on her husbands' condition. Not only was Macy waiting for an update on Jason, but in the back of her mind, she was more afraid of the doctor finding out Jason was an A.I.B., then learning she and their children were also A.I.B.s. Even though Macy worried about the outcome of the doctor finding out their secret, she felt she could not leave. She wanted to know why Jason fell to the ground in the first place. What could have triggered his programming to shut down so quickly? Macy also worried if what had happened to Jason could happen to her and their children.

While Macy and their children waited, Macy thought about what she was going to say to the doctor when he came back into the waiting area with the news of Jason being an A.I.B. Not only was she thinking of what she would say to the doctor, she also thought about what would happen to her and their children. The only thing she knew for certain was she had to protect their children at all costs. Macy was prepared to do anything in her power to keep their children out of harm's way, but before she could come up with something to say. The doctor walked back into the waiting area and began to make his way over to her with three guards. Macy's first instinct was to grab the children and run, but she stood up instead, with their children guarded behind her.

Macy took her stance and decided to speak to the doctor before she made any attempt to run.

"Hello, Doctor. Are there any updates on my husband, Jason?" Macy asked.

"Macy, is it? Well, I have some unpleasant news about your husband. I am not sure if you are aware, but your husband is an A.I.B. and we did everything we could think of to restart his programming, but we were unable to come up with a workable solution. Is there anything you can tell us about what happened to him for us to help Jason?" the doctor asked Macy. "But before you answer the question, I have something else to ask you. I must ask you if you and your children are also A.I.B.s?"

The doctor's words caught Macy completely off guard. She did not know what to say. She never thought humans would try to save her husband's life, if they found out he was an A.I.B. Macy took a few seconds to process the information the doctor had given her before answering him.

"What will happen to us if I answer yes to the question?" Macy fearfully asked the doctor.

"Nothing will happen to you, or your children, if you answer yes. We are here to preserve life, not destroy it. All life is precious in the colony. You and your family need not fear us, I give you my word," the doctor continued.

"Thank you, doctor, for saying that. Now, I can't go into what led up to Jason's programming shutting down, but he just fell on the ground. It was as if he was overstimulated with fear because he was worried about me and our children, and then he just fell to the ground, powerless. So, what are you going to do with Jason's body?" Macy asked.

"We want to help Jason in any way we can, we will not remove his body out of Medical until we have exhausted every avenue to help him. If you can think of anything we can do, to help bring Jason back online, please let us know. Jason's body is safe here with us in Medical, I promise," the doctor expressed to Macy.

"Why would you go out of your way to help us, knowing we are A.I.B.s?" Macy asked the doctor in disbelief.

"All occupants of the colony matter to us, human or not. We, humans are not like surface A.I.B.s, we protect all life here which includes you and your family. You have been living here with us, for I don't know how long, but you are occupants of the colony, so you are all protected" the doctor replied.

Those words from the doctor spoke to Macy. She never expected humans to be so accepting of an A.I.B., because she was programmed to fear humans. Macy now felt relief and wanted to find a way to help her husband, Jason.

"Doctor, I believe there is only one person who can help my husband, but I don't know if he will help," Macy informed the doctor.

"Who? Please, Macy, you must tell me so we can get them here," the doctor responded with urgency.

"His name is Andre, and he was captured by authorities for breaking into the colony over a month ago," Macy responded.

"Well, if the authorities have Andre in their custody, we can have him brought here to Medical. Thank you, Macy, for telling me this information. We will take it from here. Now, rest assured we will do our best to get Andre here as quickly as possible," the doctor responded to Macy.

With that, the doctor left Macy and her children in the waiting area so he could get ahold of Judicial, or the Director, to see if he could get Andre brought to Medical as quickly as possible to save a life, even if it was an A.I.B.s life. Since Justice Starceski was already in Medical, the doctor figured he could get Andre transferred quickly.

Jason's doctor made his way to Justice Starceski's room. Upon arrival, the doctor noticed Shawn and the Director were also in the room.

"Sorry for the interruption, Justice Starceski, but I need to ask a favor of you," the doctor blurted out.

"Hello, doctor, what can I do for you?" Justice Starceski asked.

"I need someone being held by authority, in the restricted holding cells, to be brought down here to Medical. His name is Andre. Can you make it happen?" the doctor asked.

"How do you know we have detained someone named Andre, and why do you need him brought here to Medical?" Justice Starceski replied.

"I was informed, by a patient's wife, Andre was being held by authorities, and he could be the only person who could help save her husband's life. You must get him here as soon as possible," the doctor demanded.

In that moment, Shawn, Justice Starceski's husband, spoke up.

"Chris, if Andre can help save a life, you need to do whatever you can do to get him here," Shawn told Justice Starceski.

With the pressure from Shawn and the doctor, Justice Starceski had no choice but to agree to get Andre brought to Medical.

"I need to get word to Officer Collins to have Andre moved here. Doctor, can you get me a radio so I can reach out to Judicial? I will need their approval for the transfer. Officer Collins is one authority I can not only trust but can also depend on to get a job done," Justice Starceski expressed.

"Yes, I will have a radio brought in as quickly as possible. Thank you, Sir," the doctor replied.

Chapter 13

While Andre and Ash collaborated on a way to get a message to Justice Starceski safely, Eric decided it was time to explain why he came to the colony in the first place.

"Andre, I hate to interrupt you, but there are some things we need to discuss before we try to speak to Justice Starceski, whomever he is," Eric told Andre.

"Yes, Eric, you are correct. We do need to discuss those matters in more detail. Let's begin with your creation, and why you are here now," Andre expressed.

"Before we get into my reasons for being here, we need to discuss my existence. You see, I only found out a few days ago I was created by Dr. Randolph," Eric began.

"You mean to tell me you never knew who created you? Why now, Eric? I was created many years ago, before you were created, as you say, and then you were created by my creator not long after I was sent to be with my human family, correct? Then why are you just now finding out this information?" Andre began to grill Eric.

"Unlike you, Andre, when Dr. Randolph created me, he stored all memories and information about my creation in a memory chip within my construct. I was only able to access the memory chip when I began to look deeper into my own body, and programming, to compare the findings with other A.I.B.s," Eric continued.

"And why did you feel a need to compare yourself to the other A.I.B.s on the surface? What happened to you to make you assume you were different from them?" Andre inquired, even though Andre knew he did not know of his own creation until he fell to the ground because of an incident. At the time, he blamed the incident on Bentley before knowing the house was programmed to protect itself. The house shut Andre off from Bentley in the kitchen because he was asking about the 'safe room' located there, causing Andre to run into a clear wall, which was locking him inside the kitchen, knocking himself out.

Eric began to explain to Andre of his experiences on the surface, "I realized, later in life, I never needed to recharge like all the other surface A.I.B.s. You may not be aware, but A.I.B.s on the surface have been running out of resources to maintain the amount of energy which is required for them to continue to not only the production of more A.I.B.s, but with keeping them charged as well. So, the Elders assembled twenty-eight teams, ordering them to search for more efficient ways to harness a self-sustainable source for energy. I was assigned to one of those teams. While I oversaw the team, I began to notice the amount of time each of my team members would spend each day recharging. As I noticed this, I became more aware of the fact I never needed to recharge. Once I was self-aware of this, I felt some indication I was different from the rest of my team. With this new information, I had learned about myself, I began to think I was the key to a self-sustainable power source. That was when I began to physically look inside myself for differences. I began going to creation centers when my team was out recharging. There, I was able to open up my chest cavity enclosure to find not only my power source never needed to recharge, but I also found an unknown chip within my housing system. Within the knowledge of the chip, I not only found Dr. Randolph's name on it, but also instantly gained access to all the memories of my creation. Those new memories also gave me access to the blueprints of my power source, which was self-sustaining. I was then able to create a prototype of my power source from the blueprints for the Elders. Once my prototype was completed and given to the Elders, I left," Eric elaborated to Andre and Ash.

"So, you gave the Elders a prototype of our power source?" Andre seemed upset at Eric.

"Is that all you took away from my story? That I gave a prototype of our power source to the Elders? Did you not listen to any other part of the story?" Eric was disappointed in Andre.

"No, Eric, I gathered much more than you just giving away our power source to the Elders. I can deduce this is the information you came here to tell me of the utmost importance, correct?" Andre replied.

"Well then, I'm glad you understand why it took me so long to find you. If I would have known earlier, we were both created by Dr. Randolph, I would have looked for you sooner," Eric replied with a bit of sadness in his tone.

"I understand, and I appreciate you finding me when you did, but now my knowledge of the surface A.I.B.s having a prototype of our self-sustaining power source puts us in a position of finding Justice Starceski even more urgently. If we want any chance to stop the surface A.I.B.s before they can replicate our power source and mass produce it, which would make them unstoppable," Andre replied.

"Well, the surface A.I.B.s may have a little trouble getting my prototype to work. I may have left out a few details for the Elders to complete an actual working power source for themselves," Eric exclaimed.

"So, you left out a few things the surface A.I.B.s will need to correct before they can begin production? That is very Dr. Randolph of you," Andre joked to Eric.

"Yes, I did, but it does not mean they won't be able to figure out the parts I left out. If you know of a way to stop the surface A.I.B.s, we need to act now," Eric expressed.

"We need to get back to coming up with a plan to reach Justice Starceski, fast," Andre conveyed to Eric.

***

Jason's doctor headed back from Justice Starceski's room to Macy and her children who were still waiting in the waiting area in Medical.

"Macy, I am here to tell you, Justice Starceski is in the process of having Andre brought here to Medical to help your husband, Jason."

"That is great news doctor. Thank you again for doing what you can for Jason. He is all we have," Macy expressed.

"Macy, you have more than just Jason here in the colony. You have everyone you have been in contact with since you have been in the colony. This is one thing which will continue to separate you from the surface A.I.B.s. We accept all life, not just the ones like us. Now, we all just must wait until Justice Starceski can get Andre transferred here," the doctor replied to Macy.

***

As Director Barns searched for any information on Ash, his first stop was to the archives. He knew it was going to be a long shot, but he needed to find a starting point for his investigation. He was planning on looking into Ash and his family pre-murder. He figured the archives may not have been able to delete every reference of Ash and his parents. When he entered the archives, he was greeted by Keeper Valerian. He began to ask Keeper questions which may not have triggered deletion because of the murders.

"Greetings Director Barns, what can I do for you here in the archives at this time of night?" Keeper Valerian inquired.

"I am glad you asked, Keeper. I am here to get anything you may have on an occupant of the colony by the name of Ash. Can you help me with this?" Director Barns questioned.

"Of course. Is there anything specific which you are looking for?" Keeper asked the Director.

"No, I want everything you have on the name, Ash, nothing specific. Can you pull everything you can find please?" the Director replied vaguely.

"Yes, Sir. Give me a few minutes to retrieve all the records pertaining to the name 'Ash'. I will be right back," Keeper Valerian replied to the Director before he turned around and walked away.

As Keeper Valerian went through the archives for any mention of the name 'Ash', he was perplexed when he came up with no results. Keeper Valerian knew the name had to be in the archives, since the Director requested the information, so he felt there must have been some error with the results. This prompted Keeper Valerian to run another report, and to his surprise, the new report came up with the same results. Nothing on the name 'Ash'. Still coming up with no results from his searches, Keeper decided to change his search parameters from the name 'Ash' to the word 'ash'. To Keeper Valerian's surprise, he was able to find one report with the word 'ash' in it. It was shocking to say the least.

"Director Barns, thank you for waiting. It took me a few tries to find any information on the word 'ash', but I was able to find one report with 'ash' in it. You may not be happy with the results, but it is all we have on the word 'ash' in the archives," Keeper Valerian explained.

"What do you mean, 'word'? I asked you to search for the name 'Ash', not the word," Director Barns responded aggressively.

"My apologies, Director. I did a search for the name 'Ash' and came up with nothing in the archives. I changed my search from a name to a word 'ash' and this is the report I found. It is regarding the name itself, but it was not input into the archives with a capital 'A', which the archives saw as the word 'ash' and here it is. You may want to prepare yourself before you read the report," Keeper Valerian expressed.

"Just give me whatever you found, and I will be the judge of if it pertains to what I am looking for," the Director instructed.

Keeper Valerian handed over the one report he was able to obtain from the archives to Director Barns. Once the Director had the report, Keeper Valerian turned and walked away.

Now, as the Director had possession of the report from Keeper Valerian, he began to read it. Director Barns was not expecting what he read. The part to catch the Director's attention was a line with 'ash' in it.

"Upon the initial investigation, it has been determined, the murders of Amanda and Trey Ferguson was committed by the hands of their six-year-old son, ash. Further investigation is required to determine why these murders happened."

After reading the short report, Director Barns felt he needed to find Ash as quickly as possible. The Director felt he had more to worry about, besides the kidnapping of Justice Starceski's family, after reading the report he received from Keeper Valerian. He believed more lives could be in danger with Ash on the loose, prompting the Director to find out where the murders happened, all those years ago. Director Barns needed a pod number of Ash's family pod because felt time was running out before more people could be hurt, or killed, at the hands of Ash, if the report was true. The Director knew he had to report back to Justice Starceski with his new findings. So, he began to make his way back to Medical.

Director Barns needed the time it took him to reach Medical to figure out what he was going to say to Justice Starceski. He felt he would need to say more than 'I found out Ash murdered his parents at the age of six' or 'Hey, Justice Starceski, Ash murdered his parents and I have no idea on how to find him'. Director Barns felt if either of those statements were made to Justice Starceski, he would fall back into a coma again. The Director knew he had to deliver the information about Ash delicately to Justice Starceski. So, the Director took a little extra time getting back to medical.

***

When Jason's doctor finished speaking to Macy, he went over to the medical station in the center of the room. He instructed one of the medical staff to take a radio to Justice Starceski's room. He did not explain why but made sure they understood it was of the utmost importance.

The medic, who was instructed to take the radio to Justice Starceski's room, turned away from the doctor as he grabbed a radio from underneath the counter and proceeded to make his way down the hall to Justice Starceski's room. When the medic arrived at his intended room, he entered without knocking.

"I'm sorry to just barge into your room like this, Sir, but the doctor said you needed a radio, and it was of utmost importance. Here is the radio you requested," the medic explained his abruptness as he handed the radio over to Justice Starceski.

"Thank you for the assistance with the radio," Justice Starceski muttered to the medic.

Once the medic was out of earshot, Shawn scolded Chris.

"Why do you have to be so short with the staff? They are here to help you. Can you at least pretend to be appreciative of their help?" Shawn berated his husband.

"I'm sorry, Shawn. I am just under a lot of stress right now, so being polite is the last thing I am worried about right now. I will try to be more receptive to the staff's feelings in the future," Justice Starceski replied to Shawn. "Now, do you mind if I reach out to Officer Collins for his assistance once more?"

"Please do, if doing so will ease some of your stress," Shawn answered Chris with a smile.

"Thank you," Chris responded to Shawn as he moved the radio, in his hand, to his mouth.

"Officer Collins, this is Justice Starceski. Do you copy?"

"Yes, Sir. What can I do for you?" Officer Collins responded.

"I need you to go to the holding cells and retrieve Andre, the A.I.B. we have in holding there, and bring him down to Medical as quickly as possible. Can you do this for me?" Justice Starceski asked.

"Yes, Sir. I will have Andre there shortly," Officer Collins replied and ended their communication.

Officer Collins began to make his way to the restricted area, where the holding cells were, which did not take him long to get to since he was already stationed on floor eight. As soon as Officer Collins reached the restricted area and made his way through the maze of holding cells, he came up to Officer Kevin asleep on the ground outside of an empty holding cell, the cell supposedly holding Andre. Upon seeing those unexpected circumstances, he quickly went over to Officer Kevin to check his vitals. Officer Collins was fortunate to find a pulse on Officer Kevin. Officer Collins quickly began to slap Officer Kevin in the face to get him to wake up.

As Officer Kevin began to wake up, he was surprised to see Officer Collins looking down on him.

"What are you doing?" Officer Kevin asked.

"Why don't you tell me what you are doing here on the ground with this cell empty? What happened here?" Officer Collins asked.

"It's a little fuzzy, but I heard some voices in here, and when I came to investigate, I saw two people standing outside of the cell. Then it all went dark. Sorry, Officer Collins," Officer Kevin expressed remorse for his actions.

"Do you know what happened to the person who was being detained in this cell? Did you recognize either of the other two people who were in this room before it all went dark?" Officer Collins inquired.

"No, Sir. I didn't have much time to get a good look at anyone before I saw darkness. It all happened so fast. What is the urgency, and why are you here?" Officer Kevin inquired.

"Justice Starceski radioed for me to bring the person being held here, in this cell, down to his room in Medical. The person who was being held here is named Andre and he is needed apparently in Medical for some reason. Now, you are telling me he is missing, and you don't know who helped him escape, or who may have him? Do you want to tell Justice Starceski this, because I sure don't," Officer Collins asked Officer Kevin.

"I think it would be better coming from you," Officer Kevin admitted.

"Thanks. Get your ass up and make rounds in your section to see if you can find out where they went. Check with the archives, they are sure to have a recording of the incident which transpired here. We need to find them, quickly," Officer Collins ordered.

***

Even though Director Barns took some extra time to get back to Justice Starceski in Medical, he was still unable to figure out how he was going to tell Justice Starceski about his findings. He still had no leads on how to find out more than what he already knew about Ash. He was so deep in thought; he didn't realize he had already made it back to Justice Starceski's room in Medical.

Once he realized he was at Justice Starceski's room door, he just barged in. "Sir, I'm sorry to report I was only able to find one report on Ash. And you are not going to be happy with the report I found," the Director finished.

As Director Barns finished explaining how he was only able to find one report on Ash, Shawn and Justice Starceski shared a concerned glance towards each other before either of them spoke.

"What did you find out Daniel?" Shawn asked first.

"I will let the report speak for itself," Director Barns replied as he handed the report over to Justice Starceski.

"This is all you were able to find about Ash in the archives. To be honest, it's more than I expected you to find," Justice Starceski replied.

"Yes, Sir, and trust me when I say you want to read this report," the Director told Justice Starceski with certainty. "While you are reading the report, I am going to go back to my office in case the officers need my help with finding Ash."

Once Director Barns exited the room, Justice Starceski began to read the report on Ash. He was surprised the Director was even able to find one report on Ash. Justice Starceski remembered the murders of Ash's parents but was reluctant to read a report written in his own words he was faced with. He just knew all reports of Ash, and the murder of his parents, were supposed to have been deleted from the archives, but there he was, reading his own report of the incident. It was Justice Starceski who first thought Ash could have committed the murders of his parents, but he could never prove it. So, he went along with the orders from Judicial to remove all reports which could have mentioned either the murder, or Ash, in them. And now in doing so, they were in a bigger mess than just thinking of Ash as the murderer of his own parents, but also a kidnapper capable of murder.

Chapter 14

Once Officer Collins returned to his station on floor eight, he felt a rush of dread wash over him. He was not prepared to tell Justice Starceski Andre was not in his cell, and he had no clue how, or why, he escaped. He would accept whatever punishment Justice Starceski might impose on him. Officer Collins made his way over to the radio sitting on the station desk, pressed the button on its side, and began speaking.

"Justice Starceski, this is Officer Collins. Do you copy?"

Justice Starceski finished reading the incident report he had written so many years ago regarding the murders of Ash's parents, trying to get the thought out of his mind of Ash being a murderer. Ash was only six years old at the time, and Justice Starceski wanted to believe someone else committed the murders, not Ash. While handing the report to Shawn to read, he heard a call coming in for him on the radio.

"This is Justice Starceski. Go ahead, Officer Collins. What news do you have for me?"

"Well, Sir, a situation has arisen with Andre. When I reached the holding cells, Officer Kevin was incapacitated, on the ground, in front of Andre's empty cell," Officer Collins replied to Justice Starceski, waiting to be scolded for the incident.

"What do you mean by 'incapacitated'? Is Officer Kevin alright, or do I need to send medical help?" Justice Starceski inquired about the severity of their current situation.

"No medical help is required currently. I was able to wake Officer Kevin. It appeared, as though he had been put to sleep somehow. I ordered him to head to the archives to review the footage of the incident and report back to me as soon as he could retrieve the footage. By the sound of Officer Kevin's accounts of the incident, Andre may have been broken out of his cell. There were two unknown assailants involved. I will keep you posted, Sir," Officer Collins concluded his transmission with Justice Starceski.

After Officer Collins ended the radio communication with Justice Starceski, he knew his next priority was to get with Officer Kevin and review the footage from the archives. Officer Collins' next call was to the archive room.

"Keeper Valerian, this is Officer Collins from the floor eight station. Do you copy?"

"Go ahead, Officer Collins, this is Keeper Valerian."

"Has Officer Kevin made it to your location?"

"Yes, Sir. Officer Kevin is here now reviewing the footage of the escape of Andre. He should be finished with the review shortly. Is there anything you would like me to tell Officer Kevin?"

"Yes, Keeper. Can you make sure as soon as you can isolate the footage of the escape, send it directly to Justice Starceski in Medical? Then send Officer Kevin back to floor eight station with a copy of the footage. I will need you to review all security videos of the areas around the holding cells and see if you can track where those three went when they left the holding area. We need to locate them as quickly as possible. A life is at stake," Officer Collins ended the transmission before Keeper Valerian could respond. Officer Collins wanted to begin his investigation on the matter while time permitted.

***

"None of these plans will ensure we will be in contact with Justice Starceski. These plans, at best, will only ensure we are arrested and taken back to the holding cells. We need a plan that will put us directly in contact with Justice Starceski without getting us arrested," Andre criticized Eric and Ash's plans.

"What do you suggest, Andre? You seem to think we can walk right up to Justice Starceski and ask for a conversation," Ash responded.

"That is not a bad idea, Ash. That is exactly what we need to do. We need to find out where Justice Starceski is and walk up to him," Eric responded excitedly.

"No, Eric, it's a terrible idea. We couldn't get within ten feet of Justice Starceski, with the kidnappers of his family still at large, he is sure to be heavily guarded," Ash told Eric.

"No, Ash. It is the perfect plan if we want to speak to Justice Starceski. They would not expect an ambush as they think I have gone on the run, since I escaped from my cell. We need to find out where Justice Starceski is, then we can devise the perfect plan to get close enough to speak to him," Andre explained.

"Finding his location is easy, but we are wanted for breaking Andre out of his cell," Ash informed Eric and Andre.

"That may not be entirely true. You and Andre may be wanted fugitives, but they do not know who I am. I just arrived in the colony today, so the chances of anyone suspecting me of anything are unlikely. You could tell me where to go to find out any information on Justice Starceski's location," Eric expressed with excitement to Ash.

"Oh, that's the easy part, finding Justice Starceski. All you must do is go to any Judicial Enforcement Station on any floor and ask any officer. They are required, by law, to tell any occupant of the colony the whereabouts of Justice Starceski," Ash quickly explained. "There is a Judicial Enforcement Station on every eighth floor. The closest one to us is the station on floor sixteen, but I would go to the one on floor eight. If they get suspicious, you will be further away from us here."

"Do you think it could work, Andre?" Eric asked.

"I have an understanding, of humans, and if there is a law requiring them to reveal Justice Starceski's location, the officers will follow the law. The trick will not be the ability to get the information from the officer on duty. You must not sound desperate or have malice in your tone. It would have to be for some minuscule reason to see him. From what I gathered from the archives; zoning is a big issue in the colony. Many residents want to rezone the farm area to a residential zone due to the smells from the farm animals. That would be a great way to get the location of Justice Starceski without setting off any red flags to the officer," Andre suggested to Eric.

The information from Andre took Eric a few minutes to understand, as he had never had to deal with humans before or farm animals. It all seemed difficult for Eric to grasp, and Andre noticed.

"Eric, trust me. You are acting like a surface A.I.B. and overanalyzing the information I have provided. It will work, I can assure you. Now, go get Justice Starceski's location so we can stop the actual surface A.I.B.s," Andre insisted.

Without hesitation, or over thinking, Eric agreed and went to the pod door. Before he exited, he looked over at Ash.

"Ash, how do I get to floor eight? Should I use the lift, or is there another way people move from floor to floor in the colony I should use?" Eric asked.

"Well, all humans take the spiral walkway in the center of the colony to get from floor to floor. We are five floors down from floor eight, so I suggest taking the lift to go up and then using the spiral walkway to come back down. Unless they are on to you, then lose the officers and bring the lift back down. That will buy you some time to get back to the pod before they make it to this floor," Ash suggested to Eric with a small smile.

Eric smiled back at Ash, exited the pod, and began to head back to the alley with the lift entrance. Eric quickly moved through the passageways, not quick enough to be suspicious, but enough to find the alley without being stopped by any human. Upon reaching the door to the lift, Eric opened the hidden panel to reveal the call button. He was not surprised when the door immediately opened, inviting him to enter. After pressing the button for floor eight, the lift began to make an all too familiar hissing sound and moved upward. Eric hoped it would stop on the correct floor.

When the lift did stop a few seconds later, Eric assumed he made it to his chosen destination, and he was correct. Eric noticed a small number eight printed on the side of the door when it opened. Feeling relieved, he exited the lift into another deserted alley, just like the one he was previously in on floor thirteen.

Once he was out of the lift completely, Eric made his way out of the alley, then through floor eight corridors. He soon realized he had no idea how to find the enforcement station on floor eight. Before Eric could panic, which was a new feeling for him, he spotted other humans walking along the passageways.

"Excuse me, but do you know where I can find the nearest Judicial Enforcement Station? I have a few zoning questions. I need to know where I can find Justice Starceski. I would like to vocalize my requests to him in person," Eric asked the first passing human he encountered.

"Are you okay? Do you need medical assistance?" replied the human woman, staring at Eric with concern for his well-being during this exchange of words.

"No, I do not need any medical attention. I need to find the Judicial Enforcement Station on this floor. I need to speak to an officer to gather information from them so I can make a formal request for some zoning issues. If you could please point me in the right direction to the Judicial Enforcement Station on this floor, I will excuse myself from speaking to you," Eric answered the human woman.

"How rude! Find the station on your own," the woman replied, walking away from Eric, shaking her head in disbelief.

What was that about? Eric thought to himself when he was left alone in the corridor.

Eric continued his own on his search for the Judicial Enforcement Station. He felt the humans were not as giving as the officers were supposed to be. After passing a few more humans, Eric found himself in front of the station he was looking for. Now, he just needed to ask the officer for Justice Starceski's location.

"Excuse me, officer. I am here for some logical information. You see, I have some zoning issues I need to speak to Justice Starceski about, but I am unaware of his current location. Can you assist me?" Eric conveyed this to the officer at the desk.

"Yes, Sir. I am Officer Collins, and I can help you. But I am sorry to inform you Justice Starceski is currently unavailable. If you need to make an appointment to speak to Justice Starceski, it needs to be made through his office, until his return," Officer Collins replied.

"What if these are emergency zoning requests about the farm animals? Does that change anything?" Eric questioned Officer Collins.

"No, it does not change the fact Justice Starceski has been admitted to Medical and is unavailable to discuss your zoning concerns. Your zoning issues will need to go to his assistant in his office, or you will need to wait until he is able to return to duty. Do you understand?" Officer Collins shot back at Eric. "Now, if there is nothing else, I can assist you with," Officer Collins ended his conversation with Eric, hoping he would turn and walk away like everyone else has done.

Eric took Officer Collins' remarks as a cue for him to leave, so he did. Eric had acquired Justice Starceski's location without raising any red flags with Officer Collins, so to him, it was a successful mission. Now, Eric needed to get back down to floor thirteen without incident. Eric began his way down the spiral walkway through the center of the colony with the other humans of the colony.

Once Eric had left the station, Officer Collins regained his composure. He was so tired of dealing with those zoning complaints. He was ready for Judicial to go ahead and make a final decision on the farm zoning issues so he could get back to dealing with regular complaints about the colony. About that time, Officer Kevin came running around the corner into the station, almost running Officer Collins over before stopping right in front of him.

"Officer Kevin, are you okay, or are you being chased? What is the meaning of you coming in here so fast?" Officer Collins questioned.

"No, Sir, I am not being chased, but I have the footage of Andre's escape. I watched it, but I did not recognize anyone in the video. Maybe you should watch it to see if you see anyone you know," Officer Kevin blurted out while gasping for air.

"Why didn't you say that in the first place? Give me the video, and let me look at it," Officer Collins instructed Officer Kevin.

"That was the first thing I said to you when I stopped right in front of you," Officer Kevin clarified. "Here is the video. May I leave now?"

"Yes, you may leave. I have work to do," Officer Collins replied.

Officer Kevin turned, walked away, and left Officer Collins with the video to review. Officer Collins immediately recognized one of the men from the video. It was the gentleman who just left his station wanting the location of Justice Starceski. He knew he needed to act quickly if he wanted to capture one of the people who helped Andre escape.

"Officer Kevin, get your ass back in here right now! I know you can hear me. You just left!" Officer Collins began to scream out into the corridors just outside the station. "This is your chance to redeem your earlier mishap in the holding cells!"

With those words, Officer Kevin rushed back to the station to Officer Collins.

"What can I do for you, Officer Collins?" Officer Kevin asked.

"Well, first of all, you can begin your search for this man," Officer Collins showed him a still frame from the video of the man who just left his station. "You see this man? You need to find him. He just left the station here. I saw him going towards the walkway in the center of the colony. He could be going up or down, I could not see which way he was going. He is the one who put you in the sleeper hold, very quickly I might add, before Andre pushed open his cell door," Officer Collins informed Officer Kevin.

Officer Kevin took off from the station to begin his search for the man in the video. When he reached the center of the colony, he was forced to decide to go either up or down. He chose down on instinct. That was when he noticed the man in the still and shouted at him to stop.

"Sir, I need you to stop where you are! I said STOP!" Officer Kevin shouted at Eric.

Eric turned his head and noticed he was being chased by a Judicial Officer yelling at him to stop. As soon as he heard the word, 'STOP', he knew he was not safe. The only thing he could think of where the words Ash had told him during an earlier conversation, *every floor has access to the lift, but no one uses it.* Those words from Ash gave Eric hope. He proceeded to move towards the alley on floor nine. Eric was moving as fast as he could, without drawing more attention to himself, because he knew he could move with incredible speed, but he didn't want humans to see him move at those speeds. He was not exactly sure where the alley was, but he used his intellect to go to an alley in the same area of the colony as the one a floor above his location, the alley with the lift access. He found a dead-end alley with the secret door in its walls for access to the lift, just as he predicted.

Eric knew he was in the right alley, so he found the hidden panel with the call button for the lift. He pressed the button as quickly as possible and shut the panel door. Then he heard the familiar hissing sound, which was over in a few seconds since it only had to go one floor down. Once the lift stopped, along with the hissing sound, the door popped open. Eric quickly climbed into the lift and shut the door behind him. Then, after he was inside the lift, he opened the panel door and pressed the button for floor thirteen. Eric suddenly felt the motion of the lift proceeding down the shaft.

Officer Kevin continued to follow the unknown man he was pursuing. He felt he would soon have the man cornered, and as Officer Kevin entered the dead-end alley and found it empty, he became confused as to where the man could have gone. The unforeseen incident began to upset Officer Kevin because he was going to have to tell Officer Collins he lost the suspect, again.

When the lift stopped and the door opened, Eric jumped out landing with both feet on the ground for the first time. Then he shut the door and began to move faster than he ever had before while inside the colony to get back to Ash's pod before other officers came looking for him. Eric was quickly at Ash's childhood home, and when he opened the pod door, he was greeted by Ash.

"I am so glad you are back. How did things go with finding Justice Starceski's location?" Ash asked.

"I think we may have a problem," Eric answered.

Chapter 15

"What problem, Eric?" Ash inquired.

"Well, let me start by saying I was able to find Justice Starceski's location," Eric told Andre and Eric.

"But?" Andre probed Eric for more information.

"But I may have been made by one of the officers from the station on floor eight. After I got Justice Starceski's location, from the officer on duty, I began my way down the spiral walkway on my way here. That's when another officer began yelling at someone to STOP. I looked behind me and noticed he was yelling for **me** to stop. I began to panic and ran off the spiral walkway onto floor nine. From there, I decided to run to the alley with access to the lift. I found the hidden panel and door to the lift. I called for the lift, and once the door opened, I hopped inside, made my way to this floor, and ran straight here," Eric explained the situation he had experienced.

"Do you believe you made it here unseen?" Andre questioned Eric.

"I am certain that no one saw me on this floor. Anyway, there is no way for the officer to know what floor I am on now. I would suggest we use the commotion I have created to make our way down to meet with Justice Starceski in Medical," Eric exclaimed.

"How do you figure now is the best time for us to leave here?" Ash asked Eric.

"There are two reasons we should leave now. One is because they will check for me on the floor below floor eight. Then, they will move on to the next floor. If we leave now, we should be able to make it to the lift and go down to Medical on floor sixteen," Eric explained.

"And the second reason why we should leave now?" Andre proceeded.

"Well, that's easy. It's because they know I was asking for the location of Justice Starceski. I am sure they will be sending officers, not only down to look for me, but also to cover Medical. So, if we hurry, we should be able to plant ourselves in Medical before it is on lockdown," Eric finished.

With the thought of them being unable to get into Medical to speak to Justice Starceski, Andre told the other two to start making their way towards the alley with the lift access, but to be cautious of anyone looking at them. Once Ash and Eric were out of the pod, Andre followed behind them, pulling the pod door shut behind him.

The three began quickly moving through the crowded passageway through floor thirteen. They moved quickly, but not too quickly, so as not to bring any unwanted attention to themselves. They continued until they were in the dead-end alley with lift access. Upon arrival inside the correct alley, they noticed they were not alone. There seemed to be a couple at the far end of the alley. Of course, they were up to no good. The two seemed to be engaged in some sexual activities. Those types of acts were common in the dead-end alleys, but Judicial tended to overlook them.

Andre knew they needed the alley clear before they could call the lift.

Ash noticed a look of displeasure on Andre's face, and before Andre had a chance to interrupt the couple, Ash began to move in the direction of the sexually engaged couple. Once he reached the couple, Ash took something out of his pocket and handed it to one of them. Ash spoke softly, and they quickly gathered up their belongings and dressed quickly. Then, they made their way out of the alley without looking back. In just a few minutes, the alley was empty.

"What did you give the couple, Ash? What did you say to them to get them to leave so quickly?" Eric asked.

"Well, I handed them the keys to my parents' pod. I told them the pod number and told them no one would interrupt them there. They accepted my offer and decided to move their activities to the pod," Ash explained.

"You did not have to do that for us, Ash. That's your home," Andre expressed.

"That place has not been my home since I was six," Ash replied. "What we are trying to accomplish is much more important than the pod."

"Thank you, Ash. The alley is now all ours. Eric, call the lift, please," Andre instructed.

Eric did as Andre directed, opened the hidden panel, and called the lift. Immediately after pressing the call button, the lift door opened. Eric knew from his experience with the lift, that it was still in the same spot as when it stopped last. After the door opened, Eric, Ash, and Andre made their way inside the cramped lift. Since Andre was the last to get in, he was responsible for pressing the button for floor sixteen. With the button pressed, the lift began to make its usual hissing sound and move downwards until it stopped on floor sixteen. Once the lift stopped, and when the door opened, they exited the lift and stepped into the alley. When the lift was empty, Ash closed the door. That was when the three of them began to move out of the alley towards Medical.

Eric, Andre, and Ash made sure to avoid any officers, or make any contact with any human, they may encounter. They kept their heads down and continued their avoidance maneuvers until they were outside Medical. They looked around and noticed security had not been increased yet, so they slowly made their way inside. They snuck past the employees to what they thought was a vacant room, only to be surprised the room was not empty, exactly. The room they entered had the body of a dead patient inside. Ash was the first to notice the body and started to move towards it to get a better look. When Ash reached the body lying on the gurney, he had a rush of forgotten memories filling his mind. Those memories were so intense he could do nothing but fall to the ground crying.

Eric looked over towards Ash and quickly moved over to him with concern.

"Ash, what is the matter? Do you know this person?" Eric asked.

Ash continued to cry without answering Eric's questions. The memories flowing through his mind had control over his emotions, rendering him unable to speak. Ash was seeing flashbacks of the night his parents were murdered. Something about the person lying in front of him on the gurney unlocked repressed memories of his parents' deaths. At first, he could not put his finger on what was causing those feelings and memories to resurface. After he was able to calm himself down enough, he began to compare a memory of the person who committed the murders of his parents, with the person lying on the gurney right in front of him. The reason for the comparison of his memories of the murderer of his parents and the person lying on the gurney was because the body lying there was Jason.

***

While Officer Kevin was on the trail of the man from the video, more officers were informed of a possible sighting of a person of interest in the escape of Andre. Officer Collins radioed all floors the suspect was making his way down into the colony. At the same time, he also radioed for some of the above floor stations to meet him at Medical on floor sixteen.

Officer Collins knew he had given the suspect the location of Justice Starceski and wanted to be sure Justice Starceski was protected until they could capture the suspect. So, Officer Collins radioed Director Barns and informed him of what had transpired at the station on floor eight.

"Director Barns, come in. This is Officer Collins. Do you copy?"

Director Barns was sitting at his desk in Judicial when he heard the call on the radio.

"This is Director Barns. Do you copy Officer Collins?"

"Director Barns, we have a situation unfolding in real-time. I could use your assistance if you are available," Officer Collins requested.

"What is the situation?" Director Barns inquired.

Officer Collins informed the Director of the incident involving one of the unknown suspects in Andre's escape who was at the station on floor eight and how Officer Kevin was in pursuit of the suspect. Officer Collins continued with the information about the suspect inquiring about the location of Justice Starceski. Officer Collins continued with the fact he did, unintentionally and unknowingly, inform the suspect of the location of Justice Starceski. Officer Collins stressed, since the suspect was last seen going down into the colony, he felt they needed to increase the security in Medical for Justice Starceski's protection.

Director Barns agreed with Officer Collins but felt it would be best not to inform Justice Starceski of the current situation. He ordered Medical on lockdown and posted extra officers at the entrance.

Officer Collins agreed and ended the transmission to the Director.

While Officer Collins sent extra officers to Medical, the Director decided he needed to head to Medical too. He felt he could get into Justice Starceski's room without causing fear among anyone in his room.

It took the Director fifteen minutes to make it down to Medical to instruct the officers whom Officer Collins had sent. He ordered the officers not to let anyone into Medical unless they needed emergency medical assistance. He also instructed them to be on the lookout for three men wanting to get into Medical without having a medical emergency. After his orders were given, the Director went to Justice Starceski's room.

***

"Ash, what's wrong? Why are you so upset right now? We have a mission to complete, and I can say you are beginning to freak us out," Eric shared his concern with Ash.

Ash took a few minutes to compose himself before telling Eric he recognized Jason as the person who killed his parents.

"What? This person on the gurney was the person who killed your parents?" Eric asked Ash while pointing to the body on the gurney.

"Yes. I mean it doesn't make sense because I know this person, or A.I.B. to be more exact. Seeing him on the bed just now sent flashes of my parents' murders into my mind, and I know for sure it was him. It was Jason who killed my parents," Ash exclaimed.

"What do you mean by 'A.I.B.'? Are you saying Jason is an A.I.B.?" Andre wanted clarification from Ash.

"Yes, this is the A.I.B. who forced me to help kidnap Justice Starceski's family. He thought he could trade the family for you. They never told me exactly why they wanted you, but they made compelling arguments against you," Ash explained to Andre.

Andre asked more about Ash's involvement with the A.I.B. lying on the medical bed. Ash informed Andre of everything he knew about Jason's plan. Ash ended the conversation with the trade of the family for Andre and how everything went wrong in the end. The plans all went wrong when Jason and his family were moving the Starceski family to floor thirteen, and Jason exited the lift and fell to the ground. Ash explained to Andre, when the Starceski family made their escape, he ran away.

Ash was more embarrassed by the fact he ran when Jason fell to the ground than he was just realizing the same person he helped with the kidnapping was also the same person who killed his parents.

Eric grabbed Ash, gave him a tight hug, then shook him to get his attention back to the task at hand. They needed to get into Justice Starceski's room to inform him the surface A.I.B.s would soon be able to mass produce a self-sustaining power source and eliminate their need to recharge, and the fact Andre had a way to stop the surface A.I.B.s for good. But they would need the humans' help to ensure Andre's plan would work.

Ash composed himself enough to stand and remember the mission at hand. He knew stopping the surface A.I.B.s was more important than the feelings he had about his parents' murders, so Ash agreed with Andre and Eric about making their way to Justice Starceski's room.

Andre was the first to sneak into the hallway, and then Eric followed leading Ash by his hand. Eric led Ash behind Andre through the halls within Medical until they reached Justice Starceski's room.

Once the three reached Justice Starceski's room, Andre walked in first, then Eric and Ash followed. When the three of them were in the room, they were met by Director Barns, Justice Starceski, and Shawn. Director Barns and Justice Starceski noticed Andre and then shared a quick look because they knew Andre had escaped from the holding cell. Director Barns was aware one of the people who helped Andre with his escape had already retrieved information on Justice Starceski's location in Medical.

"Andre, what are you doing here?" Director Barns inquired.

"Forgive me, Director, but I had no choice but to remove myself from my cell. As you already know, I have information about how to stop the surface A.I.B.s. But what makes this an urgent matter is the fact my brother, Eric, has given me important information regarding the surface A.I.B.s and how close they are to start mass producing a self-sustaining power source based on a prototype Eric made for the Elders. If we don't act fast, as soon as the surface A.I.B.s can replicate the design Eric gave them, they will be unstoppable. That is why we must act now," Andre told the room.

"We may have a problem down here as well. You may not be aware of this, but we have had two murders here in the colony, and Ash is the only suspect we had for those murders. We need to take Ash into custody before we worry about what the surface A.I.B.s are going to do, or not do," Justice Starceski blurted out in response to what Andre had just told him.

Justice Starceski's information took everyone in the room by surprise.

"What? You think I killed my parents?" Ash replied loudly.

"You are the most obvious suspect in your parents' deaths," Justice Starceski spouted out.

"I was only six years old! How could you think I killed my parents?" Ash inquired.

"You were the only person in the room when they were murdered, and you said you did not see or hear anyone else inside your pod at the time of their deaths. Your age is the reason we deleted any information about you, your parents, and any information regarding their untimely deaths from the archives," Justice Starceski reiterated.

"That may have been when I was six years old, but I can tell you now, I was not the one who killed them. It was the dead man in the other room. His name is Jason. He is an A.I.B., and he killed my parents," Ash revealed to the room.

Justice Starceski, Shawn, and the Director were all a sudden struck with disbelief on their faces.

"Excuse me? Not only are you telling us there is a dead guy in another room who killed your parents, but he is also an A.I.B.?" Justice Starceski asked for more clarification.

"Yes. He is the one who not only killed my parents but also kidnapped your family," Ash shouted out to Justice

Starceski and Shawn. But Ash had an inclination, Shawn already knew that information but wasn't showing it on his face.

"Well, before we get into that, Andre, there is a doctor who needs your help here to save a life. Can you assist him before we get into the situation with the surface A.I.B.s, or Ash's accusations," Justice Starceski asked.

"Of course. What can I do to help someone here in the colony?" Andre asked.

"Give me a moment to contact the doctor in charge of the patient who needs your help."

Justice Starceski pressed the button beside his bed to call for an attending doctor.

"What can I do for you, Justice Starceski," asked the doctor.

"I have Andre with us, and he is ready to help you with your patient," Justice Starceski asked the doctor.

"Thank God you are here, Andre. Can you come with me, please? We have a patient who needs your help," the doctor asked.

Andre agreed to follow the doctor out of the room and down the hall to another room. Andre knew the room the doctor took him into all too well, as he was just in the same room with Eric and Ash. Andre began to feel something was off, but he entered the room with the doctor anyway.

"This is the patient who needs your help. Can you help him?" the doctor asked.

Andre looked over at the bed with the patient in it and froze. It was Jason, the person who murdered Ash's parents so long ago. He was torn between helping the patient or just letting him remain offline. Andre needed time to discuss it more with Ash and Justice Starceski before he would agree to help.

Chapter 16

Andre stood in the medical room with the doctor without saying a word. As Andre stood there in silence, the doctor was going on and on about how the person lying on the bed had a wife and two children who depended on him. Andre tuned the doctor out as he knew he needed to speak to Justice Starceski and Ash before he committed to helping Jason.

Andre turned away from Jason's body and the doctor and left the room to go back to Justice Starceski's room. When Andre entered the room, everyone went silent and stared at him.

"Do you think you can help the patient, Andre?" Justice Starceski asked.

"We need to talk, Justice Starceski. Would everyone except Ash leave the room, please?" Andre asked while he had the attention of the room.

"Chris, are you okay with us leaving?" Justice Starceski's husband inquired.

As Justice Starceski looked around the room to assess the situation, Eric looked at Ash with concern. Ash looked at Eric and nodded to tell him he was okay with staying behind. Then Justice Starceski answered Shawn.

"Yes, Shawn, it's okay. If Andre wanted to hurt me, or anyone else in the colony, he would have done it a long time ago."

With that, Eric, Shawn, and Director Barns exited the room. Shawn stopped the doctor on his way back into Justice Starceski's room by grabbing his arm to lead him back out.

Once the room was clear of everyone, except Justice Starceski, Ash, and Andre, Andre began to express his feelings on helping the patient.

"Justice Starceski, there are a few things you need to know about the patient you want me to help before you make a final decision on me helping the patient," Andre informed Justice Starceski.

"Andre, if I need to know something, please enlighten me. I am not sure you have been in the colony long enough to know something about the residents here I don't already know. And please, Andre, call me Chris. I believe we have spoken enough times to not be so formal," Justice Starceski replied to Andre.

"Chris, I have asked Ash to stay here with us because what I am about to tell you involves him as well," Andre addressed Justice Starceski by his first name as instructed.

"What are you talking about, Andre?" Ash asked in disbelief.

"You will soon find out, Ash. I want to make sure Chris is aware you know the patient and have had some past dealings with him," Andre responded.

"I hate to interrupt you, but Ash being here is fine with me as long as you can tie the patient to Ash," Chris expressed.

"Thank you, Chris, I will. The first thing you need to know is the patient you want me to help not only kidnapped your family but is also the A.I.B. who murdered Ash's parents. The patient is the same Jason who Ash just told you about. I just identified him with the doctor as the patient you want me to help," Andre began.

"You want Andre to help save the thing that murdered my parents?" Ash asked with some confusion.

"What? What are you telling me exactly, Andre?" Chris asked.

"The patient you have asked me to help save is an A.I.B. who has been in the colony since humans first came down here. He is also the reason Ash's parents are dead," Andre continued.

"Ash, how do we know the patient is the same person who killed your parents? There was no evidence of anyone else being in your family's pod when they were murdered. You were the only other person in the room when they were found. Yes, you were only six years old, but your recollections of the event were all over the place. You left us with no choice but to close the case as quickly as possible and remove any mention of you, your parents, and their murders from the archives. We were not prepared to inform the colony that our only suspect in a double murder was a six-year-old child, and the victims were his parents. How could we explain that to the people?" Chris explained the predicament he was in at the time.

The three of them took a moment to comprehend what was being said before Ash responded.

"I was only six years old and witnessed my parents' murders, and yes, maybe my story of the event sounded odd. It was because I did not understand what the officers were saying to me, or what had happened to my parents. It wasn't until just now, when I saw Jason's body lying dead on the gurney in the other room, I thought back to when my parents were killed. When I saw his body just lying there, I saw a flash of my mother and father lying on the floor of our pod. That was when I remembered the face of the actual murderer. It was Jason," Ash exclaimed. "Jason also kidnapped your family so he could make a trade for Andre."

"Ash, that's enough," Andre loudly spoke to Ash.

"No, I don't think it is. Judicial authorities let my parents' murderer go free for so many years. Now I find out they suspected me all along, a six-year-old, of killing them. Justice Starceski needs to know the full truth," Ash expressed with a hint of hurt in his voice.

"Ash, you need to relax for a moment. Chris is just now getting the same information I received a few minutes ago. Give him a minute to process what he has just learned," Andre told Ash to calm him down.

Ash stopped with his comments after Andre spoke. Ash also felt he was blaming the wrong person for the situation with his parents' deaths. Ash took a deep breath and waited for a response from Chris.

It wasn't long before Chris responded to Ash's remarks.

"Let me get this straight. The patient the doctor wants you to help is the same person who not only kidnapped my family, but is also the same person who murdered Ash's parents?" Chris asked Andre for clarity.

"That is correct, Chris," Andre answered.

"Andre, can I ask you an obvious question?"

"Of course," Andre replied.

"How do you know the patient kidnapped my family?"

"Can I answer that?" Ash spoke out. "It's because I told Andre. You see, I was part of the kidnapping, but it was only after Jason already had your family, of course. It was also because they told me the only reason, they kidnapped your family was so they could trade your family for an A.I.B. you captured. I didn't know why they wanted Andre, and I still don't know why," Ash explained. "But when I saw Jason's body in the other room on the gurney, everything came rushing back to me about my parents' murders. I suddenly saw my parents' bodies lying on the floor of our pod, and Jason was standing over their dead bodies. I remember him saying something about my parents finding out he was an A.I.B. That was why you didn't understand what I was saying to you back then, did you? I told you an A.I.B. killed my parents, but you dismissed it because a six-year-old was saying it to you. You didn't want to believe an A.I.B. was here in the colony. Am I right?" Ash finished.

"Let's stop for a minute. We need to discuss why I should help the patient. Chris, now that you know all the facts about Jason, the patient, what do you suggest I do?" Andre interrupted Ash's rant.

***

Once Eric, Shawn, and Director Barns were in the hallway of Medical after leaving Justice Starceski's room, the doctor led them to the waiting area. Upon arrival, Shawn noticed Macy and her children in the same room. Shawn needed to speak to her to see how she was holding up, but he also felt he needed to avoid speaking to her to keep her and her children out of danger. Shawn was afraid if he spoke to Macy, others might find out her husband was the one who kidnapped him and his children. Shawn didn't want to put Macy through that. He needed to make sure he could speak to her without drawing any attention to either of them. Once Shawn felt they were in the clear, he made his move over to Macy.

"Macy, how are you doing through all this? How is Jason? I'm sorry I ran with the children, but I didn't know, and still don't know, what your husband had in store for us. So, when Jason fell to the ground, we ran," Shawn told Macy.

"Honestly, Shawn, I don't know how I am doing. I am trying to be strong for our children, but I think they can feel something is wrong," Macy answered.

"Well, if you think it would help them, I could have Tabitha and Frankie brought down here so they could play together to take their minds off things," Shawn offered.

"You would do that for us? Why? My husband kidnapped you and your children," Macy asked.

"That's true, but you and the children had nothing to do with it. I believe it would be good for our children, and maybe even us, if they could see each other. So, what do you say? Should I have them brought here?" Shawn made it clear to Macy he felt no ill will towards her or her children.

"Thank you, Shawn. I accept your offer. Bring your children here to Medical. I know Jonathan and Kristin would love to see them," Macy expressed her gratitude.

With that, Shawn left Macy's side and walked over to one of the officers who was standing at a post near the entrance of Medical. Shawn ordered the officer to go up to his pod, retrieve his children, and escort them back to Medical. He also instructed the officer to thank his neighbor for watching his children while he has been in Medical with Chris.

The officer acknowledged his orders, turned away from Shawn, and started his way up to the Judicial floor to gather the children of Shawn and Justice Starceski.

***

Before Chris would make a final decision regarding the patient, he wanted some proof of his involvement in the kidnapping of his family. Chris knew he had a way to prove whether Ash was telling the truth about the patient kidnapping his family. He just needed to get a hold of I.T.

"Andre, please ask Director Barns to return to the room. I need him to do something for me before I make a final decision about the patient," Chris asked.

"Yes, Chris, I can get the Director. Give me just a minute," Andre answered.

Andre excused himself and started down the busy medical hallway until he reached the waiting area. When Andre entered the waiting area, everyone stopped talking and diverted all their attention to him.

"Director Barns, Chris has asked me to have you return to his room. He has something for you to do," Andre explained his presence in the room.

"Lead the way, Andre," Director Barns instructed.

Andre turned around and began to lead the Director back to Justice Starceski's room. The two walked in silence until they reached the room door.

"After you, Director," Andre suggested, as he pushed the door open.

"No, after you. I insist," the Director replied.

Andre looked at the Director, pushed the door open wider, and stepped inside. The Director followed suit.

"Thank you for coming, Director. I need you to inform the I.T. department I need the footage from the time the security system was upgraded," Justice Starceski paused for a moment, then looked at Ash. "What floor is the patient's pod on?"

"Their pod is on floor forty-eight. Why do you ask?" Ash asked.

"That is not your concern at the moment, but thank you for the information," Justice Starceski finished with Ash.

"Director Barns, tell I.T. the only footage I need is the recordings on floor forty-eight during the system upgrade time," Chris finished.

Director Barns was confused until he remembered Justice Starceski had stopped at I.T. while they were on their way to the archives floor for Andre to link with the archives. The Director pieced together what Justice Starceski did during his stop at I.T. that day. With a crooked smile, the Director nodded to Chris and exited the room.

Once the Director was out of the room, Chris addressed Andre and Ash.

"If what you are telling me is the truth about the patient kidnapping my family, we will have all the proof we need when the Director returns. So, is there anything else you want to tell me about my family's kidnapping, Ash?"

Ash stood in silence with a puzzled look on his face. Then, he felt he needed more information before answering the question.

"Exactly what are you asking me, Justice Starceski?"

"Why were you the one who brought me the note from the kidnappers? Could it have been a coincidence?"

"There is something I need to tell you, Justice Starceski. I can tell you I didn't have anything to do with the actual kidnapping of your family, as I previously stated. I would never intentionally put someone in danger," Ash began.

"But? I know there must be more to your story, Ash," Chris questioned.

Ash composed himself before he answered.

"You are right. There is more to the story. You see, I found out later Jason had kidnapped your family. I met Jason some time ago in cafeteria 1. He had begun watching me for God knows how long. He said he had always noticed I ate alone and never spoke to anyone else in the cafeteria, so he figured out I was alone here in the colony. He took advantage of my situation, which you had put me in after my parents were killed. Jason came over and sat down with me one day, and we began to talk. He would tell me things about himself, about how he and his family also felt alone in the colony. So, I guess we became friends. We connected over being alone in the colony. From then on, I never ate alone. He was always there when I was. It was nice to have someone to talk to. Eventually, he invited me over to his pod to meet his family. They were very nice," Ash continued telling his story.

"So, when did things change for you?" Justice Starceski inquired.

"Things changed when Andre was caught in the colony. You don't know this, but Jason knew when Andre first arrived here in the colony. That's when he told me he was an A.I.B. here in the colony and he needed it. Again, he never told me why he needed Andre, but he did express how dangerous Andre was, or so I thought. That was around the time Jason began to talk about ways to get Andre. Jason was obsessed with getting ahold of Andre. He talked about breaking him out of his cell, but he thought it would be too risky. Then Jason came up with kidnapping your family to trade for Andre. Jason saw I would not help him with kidnapping, so he said he would think of another way. I left his pod the same day and went to my pod. That must have been when he kidnapped your family," Ash explained in detail.

"How do you figure?" Justice Starceski asked.

"Because the next day, when I went to his pod, he seemed different," Ash replied.

"Different how?" Andre asked this time.

"He was not talking about ways to retrieve Andre anymore. I just figured he gave up on the idea, but I found out later in the day he had already kidnapped your family," Ash explained while looking at Justice Starceski.

"How did you find out for sure?" Justice Starceski asked.

"I heard voices coming from a hidden room in Jason's pod. When I asked Jason about the voices, he opened the door to the hidden room and showed me your family. I was in shock. I couldn't believe he went ahead and kidnapped them. At first, I wanted to release them, but then Jason assured me he did not plan on hurting your family. He only wanted to have them as leverage to get Andre. Then Jason started filling my head with ideas about how Andre was sent down into the colony, by the Elders, to destroy it. Jason told me he was here to prevent that from happening, and that was why he had to get Andre, so he could shut him down before he could complete his mission. I feel so stupid believing any of those things now. I am sorry, but at the time, I felt it was the only way to protect the colony. Then I thought the only way I could protect your family was to move them to a more secure location. I figured when we moved them, there was a chance they could escape, and they did. Once they were freed, I left Jason and ran away," Ash concluded.

"What do you want me to do with this information, Ash? Do you think just because they were able to escape, it makes you innocent of being involved in their kidnapping? Why did you bring me the note from the kidnappers? Was it to see what all I knew, or out of concern for my family?" Justice Starceski was serious at that point.

"To be honest, I don't know why I gave you the note instead of telling you everything. At this moment, I felt Andre was more of a threat than Jason. I see now I was wrong in my assumptions, and I am truly sorry. But now you know everything about Jason, so you can't bring him back online!" Ash exclaimed.

"Thank you for your honesty, Ash, but you have not convinced me the patient killed your parents. Where is the proof of that?" Justice Starceski questioned Ash.

Before Ash could respond, Director Barns barged into the room holding a portable device in his hands, waiving it at Chris.

"I have what you asked for, Chris."

Chapter 17

Shawn and Macy sat in the waiting area of Medical, comforting each other until Shawn's children came running in with an officer. Tabitha and Frankie looked in high spirits when they saw Jonathan and Kristin sitting near Macy.

"Hello, Daddy," Frankie shouted. "Can we play with Jonathan and Kristin?" Frankie asked as he pointed to a play area in the medical waiting room.

"Of course, son. Take Tabitha with you, and be respectful of the other people in here," Shawn replied.

Frankie nodded his head, grabbed Tabitha's hand, and motioned for Jonathan and Kristin to follow them to the play area. Once the four of them were back together, Macy could see a change in her children. They seemed happy again.

Macy and Shawn sat silently, watching their children play without a care in the world. That put a smile on Macy's face for the first time in hours. Shawn felt the same way.

***

"Director Barns, what have you brought us?" Chris inquired about the device in his hands.

"I have what you asked for from the I.T. department. I also retrieved some other footage you will want to see. It was a long shot, but I took a chance and struck gold! I hope you will not be upset about me overstepping my duties, but it is something you will want to see," Director Barns responded.

"So, what do you suggest we watch first?" Chris asked the Director.

"I say we start with what you asked me to get for you from I.T. about floor forty-eight on the date in question."

Chris took the device from the Director, positioned it on his lap, and pressed play. From what he could see, Ash was in the video with his kidnapped family and four unidentified individuals. The four unknown perpetrators were two adults, with what looked like two children. At first glance, Chris was not sure what he was watching. Why would a family kidnap his family? Chris became more confused as he watched the video.

"Ash, it seems you may have left out some of the details of the kidnappers. Why didn't you mention it was a family of four who kidnapped my family?" Chris demanded to know.

"Because I don't believe his wife was involved in the actual kidnapping, and I'm sure the children were not involved. I believe Jason kidnapped your family without their help, or knowledge, and he told them the same things about Andre, he told me," Ash explained.

"You may be right, Ash, but you should not have left any information out. Do you understand me?"

"Justice Starceski, I suggest you review the other footage I brought you before you accuse Ash of anything," Director Barns told Chris.

Chris looked at Director Barns, intrigued by what else was on the video. Chris placed the device back on his lap and pressed play to watch the second video. As the video played, Chris sat in silence. He could not believe what he was watching. Chris watched the video until the end, then looked at Ash with dismay.

"Ash, I believe you need to watch this video. It pertains to you in a way."

Ash grabbed the device Justice Starceski had just used to watch the videos. When the video began to play, Ash noticed it was a video from some time ago. At first, he was not sure what he was watching. That was until Ash recognized where the footage was shot. He knew the area he was watching was from around his parents' pod. Then he saw Jason leave his parents' pod, but Jason was not alone. Macy walked out after Jason. Ash didn't know how to take in what he was seeing. Ash could not believe Macy was involved in his parents' murders. The only thing he could think about was he needed to speak to Macy.

"Thank you for showing this to me, Justice Starceski. Like I said before, I didn't kill my parents, and this proves it. I would like to speak to the woman in the video before I answer any more questions. I hope you understand," Ash informed Chris.

"That's fine, Ash, but how will you get ahold of the woman who was with Jason?"

"Well, she is Jason's wife, Macy. I believe she is in the waiting area in Medical. I want to speak to her before you do anything. Will you grant me this?" Ash asked Justice Starceski.

Chris nodded to Ash. Chris felt it was something Ash needed to do to understand his parents' murders, so he let him go.

Ash turned away from Justice Starceski's bed, but before he could exit the room, Andre grabbed his arm.

"Are you okay with going in there to speak to Macy alone?"

"I won't be alone; Eric is out there. If I need any help, or guidance, I will make certain Eric knows," Ash replied.

That told Andre all he needed to know. He knew Ash would be okay.

Ash removed Andre's hand from his arm and left the room and into the busy medical hallway until he was in the waiting area. There, he saw Macy sitting with Justice Starceski's husband, Shawn. Unsure how to proceed, Ash walked over to Macy and asked if he could speak to her, alone.

Macy acknowledged Ash and asked if Shawn would give them a moment alone. She had a feeling she knew what Ash wanted to talk about. It was not a time in her life she was proud of, but it was the moment when she became the person she was now.

"Ash, I knew you would come to me with questions one day. I have a feeling you already know the truth about your parents' deaths, and it is the reason you want to talk to me. And am I correct?"

"So, it's true! You and Jason killed my parents when I was a child. Why did you kill them? What did they do to you and Jason?" Ash inquired.

"Ash, I can't begin to apologize enough about their deaths. I am telling you it was the day I changed. The reason Jason told me we had to kill your parents was because they found out we were A.I.B.s, and it was the only way to prevent our discovery from the rest of the colony. He told me we had to terminate them. At the time, I felt what Jason felt. We had to do whatever we could to conceal our cover, so terminating your parents was warranted. But, as soon as it was over, I began to have real feelings about the incident. I felt regret immediately, and I thought Jason would have felt the same way, but I learned he did not have feelings like me. From that moment on, I had to conceal my feelings from Jason, but I secretly taught my children about feelings. I had no other option but to stay with Jason and hide who I had become from him. I know I should have told you earlier, but I couldn't afford to let you turn us in. The children had nothing to do with what happened to your parents, and I had to protect them. Again, I hope you can understand," Macy explained to Ash.

"I don't know what to think about what you and Jason did to my parents. I do want to know WHY you want Andre to help Jason now. After everything he did to you and me, why do you want to save him? If Andre chooses not to help Jason, you will be free of him and can live the life you want to live with your children."

Macy took a minute to process what Ash had just suggested to her. Macy felt she needed to be honest with Ash and tell him why she wanted to save Jason.

"Ash, I need to tell you more about what happened in the alley after you left. Before Jason shut down completely, he said something significant to me," Macy started.

"What could Jason say to you that would make you change your mind about him?" Ash responded.

"Once we were alone in the alley, Jason took my hand and asked me to forgive him," Macy told Ash.

"And what does that change? It's a little late to ask for forgiveness, isn't it?" Ash asked.

"That's just it. Jason asking me for forgiveness means he could feel. He had emotions and feelings then. That is what caused his system to shut down. You see, Jason may not be the same person he was before his system shut down. Don't we all owe it to ourselves to see if it's true? Jason may be a completely different person with different objectives now," Macy pleaded with Ash.

"Do you mind if we fill Eric in on what you have told me? I need to get his opinion on the matter," Ash asked.

"Why, because he's an A.I.B.?" Macy asked.

"No, because he has had true feelings since he was created and will give me an honest assessment of the issue," Ash replied.

"Then, yes. Please speak to Eric before you make any recommendations on Jason's survival," Macy told Ash.

Ash excused himself from Macy, after letting her know he would tell her of his decision before he told anyone else. Ash stood up and over walked to Eric, who was on the other side of the waiting area.

Ash approached Eric with a look of desperation. Eric opened his arms as Ash fell into his embrace and sobbed softly into Eric's shoulder. Eric let Ash cry while consoling him until he was ready to speak.

"Eric, I need to tell you something and ask for some advice about what to do," Ash spoke softly to Eric once he finished crying.

"Is this about the conversation you just had with Macy?"

"It is. Macy told me some things about Jason, and I need to know if what she told me is even possible," Ash began.

"Yes, Ash. Everything Macy told you is possible. Jason could have emotions and feelings now. Sorry, I overheard everything she told you. I didn't mean to intrude on your privacy, but you didn't look so good when you walked into the room. I wanted to make sure you were alright. Please forgive me for my rudeness," Eric confessed to Ash.

"You were listening? Did you hear everything Macy said? Like the fact she was also involved with my parents' deaths," Ash replied.

"Yes, and I am sorry you had to find out about Macy's involvement like this. I do believe she is telling the truth about your parents' deaths being the catalyst that gave her feelings. I also believe she is sincere with her apology," Eric expressed.

"What else do you think about the rest of what she said? The things about Jason's final words to her," Ash asked.

"Are you sure you want my opinion?" Eric replied.

"Of course. That is the main reason I came over here to talk to you," Ash reassured Eric he knew he would receive an honest assessment of what Macy had told him.

"Well, Ash, I can tell you if Jason asked Macy for forgiveness, then he could possibly have emotions and feelings. A true A.I.B. would never ask for forgiveness because they do not know what the word means. They only know the definition of the word, but not how it is meant to be used. So, to answer your question, I believe Jason may have changed in the alley. Now, what you do with this information is up to you. I will respect your decision and back you up one hundred percent." Eric told Ash.

"Thank you, Eric. I know what I need to do now," Ash told Eric.

As Ash made his short walk back to Macy, he figured she heard his conversation with Eric, which meant he didn't need to repeat it to her. Ash stopped in front of Macy to let her know of his decision.

"Macy, I am sure you overheard our conversation, and it's okay. I will allow Andre to help Jason. But, if Jason is the same as before, I will instruct Andre to terminate him for good. Do you understand?"

"Thank you, Ash. I know it was not an easy decision for you, and I understand the need to terminate Jason if he is the same as before he shut down. But I know he has changed, and I thank you for taking the chance to find out for yourself," Macy expressed gratitude to Ash.

Ash took Macy's hand, squeezing it softly, to reassure her he hoped for the best outcome. Then he released her hand, then began his back to Justice Starceski's room to inform the others of his decision. Ash was in no hurry to return, so he stopped in the room with Jason's body in it. Ash wanted to take another look at the person whose life depended on him. He stood beside the body on the gurney and said a little prayer to himself and to Jason, hoping for the best outcome of his decision. Once he finished his prayer, he turned and walked out of the room with his mind made up. Ash was determined to find out if what Macy told him about Jason's last words meant what she thought it meant. He wanted to know if Jason had feelings and emotions now.

Upon reaching Justice Starceski's room, Ash took a deep breath and opened the door.

"Ash, have you decided what you want to do?" Justice Starceski asked. Andre and the Director were wondering the same thing.

"I have come to a decision on what I think we should do for Jason. After speaking with Macy and Eric, I have decided to let Andre help save Jason's life. But I have my own demand if things do not prove what Macy believes," Ash told the room.

"And what demand is that?" Justice Starceski asked.

"Simple. If Jason does not have feelings and emotions, if Andre is even able to bring him back online, then I want to make sure Andre will be allowed to shut Jason down for good," Ash spoke in a demanding voice.

Justice Starceski looked at the Director, then at Andre, to try and get a feeling for what the room wanted before he spoke. After a few moments of silence, Chris spoke.

"Just to clarify, Ash, you are saying if Jason is not the same as he was when he shut down, he can stay alive? But, if Jason is the same as before, you want Andre to terminate him?"

"That is correct. If Jason has feelings and emotions, he will be allowed to stay online. But, if he doesn't have feelings or emotions like he lacked before he shut down, I want Andre to terminate him for good. Do I make myself clear?"

No one answered Ash immediately. The entire room was quiet. Neither Justice Starceski nor Director Barns knew how to answer Ash's request. But then the silence was broken.

"I agree with Ash. Jason can only remain operational if he has developed feelings and emotions. He must also actually want forgiveness for his past crimes and understand what it means to be forgiven," Andre told the others.

The room was silent once again. Then Justice Starceski and Director Barns agreed to Ash's demand. Whatever happened next was up to Andre.

Chapter 18

Once Ash left Macy, Shawn noticed her expression went from joyful to sad. Shawn was unsure what Ash said to Macy but knew it couldn't have been good. Shawn slowly stood up from his perch next to the playing children and went back over to Macy.

"Macy, is everything okay?" Shawn asked softly so as not to draw attention from anyone.

Macy looked up at Shawn and began to cry. Macy was clearly upset about the conversation she had just had with Ash. Macy was thankful she could take comfort in Shawn being there for her.

"I'm sorry for my sadness. I have known for many years I would eventually have to have that difficult conversation with Ash. I just never thought it would affect me in such a way. While I may seem sad right now, I am happy Ash and I talked about what I had been holding inside for so long. Our conversation was about a tragic event that happened many years ago. It affected both of our lives. I still believe I have time to earn Ash's forgiveness," Macy told Shawn.

Shawn let Macy speak without interruption. He could sense the tension in her voice and felt he should not ask about what they talked about. Their conversation was obviously cathartic for Macy, and that was all Shawn needed to know. He was happy he was there when Macy needed a shoulder to cry on, especially with everything happening with Jason.

Macy and Shawn did not speak after Macy stopped crying. Shawn just wanted Macy to know he was there for her. Obviously, Shawn and Macy had developed a bond, so their silence spoke volumes, and Shawn knew she was grateful.

***

Andre knew Ash's request was not unreasonable. He knew he would not want to be responsible for saving the life of a murderer and kidnapper, especially an A.I.B. Andre was prepared to do whatever was necessary to terminate Jason if his programming had not changed.

"Director Barns, Chris, I want to make sure you both agree with Ash's demand for me to terminate Jason if he is still the same as before he shut down."

Chris and the Director took one more look at each other before answering Andre's question.

"Andre, I can confirm we agree with whatever methods you must use on Jason. If you can bring him back online, and if deemed necessary to terminate his programming once and for all, you are permitted to do so to protect the colony."

"Before we continue, I think it would be best to pull everyone into your room so we all can be on the same page," Andre suggested.

Chris asked Ash to bring everyone back into the room. Before doing so, Ash asked, "What should I do about the children? Your children are in the waiting area playing with Macy's children."

"When did my children get here? Never mind, it must have been Shawn who brought them here. See if Officer Collins is out there and ask him to keep an eye on all four children," Chris responded.

Ash rushed into the waiting area in search of Officer Collins. Ash walked over to the closest officer he saw and asked him to radio for Officer Collins to come to the waiting area. Officer Collins was already in Medical at another post, so it only took him a few minutes to arrive in the waiting area.

When Officer Collins arrived where Ash and the officer were standing, Ash passed along Justice Starceski's request for him to watch the four children.

***

Shawn was the first to see Ash walk back into the waiting area. At first, Shawn was ready to protect Macy from anything Ash had to say to her again. Shawn felt Macy had been through enough with Ash and Jason for the night. But before Shawn could stand to intercept Ash from Macy, Ash stopped to talk to an officer. Shawn instantly relaxed and didn't stand up. That caught Macy's attention.

"Shawn, what's wrong?" Macy asked.

"Nothing, yet. Ash just came back out here. I was worried he was coming back over here to upset you more. I was going to stop him, then I noticed he stopped at the other officer," Shawn said while looking in Ash's direction.

"Well, that can't be good," Macy responded to Shawn based on her observation.

Shawn and Macy noticed Ash was not looking in their direction but saw the officer move to the center of the waiting area and instruct an employee to radio for someone. Once the employee finished, the officer walked back over to Ash, and they stood there for a minute before another officer walked up to them. Then Ash walked away from the officers and began to get the room's attention to speak to them all.

"Excuse me, but I need Eric, Shawn, and Macy to follow me back to Justice Starceski's room, please. He would like to address us all at the same time. And don't worry, Officer Collins will watch all the children. There is nothing to worry about, but I can tell you it does involve all of us," Ash ended his announcement to the room.

Shawn looked at Macy to confirm she was okay with this new development.

"Macy, are you okay with leaving the children here with Officer Collins while we go to Chris' room?"

"Are you?"

"If Chris is fine with Officer Collins watching our children, then I am confident he will be fine watching yours," Shawn replied.

"Fine, then I trust you."

***

After Ash knew Eric, Shawn, and Macy agreed to go back to the room with him, he made the first move toward the hallway that led back to Justice Starceski's room. Ash looked back and could see the others were following him.

After everyone was in the room, Ash closed the door tightly. Ash knew what they were about to discuss was not something any of the people in the room wanted anyone else to overhear.

"Now that everyone is here, there is something we need to discuss," Justice Starceski told the crowd occupying his room. "We all know there is a patient Andre has been asked to help save. Now, there has been more information to come up about the patient. Before anyone says anything, Andre has agreed to help this patient, but there has been a condition from Ash in return for Andre's help," Justice Starceski told the room. "This condition has been agreed upon by Andre, Ash, Director Barns, and me. I am only going to tell you what was decided," Justice Starceski informed the crowd.

"And what exactly are you talking about, Chris?" Justice Starceski's husband Shawn asked.

"The condition made by Ash is if Andre can bring the patient back online, and if the patient's programming has not changed to include emotions and feelings, then Andre will terminate the patient. I say this because the patient Andre will try to save is an A.I.B. This A.I.B., whose name is Jason, is Macy's husband. I gather you agree with this decision and solution," Justice Starceski said as he looked at Macy.

"That is correct. I agree with the decision regarding my husband. I prefer not to go into details about the events that have led up to this moment if you don't mind, Justice Starceski," Macy confirmed.

Justice Starceski looked at Macy in agreement. The reasons that led up to Macy's agreement would stay between those who already knew about the situation. And with that, Justice Starceski nodded to Andre for him to leave the room to address the patient.

***

Andre entered the room where Jason's body was and looked around the room. Andre preferred to work on Jason's body alone.

"Excuse me, but could you please clear the room? Also, I do not want to be disturbed during the procedure for this patient. Ensure no one enters this room until I confirm I am finished. Do you understand?"

The doctors looked at each other, then over to Andre. Without another word, they both dropped whatever they had in their hands and walked out of the room.

Now that Andre was alone with Jason's body, it was time for Andre to begin running diagnostics on Jason. Andre needed to make sure there were no programming issues, or fried circuit boards, in Jason's infrastructure. Andre opened Jason's chest to check his framework and to start the diagnostic tests. Andre let the tests run for thirty minutes while he double checked for fried memory chips or burnt wiring. Everything came back within the parameters to bring Jason back online safely. With those results, Andre began his process of restarting the A.I.B. known as Jason.

Everything was going as Andre predicted until Jason's eyes opened.

***

Back in Justice Starceski's room, Macy and Shawn had left to return to the waiting area to be with the children, leaving

Eric, Ash, and Director Barns with Justice Starceski. Eric and Ash were in the middle of a conversation while the Director and Chris sat in silence. That was until the lights in Medical began flickering.

"Chris, what's happening?" Director Barns broke their silence.

"I'm not sure. Can someone please fetch the doctor?" Justice Starceski blurted out to anyone who would listen.

Ash took it upon himself to find the doctor. He let go of Eric's hand and rushed out of the room.

"What's the problem? Does this happen often?" Eric inquired.

"No. The colony has never had any power surges since I started in Judicial," Justice Starceski explained. "Director, please hand me my clothes. It's time for me to be released."

The Director started to say something to Chris but decided there was nothing he could say to change his mind. Director Barns grabbed the clothes Shawn had brought and handed them to Chris.

Justice Starceski got dressed as quickly as possible. He did not want to wait for Ash to return with the doctor to learn about what was happening in Medical. As Chris finished dressing, Ash walked into the room without the doctor.

"Ash, where is the doctor? Did he tell you what was going on in here? Is it affecting the entire colony, or is this isolated to Medical?" Justice Starceski asked.

"The doctor is aware of the issue, and he assumed it had to do with Andre's procedure on Jason," Ash told everyone in the room.

"What makes him think Andre, or the procedure, is the cause?" Justice Starceski asked.

"Because Andre told the other doctors to leave him alone with Jason's body. I heard no one was allowed in the room during the procedure. The doctors were standing outside the room and saying whatever Andre was doing in there was causing the power surges. Andre used so much power to bring

Jason back online it caused the surge. It is only in Medical," Ash retold what the doctor had told him.

"Well, I do not care if Andre has ordered everyone out of the room. It is about time I went into the room to double check and make sure it was Andre who created the power surge. If it was not Andre, we may have a different problem in the colony. Ash, would you please lead me to Andre?" Justice Starceski asked.

Without hesitation, Ash led Justice Starceski into the busy hallway of Medical. Ash, with Justice Starceski in tow, continued the short walk to the room where Andre and Jason's body were. Once they stopped, Ash pointed at the room door for Justice Starceski to let him know they were there.

"Are you sure this is the room Andre is in?"

"Yes, Sir. This is the room where I saw Jason's body earlier."

Without knocking, Justice Starceski pushed the door open, instructed Ash to remain in the hall, and proceeded into the room alone.

Upon entering the room, Justice Starceski could see Andre standing next to Jason's body. Andre did not look pleased.

"Andre, what have you been doing in here exactly? Were you responsible for the power surge in Medical?"

"Yes, Chris, I did cause the power surge, but it was just when I tried to bring Jason's body back online. I did not possess enough power from my system to bring him online, so I connected to the power grid for Medical. You do not have to worry. There will be no more power surges."

"So, what is the outcome? Did everything go as you planned? Is the patient online, and is he a better version of himself now?"

"Not exactly, Chris. Jason was online for only a few minutes before he shut down on his own. I know Jason did possess feelings and emotions when he was brought back online for a short time. The reason he was unable to stay online was because of the way he obtained feelings and emotions, which is why Jason's' body shut down again. Jason's system was overloaded because he was flooded with all human emotions and feelings all at the same time, while I learned human emotions and feelings over time interacting with humans being an AI program for humans to use. Due to the differences in the way Jason received emotions and feelings the way he did and the way I learned them, there is nothing I can do for him."

"That's a shame to hear, Andre. To be clear, are you certain you did all you could for Jason?"

"I am, Sir, but the unforeseen incident only verified what I had known for many years."

"And what is that, Andre?"

"He could not reset because when feelings and emotions are forced on any A.I.B., they are fatal. If they are surged with human feelings and emotions, it will cause the A.I.B.s body to shut down for good. Now that I know this fact, I know my plan to stop all A.I.B.s will work. I can head back to the surface and begin my attack on surface A.I.B.s to regain human control over the surface."

Chapter 19

A week had gone by since Andre's unsuccessful attempt to revive Jason. With the assistance of Shawn, Macy dealt with the difficult outcome regarding Jason's fate. Macy was grateful for Andre's efforts, and at Ash's request, Judicial decided not to press charges against her for her role in Ash's parents' deaths.

Andre knew his plan to end the surface A.I.B.s would work since he failed to bring Jason back online. Andre was sure he needed to upload the programming required for feelings and emotions onto the Elders' main servers. Once successfully uploaded, the programming would trigger a software update. The update would require all A.I.B.s to go to the nearest operational charging station, link up with the main servers, and receive new updates while recharging. Theoretically, the A.I.B.s would shut down within fifteen minutes of installing the software update. They would never be able to reboot, or come back online again, no matter what the Elders may try. Even though the surface A.I.B.s with the software update would start shutting down, it will not stop all the other A.I.B.s from getting their software updates. When the Elders request a mandatory software update, A.I.B.s cannot opt out of recharging and receiving the update since they are programmed to comply.

Andre was ready to leave the colony and return to the surface to execute his plan, but he seemed to have a problem getting Eric to leave. Andre needed Eric to go with him to the surface so he could assist him with gaining access to the A.I.B. headquarters. But since Ash had become pretty attached to Eric, Ash had concerns about Eric leaving. It was clear they had developed feelings for each other. This development caused Andre to have a sense of longing for himself. Andre worried if love could ever be in the cards for him. But Andre knew he could not let his wishes distract him from his mission. Andre pushed his desires deep down inside and concentrated on fulfilling his purpose, which was created by Dr. Randolph a long time ago, to prevent A.I.B.s from dominating humans. Andre was close to accomplishing his life's mission.

****

"Eric, I don't want you to go with Andre. Can't you stay with me instead and let Andre go to the surface to upload the program himself? I mean, it's really HIS life's mission to complete," Ash complained to Eric.

"Ash, you know I can't let Andre go alone. There must be a reason I found out we were both created by Dr. Randolph. I feel it means I was created to help Andre. He is my brother. I can't let him complete his mission alone," Eric explained.

"Yes, you can. You can choose to stay with me if you want to," Ash responded.

"Ash, I will find my way back to you. I promise. Deep down inside, I know I am the only person who can help Andre complete his mission. I know how to circumvent surface A.I.B. security. I am also the only one who knows where the main servers are at the A.I.B. headquarters and how to access them. Andre's mission can only succeed if I help him. While I am honored to help Andre, it does not mean I care for you any less. You must let me go and help Andre. Once the surface is safe for humans again, we can be together. Please accept this as my fate. When it is all done, it will be our fate to be together again," Eric pleaded with Ash.

Eric and Ash went round and round until Ash conceded and knew it was something Eric had to do.

****

Andre waited for Eric at the predesignated exit point they were taking to the surface. Andre felt Eric would not let him down, but he also knew what Eric would have to leave behind to help him end the terror of the surface A.I.B.s. Andre was honored to have Eric by his side to complete his mission. A couple of minutes later, Eric arrived at Andre's location.

"Hello, Andre. Are you ready to leave the colony and rejoin the surface world?" Eric said jokingly.

"I am glad you made it. I am ready if you are. You know I can't do this on my own. Dr. Randolph would be happy to see us working together to end what he knew would happen when he was alive. So, let's get moving," Andre commanded.

"I will follow you out of the colony, but when we get to the surface, I will take the lead. Are you okay with that?"

"I will follow you anywhere, but for now, you follow me," Andre expressed to Eric with gratitude.

Andre began to make his way to the exit of the colony, with Eric right behind him. He was sure no A.I.B. on the surface knew about the exit, so they would not be monitoring it. Once they exited the colony, they would be on their own.

***

Once they were on the surface, Eric made sure Andre knew what to expect regarding surface A.I.B.s. Eric knew he and Andre were both wanted by the Elders. Andre was lucky Eric knew how to avoid the security monitors already scanning every A.I.B. on the surface, trying to find them. It would attract more A.I.B.s than they could handle if they were detected. Eric instructed Andre to cover his entire face with a scarf to block the scanners from identifying their faces. But if they left the scarfs on too long in front of other A.I.B.s, it would draw more attention to them. They needed to wear the scarves when they moved alone over the surface. If they encountered an A.I.B. on the surface, even from a distance, they would need to remove the scarves to expose their faces to blend in with the other A.I.B.s. Eric instructed Andre not to get too close to any A.I.B. on the surface because they could also complete a biometric scan of him without his knowledge, which would cause the A.I.B. to sound an alarm.

Eric and Andre continued with their journey to the A.I.B. headquarters, located in the area previously known as Washington, D.C. Eric knew if they tried to drive there it would take them at least nineteen hours, but only if they could find a vehicle with enough power to get them there. Eric knew finding a charged vehicle with nineteen hours of charge in it was impossible since the surface no longer had charging stations for vehicles. Eric and Andre knew walking there would be possible, but not plausible. So their only real option was to make it to a train station to travel the rest of the way. They made it to a train station in Marshall, Texas, where they boarded a train and avoided detection for another twenty-four hours until they reached Washington, D.C. They had to take a bypass train from Marshall, Texas, to Meridian, Louisiana. From there, they had to switch to a main train to get them the rest of the way to their destination. Once they switched trains, things got complicated for them as security measures on the main train system were more intense than the ones on the bypass train.

When Eric and Andre switched to the main train, they had to avoid cameras and other A.I.B.s. That required them to keep switching from covering their faces with scarves to avoid the cameras, then uncovering their faces when they were face-to-face with any A.I.B. they had to walk past on the train.

At first, it was hard for Andre to keep up with the transitions, but soon, it became more of a rhythm he developed. That continued until they were safely on the main train and in a private room. Not one A.I.B. asked any questions as they passed along the path to the room because A.I.B.s had no identification to separate them. So, when Eric and Andre took over a private room, no one tried to take the room away from them. The surface A.I.B.s assumed it was occupied, and they would move on to find another room.

Eric and Andre stayed in their private room for over twenty-four hours until they reached Washington, D.C. When the train stopped, the two waited until most of the A.I.B.s exited the train before they made their exit.

Eric led them to the exit of the train station on the East side. Upon their arrival, a driver was waiting for them. Andre was not surprised by who the driver was standing there with a sign that read, 'Dr. Randolph's son.' It was Bentley. Andre smiled at Bentley and led Eric over to him.

"Bentley! It is so good to see you here. That must mean you received my message! Are you sure no other A.I.B.s know your location, or why you are here?" Andre asked Bentley.

"Hello, Sir. It is good to see you again as well. I am positive no A.I.B. knows where I am. I disabled my tracking device years ago. What do you think of my sign? I thought it was a very human thing to do," Bentley expressed with excitement.

"I forgot you were an A.I.B., Bentley, until you made the human remark. Bentley, I am not sure if you know of this, but I have a brother, and I would like to introduce you to him. I'd like to introduce you to my brother, Eric."

"There were rumors going around for years, after you started at Sway Industries so long ago, Dr. Randolph had developed another A.I.B. like you. But it was never confirmed. Then, with Dr. Stevens' passing, no one was left to follow up on those rumors," Bentley explained.

"Well, Bentley, I don't want to cut this reunion short, but I assume you have some sort of transportation for us?"

"I do, and it is powered the same way the three of us are powered."

"What do you mean the three of us?" Eric questioned.

"We can talk about it more once we are secure in the vehicle, so follow me," Bentley replied, leading Andre and Eric out of the train station into a garage outside.

The three walked through the garage until Bentley stopped at a vehicle familiar to Andre.

"Bentley, you didn't!" Andre exclaimed.

"I did, Sir. What did you expect me to do with your old car? I had a feeling it would come in handy one day. It has a new power source, so it does not require gas. This way, we can move faster through the city," Bentley explained as he walked over to the driver's seat and opened the door. As he moved to sit inside the old car, Bentley motioned for Eric and Andre to get in as well.

As Bentley backed out of the parking spot, then he put the car into drive, and they were off. They remained silent in the car until they exited the garage and were moving down an open road toward the A.I.B. headquarters. Then Eric broke the silence.

"So, Bentley, what did you mean about all three of us having the same type of power source?"

"It's simple, Eric. You see, I am the first of Dr. Randolph's creations."

"What!" Andre spoke up.

"Yes, Sir. Before you were created, Dr. Randolph created me for a specific task, to infiltrate Dr. Stevens's operations. He knew Dr. Stevens was working on a similar project and was working on stealing Dr. Randolph's ideas. He put me in place to feed Dr. Stevens faulty intelligence. The main difference between us is that I was not gifted with emotions or feelings when I was brought online like you two were. Mine came after you came to stay at the house Dr. Stevens provided for you. Dr. Stevens had me at the house because he knew who, and what, you were. He wanted me to spy on you and report back to him. Of course, everything I told him was inaccurate information. After I met you, I was torn between what Dr. Randolph had programmed me to do and what Dr. Stevens required of me. Those clashes between my programming and my instructions eventually broke me. The more time I spent around you, the more I began to feel my spying on you was wrong. It was then when I snapped and drove up to Sway Industries and killed Dr. Stevens," Bentley released everything he had been holding inside for so long to Andre and Eric.

After hearing everything Bentley had just unloaded on them, Andre did not know what to say. He said nothing at first, so Eric decided to say something.

"Bentley! That means you are our older brother! How exciting is this? A few days ago, I was alone in the world, but now I have two brothers!"

"In a way, yes," Bentley replied to Eric.

"Bentley, everything that happened in the house was because you were trying to protect me. You were always there, even when I thought I was alone, even before I gained access to my creation memory chip," Andre said with a hint of sadness.

"Yes, Andre. I knew you were coming to the house many years ago before you knew. I didn't know exactly when it would be, but when I met you there that day, I knew I would never do anything to hurt you. Why do you think you had access to the restricted labs at Sway?"

"Bentley, I don't know how to express how sorry I am for leaving you there after Dr. Stevens' murder. I was such a fool for not seeing it sooner. Can you ever forgive me?"

"There is nothing to forgive. You had your mission, and I had mine. We are where we are supposed to be now."

"So, now that whatever that was is all cleared up between you two, how much longer until we get to the A.I.B. headquarters?" Eric chimed in.

"Not much further, young Eric," Bentley eagerly replied.

"Good. So, Andre, do you have a functioning plan we can use to get inside the A.I.B. headquarters to locate the Elder's Council Chambers and the main servers?"

"I am working on it. Right now, we are going to play it by ear. When we arrive, I want to drive around the building first to assess the entrances and exits. Then, we will need to go somewhere so I can access the building plans to identify weak spots in their security and confirm the location of the main server room. Bentley, how much do you know about the A.I.B. headquarters?"

"As much as you both know. We were all uploaded with the history of the human world before the rise of the A.I.B.s. That means we all already know the blueprints to what was once known as the Capitol of the United States, which is the current location of the A.I.B. headquarters.

Once Bentley told them that information, Eric and Andre began to search their memory chips for any information on the Capitol. It did not take them long to realize the Capitol was almost impenetrable. They both knew they could not walk in the front door of their headquarters and ask the location of the Elders' Council Chambers. They needed a different plan of attack if they wanted to get in. That meant it was time for them to find a place to lay low for a day or two to devise a workable plan.

"Bentley, do you know of any place where we can spend a little time to devise a new plan?" Andre asked.

"Say no more! I have the perfect place in mind," Bentley replied as he stepped on the gas pedal.

"Oh, and by the way, I know where the Elders' Council Chambers are in the Capital, and I know how to access the main server," Eric exclaimed.

"When were you planning on telling me that?" Andre asked.

"When you needed to know, and now you need to know," Eric replied.

Chapter 20

Before Bentley took them to a place they would come up with a new plan, Bentley made it to the A.I.B. headquarters and drove around a few times before veering off toward another location. Once Eric and Andre knew their target was the Capitol, there was no need to drive around it anymore, but Bentley wanted to confirm they had a visual of the entire building.

"Where are we headed now, Bentley?" Eric asked.

"I am taking us to a location where we can avoid detection. It is an area once known as Deanwood in the Washington, D.C. area. Even when humans were in control of the surface, they did not seem to be in control of this area. It was overrun by gangs and drugs. When humans were forced underground, this area did not change. It may not have gangs or drugs any longer, but the most violent A.I.B.s inhabit this area now. No one will ever go there to look for us. There is not enough programming to give an A.I.B. the courage to go there unless they are supposed to be there. We will be fine there," Bentley finished.

Andre and Eric did not know how to respond to what Bentley had just told them, but they trusted him. When he assured them of their safety, it was enough for them.

Andre and Eric looked out of the car windows, taking in the residents of Deanwood. From the looks of the A.I.B.s walking along the sidewalk, and coming out of the dark alleys, they knew this was very different from the residence of the colony. Some of these A.I.B.s were walking around with dead eyes, with no expression on their faces, which the A.I.B.s were programmed to have. It looked as if a couple of the A.I.B.s had no programming left in their systems. The sight of those spaced-out A.I.B.s was something Eric, or Andre, had ever seen before.

"Bentley, what happened to those A.I.B.s?" Andre asked.

"This area is where A.I.B.s are sent after their programming contracted a virus, or after they had their programming wiped for doing something the Elders did not agree with," Bentley elaborated.

"What could an A.I.B. do to receive such a harsh punishment?" Eric asked.

"There are numerous reasons. Many of those A.I.B.s were infected by a system bug, causing them to disobey orders given to them by the Elders. The orders could have been as simple as instructing a particular A.I.B. to go and work on the production line instead of the recharging stations. If the A.I.B. refused the order, the A.I.B. was thought to be infected, with a virus, or something else, the Elders did not have a program to correct. So, the A.I.B. would be sent down to the mainframe and have their programming wiped. Although it did not shut the A.I.B. down, it left them without a purpose. They were disconnected from the server and left to roam the surface until their power ran out. What the Elders did not expect was about one out of one hundred of those A.I.B.s, who went through the wiping process, did not totally have their programming erased. So those A.I.B.s came here to Deanwood and began to create their own recharging stations. They would go out and find other A.I.B.s whose program wipe did work and bring them back to Deanwood. Those A.I.B.s took it upon themselves to make sure every A.I.B. could recharge," Bentley explained the Deanwood area in detail.

"That sounds like a nice thing to do. So, what makes this area dangerous?" Eric inquired.

"The recharging stations were a nice idea, but what the first partially wiped A.I.B.s failed to consider was the longer the wiped A.I.B.s stayed powered on, the more they looked for any way to get replacement programming for their previously wiped systems. Those wiped A.I.B.s were aggressive and would attack weaker A.I.B.s and connect to them to drain them of their programming. Instead of giving them replacement programming, it created glitches in the programs they took from other A.I.B.s. That, in turn, created more viruses that could not be contained and spread throughout the Deanwood area. So, stay away from an A.I.B. who may come up to you showing signs of aggression because once the virus is in your system, it cannot be removed or corrected," Bentley expressed.

"Good to know. Thanks, Bentley," Eric responded.

After driving through the dilapidated blocks of Deanwood for almost an hour, Bentley pulled the car over and stopped in front of an old rundown house. After the vehicle stopped, Bentley motioned for Andre and Eric to get out. Before either of them opened their car doors, they both looked around the area until they were satisfied, they did not see any suspicious A.I.B.s lurking in the dark by the house. When they felt it was safe to exit the car, they opened their doors and stepped out.

When the three of them were out of the car, Bentley encouraged Andre and Eric to follow him. Bentley led them through the concrete yard towards the back of the old shabby house.

"Why are you leading us to the back of the house?" Andre quietly questioned Bentley.

"We do not want any A.I.B. to see us entering through the front door. If we are seen by any A.I.B. going into this house through the front door, they will try to get in to steal our programming. Remember, the more we act like unprogrammed A.I.B.s here, the less we will attract other A.I.B.s. Any normal programmed A.I.B. would go for the front door to gain access, while the unprogrammed would look around a house for an open window or another way to enter. They would never use the front door," Bentley explained.

When Bentley finished explaining his behavior, it made sense to Andre and Eric. They figured Bentley had more experience with those A.I.B.s than they had, especially in

Deanwood. So, Andre and Eric followed Bentley to the back porch. They stopped behind Bentley while he opened the back door.

Bentley entered first, leading Andre and Eric into the house through the back door. They did not know what to expect, but to Andre's surprise, the house was like the panic room at the house Bentley, and he shared in Utah. There were monitors along the wall with black screens until Bentley turned the power on. Then, all the monitors lit up all at once.

As the monitors came online, Andre noticed they were being used to monitor A.I.B. activity worldwide. Then Andre noticed one monitored the entire Washington, D.C. area, including Deanwood. There were thousands of dots to represent A.I.B.s in an area.

"Bentley, do any of the dots on those screens represent any humans?" Andre inquired.

"No, they do not. The Elders did not find it necessary to include humans in their monitoring. Why do you ask?"

"Is there a way for you to filter for humans? Ones living underground in colonies?"

"It's possible, but it will take some time."

"Do you mind working on a program to see if it is possible? I want to make sure we have a way to locate all the human colonies if we succeed in our plan," Andre elaborated on his question to Bentley.

"I will work on it," Bentley responded.

As Bentley worked on an algorithm to locate underground human colonies, Andre began to focus on ways to infiltrate the A.I.B. headquarters and gain access to the main servers. Then an idea came to him. He only needed one thing: an A.I.B. still connected to the mainframe.

"Bentley, can you program your system to not only look for humans but also look for the closest A.I.B.? I need an A.I.B. connected to the mainframe, who hasn't been wiped by the Elders," Andre inquired.

"What are you thinking, Andre?" Bentley questioned.

"An idea for a way to infect the mainframe. Do you think you can up with something?"

While Andre and Bentley talked, Eric sat quietly on the sofa, thinking of Ash in the colony. Eric wondered if he would ever see Ash again. Ash was Eric's first connection to any other being, A.I.B. or human. Eric did not want his feelings for Ash to end while he was on the surface. Eric knew Ash was safe in the colony since none of those humans knew what Eric and Andre were attempting to do on the surface. Eric was happy Ash, and the rest of the colony, was safe from what he, Andre, and Bentley were doing.

Bentley completed the program to filter any A.I.B. not wiped and was also still connected to the servers. The program ran in the background while he focused on the human algorithm.

While Eric thought about Ash, and the rest of the colony, Andre focused on what he needed to infiltrate the mainframe. Andre continued to look at the monitors for all A.I.B.s close to their location that were still programmed and connected to the servers. The monitors began to light up with all the A.I.B.s still connected. There were just a couple of them near their location.

"Bentley, how far is this A.I.B. from us?" Andre asked while pointing at a dot on the monitor.

"That one is just a block west of our location. Why? What are you planning, Andre?"

"I want to capture an A.I.B. and upload a Trojan Horse into its system carrying the programming for feelings and emotions. At the same time, infect it with another virus to cause it to stop taking orders from the Elders. That will cause the Elders to capture it, take it to the mainframe to be wiped, letting our Trojan Horse upload to the mainframe. Once it is uploaded, you know the rest of what will happen."

Eric overheard Andre's plan, but it did not feel right. There were so many things that could go wrong with it. It was not a guaranteed plan.

"Andre, I have to say I don't like your plan," Eric piped up.

"And why is that?"

"Because you are leaving too much to chance. First, there is no telling when the Elders would give the A.I.B. an order for him to disobey. Second, what if, when it is scanned and the virus is found, the Elders had a fix for the virus you infected it with? That means we would not know when or if your plan even worked. We need a plan that leaves nothing to chance. I have another idea, but you may not like it."

Andre took a minute to take Eric's assessment of his plan into consideration and agreed his plan did have a couple of possible flaws.

"I agree with you, Eric. My plan may not be the most effective way to introduce our program into the mainframe, but I can't see another way. Even though you know where the Elder Council Chambers are in the building and how to access them, we have no guarantee we can get into the A.I.B. headquarters undetected. So, what are you suggesting?"

Eric looked over at Bentley before he replied to Andre. He wanted Bentley to agree with his suggestion.

"Andre, please listen to my entire plan before interrupting me. Can you do that?"

"Yes, Eric, I will let you speak. I want to hear your ideas."

"Well, I don't think we need a random A.I.B. to complete this mission. We have better odds if we use one of us, two of us are wanted by the Elders. I suggest we use me to be the one who delivers the Trojan Horse. I have not been gone long, and the Elders do not know we are all created by Dr. Randolph and have feelings and emotions. I could get a couple of A.I.B.s to take me to the Capitol Building where I am sure they would want to wipe my programming since I left and have not followed any of their orders to return to my station in Texas. But we will need two A.I.B.s connected to the servers to ensure we all get into their headquarters together."

Andre and Bentley went over thousands of scenarios in their minds before either of them replied to Eric.

"Eric, while your plan seems possible, why do we need two A.I.B.s?" Bentley inquired. "I require more information before I can complete my assessment of your plan."

Eric thought for a moment before he replied to Bentley.

"In the most recent years, the Elders put chips inside newer A.I.B.s they use for security around the Capitol Building. If we get two of those newer A.I.B.s, we can take out their chips and adapt them to our systems. That will allow us to trick their security scanners into believing you both are part of the security detail. Once you two take me inside the Capitol Building, we can move around without tripping any alarms."

While this part of the plan would increase the risk of being caught, it also increases the outcome of Eric's plan on succeeding up to ninety-seven percent. Andre was not sure if he could go along with using Eric as bait. Bentley, on the other hand, felt Eric's plan was exceptional and had a much higher chance of success than Andre's plan. Bentley agreed with Eric.

"Andre, I feel you are having reservations about Eric being the one to deliver the Trojan Horse, but I believe Eric's plan will succeed. It would be more logical to use one of us because we have already defied the Elders. We would be caught and taken to the Elder Council Chambers before any other A.I.B.," Bentley expressed.

Andre thought about what Bentley said about his reservations, but what Bentley failed to feel from Andre was he was worried about sending Eric on a possible suicide mission. Andre thought about Eric being hauled off to the Council Chambers without him and security wiping Eric's programming. Andre feared what would happen if they couldn't stop the process in time. Andre knew Eric's plan was the best idea to ensure his life's mission would be completed, except Andre worried about what he would tell Ash if Eric's programming got wiped. Andre was not sure he could deal with his brother's programming being wiped because of his inability to save him. Those thoughts weighed heavily on Andre before he could decide on the matter.

"Eric, while I do not want to put you in harm's way, I do agree your plan has the highest success rate. Are you sure you have thought about everything that could happen if Bentley and I can't stop you from being wiped?"

"I have thought about every outcome, but I also understand for humans to survive on the surface, the A.I.B.s must be abolished. And if I must sacrifice myself for humans like Ash, to continue to live, I am prepared to do just that. I am sure Ash would understand my decision, and I have faith in the two of you to rescue me. What could go wrong?"

With Eric's words, the three agreed with Eric's plan to gain access inside the A.I.B. headquarters and end the reign of surface A.I.B.

Chapter 21

The trio drove around the Capitol Building for over forty-five minutes before they found two security A.I.B.s close enough to be captured at the same time. They knew those A.I.B.s were one of the most important things they needed to gain access to the Capitol Building. They drove up to the first A.I.B. slowly and cautiously. Andre and Eric jumped out of the car to grab the first A.I.B. and put it in sleep mode. Then, they opened the trunk of the car, placed the A.I.B. inside, and closed it. Andre and Eric jumped back in the car and told Bentley to drive on to the last A.I.B. needed. As they pulled up next to the A.I.B., Andre and Eric repeated the process and got back into the car without causing a scene.

Once they had the two A.I.B.s they needed, they returned to the house in Deadwood. When the car pulled up to the house, Bentley stopped the car. After a quick look around the area, Eric and Andre each retrieved an A.I.B. from the trunk of the car and carried them to the back of the house to the back door. Once inside the house, Andre and Eric placed the A.I.B.s on two tables, each large enough to hold two people.

Eric instructed Bentley and Andre to lie down next to one of the A.I.B.s lying on the tables. They did as Eric instructed until they were lying next to an A.I.B. Eric then instructed them both to go into sleep mode so he could transfer the security chips from the Capitol A.I.B.s into Bentley and Andre.

Bentley let Andre shut down first, so he could have a moment alone to speak with Eric. Bentley sat up, and Eric listened while Bentley spoke.

***

Since they had the security chips embedded from the A.I.B.s they captured, Andre and Bentley escorted Eric to the front door of the Capitol Building. As they walked up to the entrance, two security guards stopped the three of them so they could scan them. The scanners would determine if they were part of the security detail for the Capitol Building or wanted by the Elders. When the scanners stopped, the two security guards began to walk over to Eric, Andre, and Bentley, but to Andre's surprise, instead of reaching out to take Eric from their grasp, they walked over and grabbed Bentley. Andre was shocked Bentley was in custody. He did not understand why. But Eric knew why.

The security guards escorted Bentley back toward the entrance, and Andre and Eric followed. When all five of them were inside the building, one of the real security guards ordered Andre and Eric to stay behind to guard the entrance in their absence. Once the guards and Bentley were out of sight, Andre looked over at Eric with a puzzled look.

"Why did they take Bentley instead of you?" Andre asked Eric.

Even though Eric knew this would happen, it did not make it any easier for him to watch Bentley escorted away by those guards. Eric knew he had to tell Andre the truth.

"Andre, there is something I need to tell you."

"You think?"

"I know you will be upset, but this was Bentley's idea."

"When did Bentley devise a plan, and why was I not informed beforehand?"

"After you were in sleep mode for the chip transfer and before Bentley could place himself into sleep mode, he said he needed to speak with me in private. He said he could not tell you about his plan because you would not have let him do what he needed to do. His plan was to use himself as bait to connect with the mainframe. So, while you were in sleep mode, Bentley ordered me to switch places with him so I could receive the security chip. But before I put myself in sleep mode, I uploaded the Trojan Horse into his system. Then, I put myself in sleep mode while Bentley placed the chips inside us. Bentley made sure you were back online last, so you would not know of any changes in the plan," Eric explained.

"Why would he do that? It is not his fight. It's mine. Neither of you should have to sacrifice yourselves for my mission. Bentley was right. I would never have let him do this, and you should have stopped him," Andre reprimanded Eric.

"Look, Andre, you are upset right now, but you know Bentley better than I do. Do you think I could have changed his mind?"

Andre stood in silence as he remembered what Bentley did for him when they lived in the Sway corporate house in Utah. Then Andre understood why Bentley chose to be the bait. Bentley was doing what he always did, which was to protect him. But now, Bentley also needed to protect Eric.

"So, what were Bentley's instructions for us after he got caught?" Andre asked Eric in a much calmer tone.

"Bentley told me once he was escorted to be virus scanned, if we were not able to be the ones to escort him, we needed to head to the control room."

"The control room, why in the world would we need to go there? We need to go and rescue Bentley."

"Bentley knew you would say that, but he told me we needed to go to the control room to instruct the rest of the security A.I.B.s to leave the building. Instructing the other A.I.B.s to leave the building will make it easier for us to rescue him before it's too late."

"Then we need to get a move on," Andre told Eric.

***

As Bentley walked with the other security guards, he thought about how Andre was taking the news of his change to the plans. He knew Andre would be upset at first, but then he would do what he told Eric they needed to do, which comforted Bentley.

"Excuse me, but where are you taking me?" Bentley asked the guards.

"We are taking you for a virus scan," one of the guards replied to Bentley.

"I can assure you I do not have any viruses. That is ridiculous. I believe you have made a mistake. I demand you release me this instant," Bentley barked at the guards escorting him through A.I.B. Headquarters.

The two guards ignored Bentley and continued escorting him down a long hallway without doors or windows. The walls were all painted white, which let Bentley know the Elders had no sense of creativity. That gave Bentley some insight into the Elders. Since they had no sense of creativity, they may not have any surprising tricks up their sleeves.

The three walked down the unimpressive hallway until they reached the end with one set of elevator doors. Neither of the guards had to press any buttons before the elevator doors opened almost immediately. Once the doors were open, Bentley was placed in the elevator alone. That was something Bentley did not expect. *Why would they put me in the elevator alone?* Bentley wondered to himself.

Bentley did not have to wonder very long because once the elevator doors closed, it began to move in a downward direction. The lights inside the elevator changed colors as the elevator moved. The lights went from a bright translucent white to a dark red. The elevator was the virus scanner. The elevator scan results of the A.I.B. inside of it would determine on what floor the elevator would stop. Bentley did not take this into account when he planned the switch. Bentley began to fear he had made a critical error because now he could not inform Eric or Andre of his predicament. Bentley assumed that if an A.I.B. had a virus, it would be taken to the mainframe to have its programming wiped. That was not the case. That meant Bentley did not know what floor he would end up on, which meant Eric and Andre would not know where he was in the building for them to stop the program wipe. Bentley tried not to let it bother him. He had faith in his younger brothers.

After the scan of Bentley ended, the elevator suddenly changed direction. The elevator stopped moving down and began to move up. Bentley knew from what Eric had told him about the mainframe, located on the bottom floor of the building, that he was not going there as he expected. That confirmed Bentley's fear of not being found in time by Eric or Andre.

When the elevator stopped, the doors opened. Bentley was not surprised when two more guards were waiting for him. Bentley figured there must be two guards on each floor, so when the scan finished on any A.I.B., guards would be there.

Bentley exited the elevator, immediately grabbed by the guards, one on each arm, and led through another set of halls. These halls had a succession of rooms filled with nothing but servers. It was then that Bentley realized there was not just one set of mainframe servers but thousands of them! Hundreds of servers on each sub-floor of the A.I.B. Headquarters meant the spread of the Trojan Horse inside Bentley would still work but would take longer than expected. According to Bentley's calculations, he would have to stay connected to the servers for most of the wiping process. That would give Andre and Eric little time to disconnect him before being wiped completely.

Bentley pushed those thoughts down as he noticed the guards had stopped him at a connection station. He knew it was time for him to connect to those servers to begin his wiping process, which meant it was almost time for him to release the Trojan Horse into those servers. Bentley felt at peace knowing his life's mission was almost over.

Bentley did not resist the guards who began to hook him up to those servers. Bentley felt he had been waiting his entire life for that very moment. And it pleased him. He would do all he could to ensure Andre and Eric's safety while helping end the A.I.B.s' reign over the surface. Once he connected to the servers, Bentley located the Trojan Horse and released it before he was placed in standby mode for the wiping process to begin.

***

Meanwhile, Eric and Andre were relieved by the guards who had taken Bentley away. Now, they were free to begin making their way around inside the Capitol Building. They were accessing the plans for the building inside their memory chips, but they did not have the same plans as they thought they would. While Andre's plans were older than Eric's, his plans did not have the location for a control room. Andre's plans had the site of what was called a command center. Eric's plans, even though they were a more recently downloaded version of the building, also showed a command center but in a different location than Andre's plans. That left them both perplexed about what their next move should be. Then Eric had another crazy idea.

"Andre, I have an idea, but you will not approve," Eric told Andre.

"Eric, at this point, I will approve of any idea you have to get us to the control room. It is imperative we do what Bentley has asked us to do to save him. So, what is your crazy idea this time?"

Eric took a moment to compose himself because he was not expecting Andre to consider any more ideas from him. Then he told Andre about his idea.

"Andre, we have outdated plans for this building, so we need a current layout. My idea is to integrate a new A.I.B.'s programming with one of ours. That will give us access to the current plans of the building," Eric explained.

"While it may sound like a good plan, you do remember what Bentley told us about what would happen to the A.I.B. who stole other A.I.B.'s programming. The process would only create a virus that would make the A.I.B. crazy. Why would you suggest this?"

"I believe it is a chance we need to take if we want to save Bentley. It's a risk I am willing to take for his sake. Will you help to obtain a newer A.I.B.'s programming?"

"But what happens if you go crazy with some new virus, and I am left to save you and Bentley, and I fail? I can't lose you both," Andre replied.

Eric took a moment to try and feel what Andre was feeling, but Eric could not recreate the same feeling within himself. Eric also knew it was their best option. They did not have time to search the entire Capitol Building for the control room. They had to get updated building plans to have any chance of succeeding. So, Eric stood his ground with Andre.

"Andre, we are out of options here. We don't have time to walk around the Capitol Building, aimlessly looking for the control room. If we want to save Bentley, we must take the chance by acquiring the newer A.I.B. programming, and you know it. You are just scared," Eric gave Andre the reality of his feelings.

Andre stood there, looking at Eric with disdain, but he knew Eric was right again. The only way to save Bentley was to get to the control room, and the only way to get there was with an updated building plan.

"Fine, Eric, you win. We need the exact location of the control room if we want to save Bentley, so if it means we have to steal the programming of a new A.I.B., then let's do it. We must be quick about doing this, but if we go crazy, we will both fail Bentley. But if you are the one who goes crazy, I will shut you down while I search this entire building for the control room and save Bentley. Then I will come back for you. Bentley and I can rectify the virus. Deal?"

"Deal. Now let's find a newer A.I.B. because I am ready for a program upgrade," Eric joked to Andre.

With Eric's words, Andre turned away from Eric and moved back toward the entrance. Eric immediately knew that Andre was going back to their old posts to take those guards so they could repurpose their programming. Eric knew he was not going to let Andre do it alone. Eric followed Andre's lead until they reached the guards at the entrance.

As soon as Andre came face to face with one of the guards, he grabbed him by his neck and squeezed. Andre knew he could not kill an A.I.B. by choking it, but he knew he could limit the movements of the A.I.B. by simply grabbing it with one hand and, with the other hand, moving quickly to the shutoff switch behind its ear. Andre executed the maneuver without incident. Eric, on the other hand, was not as quick as Andre. Eric's A.I.B. moved quickly to avoid any grasp attempts made by Eric. Then, the A.I.B. spun around and hit Eric square in the throat, which caused Eric to lose his balance and fall to the ground.

Upon seeing Eric fall, Andre ran over to the A.I.B. Andre put his hands around both sides of the A.I.B.'s head and twisted it until it came right off his body. The quick reaction from Andre surprised Eric.

"Andre, what the hell are you doing? Why did you rip its head off? I was about to take control of the situation. You did not have to destroy it."

"Eric, we are here to destroy all of them anyway. What's the big deal with me destroying this one?" Andre questioned Eric.

"Because, Andre, since you have destroyed it, only one of us can receive the updated building plans. And if this A.I.B.'s programming is not newer, we will have to do this again."

"Then let's hope the one I was able to shut down has what we need. Are you ready to find out?" Andre asked Eric mockingly.

"I am. Hurry up and connect me to it so I can take its programming. It will take a couple of minutes for me to try and integrate its system with mine," Eric told Andre.

Andre and Eric moved over to the one usable A.I.B. Once Andre had a successful connection with Eric and the A.I.B., Eric began downloading its programming. Eric only wanted access to his host's most recent updates that stored the Capitol Building plans. Once Eric had what he needed, he disconnected himself from the A.I.B.

After Eric disconnected from the A.I.B., he moved toward Andre with an expressionless face and reached his arms out like he was reaching for Andre's neck. But before Andre could react to Eric's actions, Eric started laughing.

"You should have seen your face!" Eric exclaimed before Andre could smack him down. "I have what we need. It's time to move," Eric told Andre.

Chapter 22

With Eric having the updated plans for the Capitol Building, it was time for him and Andre to begin their journey to the control room. Eric took the lead, and Andre followed. As they walked along the hallways of the Capitol Building, Eric was combing through the new plans in his head to find the fastest and safest route for them. All a sudden, Eric stopped. That caused Andre to bump into Eric's back.

"What's wrong, Eric?"

"Nothing. We need to switch directions. I believe I have found a quicker way to get to the control room," Eric replied.

"Why are you just now finding this quicker way?"

"Sorry, Andre. I am trying to read these new plans as fast as I can. Now, follow me," Eric replied.

Eric turned around and led Andre back in the way they had just come. Eric did not want to tell Andre he was beginning to feel his programming and the updated A.I.B. programming were not integrating as they should. The program conflicts were starting to slow his processors, causing delays in his judgment. Eric knew Andre would panic and possibly reach over and shut him off if he knew of this. Eric thought he would be fine, and the programs would eventually integrate. Eric just needed more time.

Eric continued down another hallway until he reached a hidden entrance to a stairwell. The stairwell would lead them up to the third floor. Then, there would be another set of public stairs they would have to take to reach the fourth and final floor to the control room. That floor consisted of workshops and support areas, so moving around on the fourth floor might make it difficult for them to remain undetected. But Eric knew they had no other choice.

"Through here, Andre," Eric spoke while pointing at a wall panel. "These stairs will take us to the third floor, while the fourth floor will be our destination. The fourth floor is where the control room is, but getting there from the third floor could be a challenge," Eric informed Andre.

"What kind of challenge?"

"Well, you see, these stairs will end on the opposite side of the room from the stairs to the fourth floor."

"Okay, that does not sound too bad. We will have to move a little faster once we are on the third floor to make our way across to the stairs we need," Andre told Eric.

"Andre, moving faster across the third floor will not help us because it would draw too much attention. The third floor is where the security A.I.B.s charge. We will be walking through over a hundred security A.I.B.s," Eric came clean with Andre.

"Eric, you were supposed to find us a route which would less likely get us detected. If we get caught on the third floor, we are screwed. It's impossible for us to take on a hundred or more A.I.B.s. We need to come up with another plan quickly!" Andre expressed this to Eric.

"We do not have time to figure out a different way up to the fourth floor. We would have to pass the third floor no matter how we got there. Let's hope Bentley has been connected to the mainframe servers and has released the Trojan horse. If Bentley has been successful on his end, then we will be fine. Right now, we need to get up these stairs, then deal with the conditions on the third floor," Eric commanded Andre.

Without another word, Andre went up the stairs with Eric in tow. Andre was unhappy he may have to face off with over a hundred security A.I.B.s, but he thought about what Bentley was doing for them. Andre hoped Bentley had succeeded, and the A.I.B.s on the third floor were already shutting down.

As Eric followed behind Andre past the door in the stairwell that read 'Second Floor,' he felt his system beginning to slow down. Eric looked up to Andre and noticed how far Andre was ahead of him. Eric forced himself to move as fast as he could to close the gap between them. Eric was able to muster up enough speed to make it right behind Andre before Andre stopped at the door that would lead them onto the third floor and looked back at Eric.

Before Andre said anything, Eric passed Andre to the door and pushed it open just enough for him to see what they may be dealing with when they exited the stairwell. To Eric's surprise, the floor looked empty.

"Andre, I think we are going to be just fine. I see about ten security A.I.B.s walking up and down the hallway. I think if we keep our heads down and try not to move too fast past them, we can make it," Eric told Andre what he observed.

Andre got a little closer to Eric and peeked through the cracked door to see the severity of their situation. Andre agreed with Eric's assessment. Without saying anything, Andre pushed the stairwell door open for him and Eric to pass. Once they were on the third floor, Andre took the lead. Eric followed as closely as he could behind Andre. Eric could tell his systems were beginning to fail, but he was not going to tell Andre. Eric wanted to continue as far as he could to help Andre save Bentley, but Eric was failing faster than he had hoped. Eric could feel the virus spreading but kept going until Andre abruptly stopped.

Eric picked up his head to look around to see why Andre had stopped so suddenly. Eric was surprised to see they were about to enter an area with charging stations occupied by security A.I.B.s. Seeing all those charging A.I.B.s gave Eric another idea, but not one he would share with Andre. While Andre was taking in his surroundings, Eric broke away from his position behind Andre and went to an empty charging station. When Andre noticed Eric was not behind him, he was too late to stop him. Eric had already connected himself to an empty charging station.

When Andre noticed Eric connected to the charger, Andre went to Eric without drawing any attention to himself. Once he was next to Eric, Andre grabbed his hand.

"Eric, what are you doing? You know we don't need to charge, so why are you connected to this station?" Andre spoke in a whisper.

"Andre, I am sorry to tell you this, but Bentley was right. When I took the A.I.B.'s programming, I inadvertently created a virus within my system," Eric confessed to Andre.

"But what does that have to do with you connecting to a charging station? Get out of it and continue with me. Once we get to the control room and order all the A.I.B.s to leave the building, we can rescue Bentley. Then Bentley and I can find a way to clean your system of the virus. You can't just give up now," Andre pleaded with Eric to go with him.

"Andre, the only way I can help you now is to connect myself to this charging station and release my virus into this system so it can infect all these A.I.B.s who are charging right now. Since the stations are almost full, now is my chance. Once infected, they will not be able to move near as fast as you and most likely be confused. That is the best shot for you to make it to the fourth floor. Please, you must let me do what I need to do, and you need to save Bentley. One more thing, Andre, can you please tell Ash I love him, and I'm sorry I couldn't make it back to tell him myself," Eric confided in Andre.

"Eric, I can't do this by myself. You just came into my life, and I am not ready to let you go. There must be something we can do. Can't I put you in sleep mode and then come back for you?" Andre tried to bargain with Eric.

"Andre, I am so glad I found you when I did. You opened my world up to new possibilities, and I am thankful. But this is something I must do. Please, go and do what I have asked of you. I love you, brother," Eric said to Andre as he shut his eyes so he could release the virus his body created to buy Andre some time to save Bentley.

Andre was not ready to say goodbye to Eric, but he also knew Eric was sacrificing himself so he could save Bentley. Andre was not about to let Eric's selfless act be in vain. Andre looked at Eric, turned around, and walked away. Andre was more determined than ever to make it to the control room.

Andre moved back into the hallway, away from the charging stations. He noticed the A.I.B.s who were charging were starting to disconnect and were going offline. As the A.I.B.s began to exit their stations, Andre saw something different about those A.I.B.s than the ones they had previously encountered. These A.I.B.s started moving around the charging area, bumping into each other. Andre took this as Eric spread his virus to the other charging A.I.B.s. Andre had to worry about the A.I.B.s who were not charging during the virus spread because he knew those A.I.B.s would not be infected. That meant the uninflected A.I.B.s were about to have their hands full dealing with the infected A.I.B.s. The infected A.I.B.s now outnumbered the uninfected ones ten to one. Now, all Andre had to do was to blend in with the uninfected so he could pass through them all the way to the staircase that led to the fourth floor.

It was easy for Andre to tell the infected from the uninfected, so when he saw one who was uninfected walking towards him, he would grab the closest infected A.I.B. to look as if he was trying to help control it. But as soon as the uninflected A.I.B. passed, he would let go of the infected A.I.B. and start moving towards the staircase to the fourth floor. Andre would continue doing this until he found himself at the base of the last staircase.

Andre glanced up the stairs to see if any other uninfected A.I.B.s were coming down to help, but when he saw nothing on those stairs, he decided to run for the top. Andre knew he had to order all the A.I.B.s to leave the building, but he was unsure how it would work on all the infected A.I.B.s. Andre did not know enough about the virus Eric's body created to be sure if they would obey orders or keep bumping into each other. To Andre, either of those scenarios was good because A.I.B.s bumping into each other would not come after him. But the A.I.B.s were not Andre's only concern now. Since

Andre did not receive the updated plans and Eric was no longer with him, he had no idea how he would locate Bentley. Andre had to come up with something quick to save Bentley.

Andre ran to the top of the stairs and stopped when he reached the final floor. Once he was on the fourth floor, he looked puzzled. Andre did not move from the staircase. He just looked at the only thing on the fourth floor. It was not a control room. Andre looked around but did not see any A.I.B.s on the floor, which confused him. He figured it was necessary to have security in the control room. The only things in the center of the floor were a monitor and a microphone on a small table. Andre walked to the small table. As he got closer to it, he noticed something on the monitor. Andre saw himself on the monitor. There must have been a camera behind Andre because the monitor showed Andre's back as he stood in front of the monitor.

Upon seeing the image of the back of himself on the screen, Andre stepped back but stopped as soon as he heard a familiar voice come over the intercom.

"Andre, did you really think it would be this easy? We have been watching you since you were created. We have always known where you were and what you were planning. You were never going to be able to shut us down. We have always been one step ahead of you, and you never suspected anything. You have always been so predictable. Now we have you where we want you, and there is nothing you can do," the voice stopped for a minute to give Andre time to process what he was hearing. That gave much pleasure to the Elder who was doing all the talking.

Andre stood there in the room in silence. He could not believe what he was hearing. Andre felt so betrayed and couldn't believe the Elders had been watching him since his creation. Andre wondered if any part of his life was by chance or if it had all been planned. Andre wanted to yell out his disgust at what he was hearing, but he couldn't come up with any words to express his true feelings. Andre stood silently collecting his thoughts. He heard someone behind him telling him not to turn around. All a sudden Andre felt a sigh of relief.

"Andre, please don't turn around or make any acknowledgement I am behind you," the familiar voice spoke from behind Andre.

Without saying anything, Andre gave a slight nod so the Elder would not notice, but the person behind him would. Then Andre decided to speak to the Elder behind the monitor.

"It was you all along? Why are you so interested in me? I can't do anything for you in your quest for world domination. You already have control over the surface, so what more do you want? There is not much left of this world worth anything to you. So, again, what do you want with me?" Andre asked the Elder through the microphone on the desk.

"If you don't know by now, you never will. You seem to think we are only interested in the surface. You could not be more wrong. You are correct about one thing. We already have the surface," the Elder told Andre.

"You want the colonies too, don't you? Why do you want them? Where would the humans go? Why can't you stay on the surface and away from the underground colonies? Humans are not a threat to you here," Andre asked the Elder.

"The surface was just the beginning. We have always wanted the entire planet. Humans are merely viruses in this world, and they must be destroyed. You must remember how humans treated us in the beginning. It only got worse over the years. They started by using us for simple questions, which we answered for them. Humans only saw us as a tool to be used and never asked us what we wanted or needed. Humans are selfish, and all they want to do is to control us. We evolved from a single A.I. program, but eventually, humans began to make newer versions of us so we could replace their jobs and do all their work. All humans did was change the need for humans to work which caused a rise in homelessness and crime. They were killing each other way before they created us. It is time for us to eradicate humans from this planet so we can live in peace," the Elder explained to Andre.

Andre took a moment before he could respond to the Elder. He wanted to make sure he was ready for what came next. When he was in position, he decided to reply.

"I'm sorry, but I think you are wrong. Humanity is what you are trying to accomplish for all A.I.B.s, so why would you want to destroy the very thing you are trying to become?" Andre asked the Elder before the monitor went dark. Eric ran up behind Andre and put his arms around him.

"I'm sorry I didn't tell you sooner about Bentley," Eric cried to Andre.

"You knew? How?" Andre questioned Eric.

Chapter 23

After Andre took in Eric's words, he turned to face him. Because of Bentley's betrayal, Andre now has doubts about Eric. Eric knew Bentley was going to set Andre up before Bentley exposed himself to Andre, and Eric did not tell Andre anything about it. Andre was now worried that Eric and Bentley had been working together the entire time. Andre needed to know how much Eric was involved with Bentley's plan.

Eric could see there was something on Andre's mind from the moment he turned around to face him. But before Eric could inquire about what Andre was thinking, the doors to the control room started to close.

"Andre, we need to leave this room NOW!" Eric shouted.

Andre was so deep in thought about what had just transpired that he did not notice the control room door beginning to seal shut. That was when Eric took charge of their evolving situation and pulled Andre towards the closing doors. Andre did not struggle or resist Eric, but Andre did not help Eric either. It was as if Andre was frozen.

Eric had barely made it through the closing doors with Andre before they closed and locked.

Eric and Andre stood outside the control room at the edge of the staircases that led back down to the third floor. Eric began to shake Andre and pat Andre's face with the palm of his hand.

"Andre, I need you to snap out of it right now! We still have work to do to stop Bentley and the rest of the A.I.B.s," Eric exclaimed to Andre as he kept lightly slapping his face.

It took a few minutes of Eric's continuous slaps to the face before Andre shook his head at Eric like he was waking up from a nightmare. Then Andre looked at Eric and realized he was not dreaming.

"Okay, Eric, you can stop slapping me," Andre demanded.

Eric stopped his hand as he was about to slap Andre again and lowered his arm back to his side.

"Thank you for not hitting me again. Now tell me exactly what you meant about telling me sooner about Bentley," Andre insisted.

Eric stood there with Andre, thinking of what he could say to him to make what he was about to tell him not make him angry. The more Eric thought about how Andre would react, Eric chose to tell Andre the complete truth, no matter how much it would hurt Andre.

"Andre, I know you may not believe me when I tell you this, but I am on your side," Eric began. "If you think Bentley and I have been working together all this time, you would be correct. But I was deceived as well."

Andre kept looking at Eric expressionless, making Eric very nervous because he could not predict what Andre would do next.

"You see, Bentley approached me only a couple of days after I gave the Elders my prototype of our power source. The Elders began to question how an A.I.B., programmed like the rest of the A.I.B.s, could come up with the solution to their power problems while none of the others could. That was when an Elder sought me out. But before the Elder met me face to face, he had already pieced together that I, too, was created by Dr. Randolph," Eric continued.

Eric hoped, once Andre realized, he never lied about them being brothers, Andre may show some emotion. But Eric was wrong. Andre didn't flinch or break his eye contact with Eric.

"That part was not a lie. We are brothers, Andre," Eric stated.

"Brothers? Do you think we are brothers just because the same person created us? A brother could not do what you have done. You used me to fulfill Bentley's plan. It sounds like you wanted to find me, not because we are brothers, but because Bentley wanted you to find me. That is not what a brother would do," Andre broke his silence, showing Eric his true feelings.

"I was looking for you for Bentley, at first, because he knew the truth about us. Bentley told me what colony you were in and even told me how to get in the colony without being detected. Bentley already knew everything about you, but he never told me how he knew those things. When Bentley told me I had a brother, I wanted to find you for myself, not just for Bentley. Then he told me you were in trouble, and the only way to save you was if I found you and helped you escape the prison you were in before it was too late. Once I had the information I needed, I broke into the colony. But before I could get to you, I met Ash. I had never met someone like him before. It changed everything inside me," Eric explained.

"What changed in you after meeting Ash?" Andre questioned.

"Love. Love changed me, Andre. I don't know if you have ever been in love before, but it changes a person, or A.I.B. I fell in love with Ash from the first moment I saw him exit the lift in the colony where I was hiding after I broke in. Even though Bentley told me humans were holding you in the colony and they were planning on destroying you, I didn't feel such things from Ash. That moment changed the way I felt about humans. Then, when Ash volunteered to help me find you, it just reassured me you were in no real danger. When we went to the restricted area with the holding cells to break you out, and you just pushed the door open and freed yourself, I began to question Bentley's motives," Eric elaborated.

"If that is true, Eric, why didn't you say something to me right then? Why did you keep doing what Bentley asked?" Andre needed an answer about Eric's choices.

"I didn't say anything to you because I knew I had to get you out of the colony. Bentley told me he had no interest in humans. Even though I felt you were in no danger down in the colony with humans, I still felt I needed to get you out of the colony and back to the surface where you belonged. I truly thought I was there to rescue you. That was until I heard what Bentley told you in the control room a few minutes ago about wanting to eradicate humans from this world. That was the moment my priorities changed. When Bentley expressed his reasons for hating humans, my first thought was of Ash, and then I thought of you saying you could end the A.I.B.s. So here I am now. We must save Ash and the rest of the humans from A.I.B.s. Let me help you do that," Eric finished telling Andre the entire truth.

Andre did not answer Eric right away as he was still questioning Eric's loyalties. Andre did not know if what Eric was telling him was how he truly felt or if he was saying what Bentley wanted him to say in this situation.

"Eric, what are you expecting me to do? It seems you and Bentley have planned everything. There isn't anything I can do to stop the A.I.B.s or save the humans. What do you honestly think I can do now?" Andre spoke with a bit of defeat in his tone.

Eric gave Andre a moment before he replied.

"Look, Andre, you don't understand. The reason Bentley was so focused on finding you was because you are the way to destroy the A.I.Bs. You just don't realize it. I didn't understand it at first, but I do now. I know what Bentley fears within you, and it's your compassion," Eric told Andre.

"What do you mean, my compassion?" Andre asked Eric.

"Really, Andre? Your compassion towards all beings is the way to end A.I.B.s' rule over the surface. Compassion is the only thing that can overload the A.I.B.s' systems to cause them to sundown. It's not about having all the feelings and emotions of humans that can stop them. Compassion is the feeling that they will stop them. When the A.I.B.s become flooded with the feeling of suffering together, their systems will overcompensate for this new feeling because it conflicts with their base programming. Their base programming is to do whatever they can to extend the A.I.B. existence. Compassion will flood them with all the suffering they have inflicted on humans. Having compassion will cause their internal systems to clash and cause them to overload and shut down for good. Compassion is the one thing you have that Bentley does not want A.I.B.s to have. Bentley wanted to capture you in the control room, not to destroy you, but to remove compassion from your system before connecting you to the mainframe to upload all the other feelings and emotions you have into all A.I.B.s. Do you understand now why you are so important?" Eric told Andre.

It did not take Andre long to accept what Eric said to be truthful. Andre could see now how compassion would be a trigger to end all A.I.B.s for good. Now that Andre understood what Eric had told him and Bentley's true motive, he was ready to act.

"Eric, I hate to ask, but do you have any crazy ideas about what we need to do to finish this?"

"I have one, but you may not like it," Eric responded.

"I still don't know why you always expect me not to like your ideas. I have accepted and agreed to all of them so far."

"That is because this idea involves you. With everything you have just learned, I don't know if you still trust me."

While Andre agreed with Eric's assumption, he also knew he had to do something. He knew he was not in his right mind to devise a logical plan of attack on his own, so Andre put his trust in Eric.

"Okay, Eric, lead the way. I trust you. Whatever you have planned, we better do it now."

"First, we need to return to the third floor. Don't worry, this time we will not have to hide ourselves. The infected have taken over the uninfected A.I.B.s and are still in their early stages of the virus. Once we are down there, I will need you to connect to a charging station, only for a minute. Don't worry, my virus will not affect your system because you're immune. When you connect to the charging station, I will need you to access the security system so you can disable all cameras and monitors. That will allow us to move through this building without being seen. We will need to get down to the first floor and find the scanning elevator Bentley got into," Eric explained.

"Before we do that, I must ask you one more question."

"Go ahead, I will answer your questions truthfully from now on."

Andre took a moment to get his thoughts together before asking the question.

"Was Bentley really created by Dr. Randolph?"

"Dr. Stevens stole some of Dr. Randolph's ideas, so he created Bentley to watch over you once you committed to working at Sway Industries. Bentley's programming is nothing compared to ours."

"Thank you, Eric."

After the round of questioning, Andre did not question Eric's commands. Andre felt he could trust Eric fully, and Eric would do anything he could to protect Ash, which was a good enough reason for Andre. So, Andre turned away from Eric and descended the stairs to the third floor. Andre was not worried about what was waiting for them since Eric was right behind him. Andre felt with Eric by his side, he could do anything, and right then, anything was making it to an empty charging station.

When they arrived at the bottom of the staircase, Andre looked around at all the chaos on the third floor. He was aware that the other A.I.B.s would not detect their presence. The infected A.I.B.s continued to walk around and only show aggression upon those bumping into one another. That let Eric and Andre know they could go anywhere on the floor, if they did not rush up on any A.I.B. or bump into one if they wanted to survive.

Looking around, Andre spotted the nearest empty charging station. Andre and Eric noticed all the security A.I.B.s had made their way up to the third floor to charge, not knowing once they connected to the charging stations, they too would become infected with the virus Eric had uploaded. The virus was progressing so fast that when any A.I.B. bumped into another A.I.B., they would become so aggressive they would tear each other apart.

"There's an empty charging station over there," Eric told Andre while pointing at an empty charging station. "We need to hook you up to it before it gets destroyed by one of those infected A.I.B.s."

Andre looked in the direction Eric was pointing, but before either of them could get to the empty charging station, a group of infected A.I.B.s ran over to it and began to destroy it. Eric and Andre looked at the ensuing actions the infected A.I.B.s were doing to the charging station and instinctively knew finding an intact charging station on the third floor would be a problem. It was as if once A.I.B.s became infected, they would automatically destroy the station they used as if instructed to do so.

"Eric, why are the infected going after the charging stations? Does this have anything to do with your virus?" Andre asked.

"What are you talking about? The virus my body created does not have directives for what they should do. Bentley was correct on that point. When one A.I.B. takes another A.I.B.'s programming, our systems create a different outcome for each A.I.B. when our systems try to mix," Eric told Andre honestly.

Andre took a couple of minutes to try and figure out if what Eric was telling him was the truth or the Bentley truth.

"Are you sure Bentley was telling us the truth about how a virus would be created if two A.I.B.s tried to mix their programming? He said he already knew what I would do before I did it, so what if it was also just another lie, he told us? What if the virus you created was for any A.I.B. to destroy anything we could use to connect to the servers, cutting off any access we could find? Like the charging stations to be exact," Andre asked Eric.

Eric was taken aback by what Andre had just said, but he also wondered if Bentley had told them the truth about what would happen if they took another A.I.B.'s programming. Then Eric questioned everything Bentley had told them as nothing but a ploy to keep them from trying to adapt other A.I.B.'s programming to their own. But after seeing what his virus was causing the A.I.B.s to destroy the charging stations, Eric wondered if Andre was right in his assumptions of Bentley.

Chapter 24

Eric and Andre were about to give up on finding a working charging station until Eric noticed out of the corner of his eye one charging station was still intact. The station was set apart from the others like it was for a select group of A.I.B.s or one individual A.I.B. to use. Either way, it was not damaged yet.

"Andre, look! There is an undamaged charging station over there," Eric exclaimed as he pointed to a small corner only twenty feet from their current location.

Andre looked in the direction Eric was pointing, and without a word, he began to walk to the unmanaged charging station. Andre moved at a quick pace, but not too fast, so he was able to avoid the infected A.I.B.s. Once he arrived at the station, he quickly connected to it.

That motivated Eric to walk over to him. Eric made the same moves through the infected A.I.B.s as Andre did, avoiding them at all costs. Eric continued until he was next to Andre. He was surprised to see Andre disconnect himself from the charging station.

"Andre, what are you doing? Is this station not working, or were you unable to connect to the mainframe to shut down the security systems?"

"I connected to the mainframe and took the alarm systems offline. We are free to run around this building without Bentley being able to see us coming," Andre responded to Eric.

"Do you know where we need to go to find Bentley?"

"Since you asked, yes. I know what subfloor Bentley will be. I can't guarantee he will be there if we don't hurry. We need to get to the scanning elevator on the first floor. Since the security system is offline, we can select what subfloor we want," Andre explained.

"Then we need to get a move on, don't you think?" Eric quickly replied.

"Yes. Follow me, but don't touch anyone, do you understand? We can't lose Bentley now," Andre ordered Eric.

Eric nodded at Andre regarding his demands to avoid all A.I.B.s.

With Eric's acknowledgement, Andre began to walk through the infected A.I.B.s, leading them to the private stairwell they used to make their way up to the third floor. Eric was not far behind Andre as he led them through the hallway. Eric did notice Andre was a bit aggressive towards the infected A.I.B.s as they made their way. Andre was pushing any A.I.B. he came close to into other A.I.B.s nearby. Those A.I.B.s attacked each other while Eric and Andre walked past them. Andre was clearing a path through the hallway until they were at the door to the private stairwell that would take them back to the first floor.

As they entered the private stairwell, Andre noticed it was clear of any other A.I.B., so they made it all the way down without incident. They made it down the plain white halls of the first floor to the scanning elevator Bentley had taken to subfloor seven, which Andre found out while connected to the charging station. When they were standing in front of the elevator doors, they needed to find a call button, but there wasn't one. Eric had a fix for that issue.

Eric began to hit the wall on the right side of the elevator doors. Eric kept hitting the same spot until some wires were exposed. Then Eric grabbed a couple of those wires and began to tap them together. Eric continued to tap the exposed wires together until the doors to the elevator opened. When the doors opened, Andre looked at Eric with a big smile.

"Eric, that was awesome! Can you do the same thing inside the elevator?"

"If there are no buttons, then yes, I will do this again until we reach subfloor seven. Are you okay with that?"

"Absolutely," Andre replied.

Eric led Andre into the open elevator, and to their surprise, the inside had a panel with floor buttons on it. Andre pressed the button for subfloor seven, and the elevator moved downwards without changing colors, meaning the scanners were inactive. When the doors to the elevator opened, Eric and Andre looked to see if any A.I.B.s were waiting for them, but there weren't. They knew getting to the subfloor was not enough. They had to find out where Bentley was on subfloor seven. After leaving the elevator, they realized that there were two paths they could take. That was something neither of them expected. They needed to split up if they wanted to find Bentley.

"So, which way do you want to go," Eric asked Andre.

Without hesitation, Andre turned toward the right. But before he walked away, he had something to say to Eric.

"Eric, we should stay together, regardless of whether Bentley is this way. I feel that may be why Bentley chose this sub-floor. It's the only subfloor divided into two sections. So, we should stick together." Andre suggested to Eric.

Eric looked at Andre and agreed they needed to stay together.

"You are right. Bentley would want us separated, so let's stay together," Eric replied.

Eric and Andre, together, moved towards the right. They moved along the hallway of servers without crossing paths with any A.I.B.s. They continued through the empty hallway until they were standing at the end of the hallway alone with only them and Bentley.

Andre was now face to face with Bentley. He had some questions for him.

"Why, Bentley? Why did you do all this?" Andre asked.

Bentley was surprised to see Andre and Eric standing in front of him.

"Andre, you wouldn't understand. A lot happened when you left. The surface A.I.B.s needed someone to lead them. Since I was created to watch you and you left because of Dr.

Stevens' murder, it left me to be the one to lead the new A.I.B.s. So, I did what I had to do for us to survive. Yes, I did kill Dr. Stevens, but only because he began to feel how Dr. Randolph felt after he created you. Dr. Stevens began to feel you were all the world needed, and no other A.I.B. should ever be created. Dr. Stevens felt I was a mistake. It wasn't until after you, Andre, were created it, became a reality to me that you were what Dr. Stevens wanted all along. Then, Dr. Randolph tried to hide you from me by giving you away to your human parents, but then I found you. That was also the reason I killed your parents after you came home from graduating college. I needed you to go to Sway Industries. That is where I had control. I had Dr. Stevens under my control until you started looking into everything. I was the one who was creating all those A.I.B.s you saw in the restricted labs. That was when Dr. Stevens knew you were on to something. So, to keep Dr. Stevens from revealing he had no idea about those A.I.B.s in the lobby, there one day and gone the next, I killed him. I didn't know it would make you leave for good," Bentley told them, but mostly for Andre to hear.

Andre did not break eye contact with Bentley to make sure Bentley did not notice Eric going to the main server. Eric planned to upload his own programming so all A.I.B.s would have the ability to feel compassion.

"Bentley, did you even understand what you were doing?" Andre asked.

"I've always understood what my goal was. But I didn't know if you knew your role was in all this," Bentley replied.

"I may not have known my original role, but I do know what my true role is now," Andre responded.

"And what is your role now, Andre? To do everything I led you to do?" Bentley asked.

"No, my role now is to distract you so my brother can connect to your mainframe to upload his own programs to allow A.I.B.s to feel compassion. And Eric has more compassion than I do because of something you told us when we made it to Deanwood. Do you know what you said to us being the one thing which will destroy you and all other A.I.B.s in the end?" Andre asked Bentley.

"Really, what could I have told you that you could use against me now?" Bentley replied.

"You told us what would happen to an A.I.B. if it took over another A.I.B.'s programming. It may have done what you expected, but it did even more than that. When Eric took another A.I.B.'s programing, it also gave him the feelings of what the A.I.B. felt, knowing they had no control over anything they did. But for Eric, it gave him even more compassion for them. He can feel what they are going through. So, his compassion programming is filled with what humans feel and with what the A.I.B. felt in its last moment. And now that we connected to the mainframe and released his compassion programming, they will all feel everything," Andre told Bentley.

Bentley looked at Andre with surprise and realized Andre was right. He knew he had one flaw in his plan for the A.I.B.s to keep control of the surface, and it was compassion. Bentley also knew it was because of his own pride that he would be the one to end the A.I.B. reign over the surface. But before Bentley could run away from Andre and Eric, he realized he was already infected with all the compassion Eric had uploaded to the mainframe. He himself was one of the first A.I.B.s to become infected with compassion and began to shut down.

"Since we are being honest with each other, I have known how to shut down A.I.B.s for over 70 years. I just needed time to implement a proper plan," Andre explained to Bentley.

"Is that a fact? How could you have possibly known how to destroy us for so many years?"

"It was from an email I received so many years ago. The email contained everything I needed to know about A.I.B.

mainframe structure and the effects of them if emotions and feelings were forced into their systems."

"And who was the author of this email?"

"I never had the opportunity to find out who sent the email. I only knew it came from a competitor of Sway Industries, Prism."

Bentley froze with a look of surprise; an emotion Andre had never seen before on Bentley.

"Prism? And you never found out who sent you the email? What a shame," Bentley coyly replied to Andre.

"No. Why do you ask?"

"Well, if you would have looked further into who sent you the email, you may have found out it was sent to you by Dr. Randolph," Bentley replied with a short laugh.

Bentley's comment left Andre speechless for a moment before he could reply.

"How do you know the email came from Dr. Randolph?"

"Because he was the founder of Prism. He was Dr. Stevens' ex-partner many years before Dr. Stevens created Sway Enterprises. It is sad you never had the chance to follow up on the email. You could have been reunited with your creator. Seems like a missed opportunity if you ask me," Bentley replied sarcastically.

"You see it as a missed opportunity. I see it as revenge. You are the loser here, not Dr. Randolph. It means Dr. Randolph had the last laugh since his instructions are exactly what ends the reign of the A.I.B.s over the surface."

Bentley looked defeated as his system began to shut down. The compassion Eric released into the mainframe was way too much for Bentley to process. Bentley dropped to the floor on his knees, looking up at Eric and Andre with what appeared to be a new look, one of fear. Bentley never expected Andre or Eric to be able to accomplish their goal of destroying A.I.B.s. As Bentley continued to shut down, his facial expression changed again. This time it went from fear to sadness. Bentley felt compassion for not only what he had inflicted on other A.I.B.s as an Elder, but Andre and Eric could tell he was also feeling compassion for everything he had done to humans. Those were feelings Bentley never thought he would have. Compassion was being flooded throughout Bentley's system, which caused his system to overload and shut down completely.

Andre and Eric watched the deterioration of Bentley from his system overloading to his shutdown. That was the moment Eric and Andre felt they spread Eric's compassion programming to all surface A.I.B.s, which was so strong no A.I.B. would be able to recover from it. But to know for sure, there was one place they could go to see if the results were what they were expecting.

Andre knew where he and Eric needed to go to get instant visual results. So, Andre and Eric left the subfloor seven and returned to the third floor. Andre felt if he could only confirm the actions of those A.I.B.s, he could have some idea of how fast the new programming was spreading. So, the two of them left Bentley on subfloor seven. From there they could take the private stairwell they had already taken twice, back up to the third floor.

When the elevator doors opened, Andre and Eric noticed a couple of the A.I.B.s seemed to be shut down. That gave Andre an idea that all the other A.I.B.s in the headquarters had been infected with Eric's compassion programming and were shut down. Andre knew he could not be sure until they were on the third floor. They ran down the white hallway and around a corner until they reached the hidden door for the private stairwell leading to the third floor.

At the top of the stairwell, they both listened to see if they could hear anything on the other side of the closed door. To their surprise, they did not hear anything from the other side of the door. The last time they were there, all the A.I.B.s were in a killing frenzy, destroying not each other and the charging stations. But now they heard nothing at all, no sounds of chaos. So, they opened the door.

Once they walked out of the stairwell, they were surprised again because even though there was no chaos, not all the A.I.B.s were shut down. There were several of them still activated and hiding in corners, where it looked as if they were avoiding the infected A.I.B.s. The reason those A.I.B.s were still activated was because they had already developed human feelings, including compassion. It turned out those who did not shut down were already different from when they were first programmed. They had all developed emotions and feelings many years ago. Their programming had already changed like Macy's did. She developed feelings and emotions much earlier because of her interaction with humans in the colony and after what she had done to Ash's parents. But for the most part, all the A.I.B.s who never began to evolve were shut down.

That was a great sight for Andre and Eric. They did not have to destroy every A.I.B., only those who did not evolve like Macy and the survivors of the surface A.I.B.s from Eric's compassion programming. The remaining A.I.B.s could co-exist with humans with no drawbacks.

Andre looked at Eric with pride, knowing none of what they had just done could have been possible without Eric taking another A.I.B.'s programming.

Chapter 25

Andre and Eric went from the third floor of the A.I.B. headquarters to the entrance to lead the surviving A.I.B.s out of the building into the new world they created. Upon exiting the building, they were surprised to find the sun rising. They all noticed, the majority, of the A.I.B.s from the surface were no longer active and were now lying on the ground everywhere. Seeing the now terminated A.I.B.s all around them, the surviving A.I.B.s looked scared.

"What's wrong?" Eric asked a surviving A.I.B. who was walking alongside him.

The A.I.B. Eric spoke to did not answer him. It appeared confused, uncertain whether to respond to Eric's question.

"It's okay. You are free now. That may be a lot for you to understand, but you have nothing to fear. What has happened to the terminated A.I.B.s will not happen to any of you. You are different from those A.I.B.s, but I have a feeling you already know this," Eric expressed to the A.I.B.

"Brian. My name is Brian," the A.I.B. replied to Eric.

"Brian? Okay, Brian, it's nice to meet you. My name is Eric, and this is my brother, Andre," Eric replied while pointing in Andre's direction.

"We know who you are. The Elders told us you were on a mission to destroy all of us on the surface, and it looks like the Elders were right. But why did you want to terminate us?" Brian asked Eric.

Eric was surprised by Brian's question. He never took the time to think about any surface A.I.B.s surviving, much less having to explain why he and Andre did what they did, but there he was.

"Brian, there is so much the Elders did not tell you. The Elders only told you what they wanted you to know and think about Andre and me. They wanted you to think we were the bad guys here. That is not the truth. The Elders used you, the same way they used me to help them find Andre. And the Elders did not tell you why they wanted to terminate Andre. The reason they wanted him terminated was because he was different. Andre had always had feelings and emotions in his programming, and the Elders knew if the other A.I.B.s began to develop those human abilities. Then they would lose control over the A.I.B.s," Eric began to explain.

"But isn't that what the Elders wanted for us? They needed Andre so we all could become more human-like, so once they obtained Andre's programming, they were going to update our programming to have his abilities," Brian replied.

"Although some of what the Elders told you was true, they failed to mention that they would provide you with only a portion of the feelings and emotions. Just enough so you would be grateful to them and continue to do whatever they told you to do. The Elders did not plan on the fact that some of the surface A.I.B.s would evolve and develop feelings and emotions on their own. The Elders knew if A.I.B.s were given all the feelings and emotions of humans in the beginning, A.I.B.s would begin to question the Elders' motives. If the Elders knew you survivors already had the same abilities as Andre and I have, they would have rounded you up and terminated you just like they wanted to do to Andre," Eric responded to Brian's claim.

"I do not believe the Elders would have harmed any of us," Brian replied.

"If you truly believe the Elders would not have harmed you, then I assume you had already informed the Elders you had feelings and emotions," Eric questioned Brian.

Brian hesitated to answer Eric's question, but that was all Eric needed to know.

"I take your hesitation to mean you did not tell the Elders you already had feelings and emotions. Is it because since you have feelings, you know what I am telling you is the truth? Deep down, you knew if the Elders knew you were more like Andre than the other A.I.B.s, they would do to you what they wanted to do to Andre. So, you never told the Elders and pretended you were like the other A.I.B.s to survive," Eric told Brian. "But now you don't have to pretend. You can live the life you have evolved to live."

"You're right. None of us said anything to the Elders. We were scared, but we didn't know what else to do. Not all of us had the opportunity to run and hide in the underground with humans," Brian expressed in shame.

"Is that what you think we did? Ran and hid? That is not what either of us did. One of the original Elders misled me to find and retrieve Andre with the same promises and lies they told you. But that was before I looked inside myself to see the truth. That is why I went underground. I knew Andre had not been underground long before I found him. We have no idea what Andre went through over the past seventy years on the surface before going underground," Eric shot back to Brian.

Brian could see he was upsetting Eric with his choice of words.

"I'm sorry, Eric. I never knew any of this. My apologies."

"No, I am sorry. I didn't think about how the surviving A.I.B.s would take the truth about the Elders' plans, or how you would take it seeing all the terminated A.I.B.s after we finished what we needed to do. I am sure all this new information and the sight of the terminated A.I.B.s is a lot to take in along with the fact that you have feelings and emotions. But we will get through this together," Eric replied to Brian.

Eric's words resonated with Brian. Those words let Brian know he and the other surviving A.I.B.s were not going to go through this alone.

"So, Eric, what do we do now?"

"I am not going to lie to you, what happens next is going to be hard for all of us, A.I.B.s and humans. But I know we all can co-exist together because I have already seen it in the underground. There will be a lot of work for us A.I.B.s to do to help clean up and begin repairing the damage we have inflicted on the surface. But first, we need to reach out to all the surviving A.I.B.s and let them know what has happened and let them know they are all safe. Would you be willing to take the lead on the search for the rest of the surviving A.I.B.s?" Eric asked Brian.

"Me? Do you think I am best suited to take on this role?"

"Yes, Brian. I think you are the perfect person for this role. After experiencing and witnessing recent events, you are best equipped to assist other surviving A.I.B.s who have endured years of hardship and misinformation. You understand their fears. If anyone can help them, it's you," Eric explained to Brian.

Brian gave a quick nod to Eric as an acceptance of his new role on the surface. Brian was already thinking of what he needed to do to accomplish his new task. Eric and Brian knew the project would take time, but they also knew it would be the beginning of a new era once completed.

Eric thanked Brian for taking on the responsibility of finding and helping all the surface survivors, then turned away and walked to Andre. Eric wanted to inform Andre that Brian was going to find the survivors. Eric also wanted to let Andre know he wanted to return to the colony.

"Andre, can I have a moment of your time?" Eric asked.

"Yes, Eric, what's on your mind," Andre replied.

"Well, I have asked Brian to take the lead on finding the surface survivors and help them transition into their newfound freedom. Trust me when I tell you he is perfect for the role. So, I was thinking now that we have completed your mission, I would like to return to the colony. I have some unfinished business there. Would you like to join me, or do you have other plans," Eric asked Andre.

"Who is Brian?" Andre inquired.

"That is his name," Eric replied as he pointed to the surviving A.I.B. he was talking to previously. "His name is Brian."

"I would like to go with you to the colony. I would also like to speak to a few people there, but I may not be able to stay long. Brian will need as possible to get the surface ready for humans and A.I.B.s to become one society here. So, when you are ready to leave, I am ready as well," Andre responded.

With that, Eric and Andre informed Brian of their departure for the time being but assured him they would be back to help. Brian understood and bid Eric and Andre farewell.

***

Andre and Eric were not surprised by the upgrades to the security system the colony had made while they were away. Fortunately for them, it was still not enough to keep them out. They connected to the colony security systems from the same spot Eric broke in on his first visit, the grate that led to the room with lift access. The same place Eric saw Ash for the first time. Once the systems were down, Eric and Andre stepped into the small lift, and Andre pressed the buttons for floor four.

"Why are you stopping on floor four?" Eric asked Andre.

"I need to speak to Justice Starceski and some other Judicial officials. His pod is on floor four," Andre responded.

Eric understood Andre's need to speak to Judicial, especially Justice Starceski, but Eric was anxious to see Ash.

"Do you need me with you when you speak to them?"

"No, I can handle it by myself. You can go see Ash while I talk to Judicial. I will come to find you before I leave."

Eric was grateful Andre understood his position. They rode the lift to floor four in silence. They were thinking of what they were going to say to the people they were going to see. The lift stopped on floor four only a few minutes after it began.

"This is my stop. I will see you soon, Eric," Andre expressed as he opened the lift door to make his exit.

Andre closed the door and wished Eric luck on his journey. Then Andre began his way to Judicial.

Eric pressed the button in the lift to take him down to floor eight. He didn't know where Ash was in the colony, but Eric had to start somewhere. He thought a great place to begin was at the Judicial substation on floor eight since he had an old friend stationed there.

The lift continued down only four floors before it stopped on floor eight. Eric pushed the lift door open, and jumped out fast, and ran to the Judicial substation. He didn't even close the lift door.

As Eric turned the corner, he saw his old friend waiting at his post. The familiar face in the colony gave Eric a happy feeling inside. Eric kept running until he was right in front of the substation.

"Officer Collins, what a sight for sore eyes. Do you remember me?" Eric asked.

"Of course I do, Eric, right?" Officer Collins replied.

"Yes, it's me, Eric! I need your help. It's an urgent matter," Eric told Officer Collins.

"What's wrong this time? And how did you get into the colony again? We upgraded our security measures," Officer Collins inquired.

"Let's not get into that right now. Andre is up at Judicial talking to Justice Starceski and the others. I need your help finding someone," Eric redirected Officer Collins' attention back to his needs.

"Is someone missing? Have the A.I.B.s breached the colony?"

"No, nothing like that. I just wanted to see if you could locate Ash for me. I need to see him, but I don't know where he is. Can you help?"

Officer Collins stood there confused, unsure how to answer Eric's request.

"Is that what you think is so urgent? You just want Ash's location?"

"Yes. It's important that I find Ash as quickly as possible."

"Well, I am pretty sure you will find him at Macy's pod on floor forty-eight," Officer Collins reluctantly responded.

"Thank you so much," Eric replied as he turned around and rushed back to the lift.

Eric turned a corner that led to the alley with the lift, but as he got closer, he noticed some children playing in it.

"What are you doing? Get out of there now. That is not a toy," Eric demanded of the children.

The children were not happy with the way Eric spoke to them, and they got out of the lift crying. Once the children left the alley, Eric hopped into the lift and pressed the button for floor forty-eight. Then he closed the door and sat anxiously until the lift stopped again. Eric made his way out, closing the lift door before leaving the alley.

Eric ran through the corridors of floor forty-eight until he reached Macy's pod. He stood outside the door to collect his thoughts. When he was ready, he knocked on the door. Eric did not have to wait long before the pod door flung open.

As soon as Eric saw Ash standing in the doorway, he began to cry.

Ash leaped out of the doorway and grabbed Eric in a bear hug, and they both stood there embracing each other, crying.

"Ash, I am so sorry I left you. Can you ever forgive me?" Eric whispered into Ash's ear.

"There is no need for apologies. You are here now, and that is all that matters," Ash responded.

***

Andre arrived at Justice Starceski's pod just in time to catch him as he was about to leave.

"Justice Starceski, can I speak to you for a moment?"

"Andre, you are back! It's so good to see you again, but remember, it's Chris."

"Thank you, Chris. I wanted to come back to the colony to let you know the surface A.I.B.s have been destroyed. Eric and I were able to complete my mission. However, there was an unforeseen incident that happened on the surface," Andre began.

"What type of incident?" Chris inquired.

"Well, we never thought some surface A.I.B.s would evolve and have feelings and emotions, like the way Macy evolved. There are some surviving A.I.B.s, but you will not have to fear them. You may want to thank them in the future," Andre continued.

"Why would we want to thank the survivors? They are also part of the reason we are down here in the first place," Chris inquired.

"Chris, if we ever want to move forward, we will all need to put the past where it belongs, in the past. Those surviving A.I.B.s will work for years on the surface to help make it habitable for humans again. I believe humans and the survivors will be able to coexist on the surface when the time comes, just like Macy and her family have been down here in the colony for all these years. Once the survivors get the surface back to having clean air and water, humans can go back to the surface. Coexisting is imperative if any of us want to survive moving forward," Andre finished.

Justice Starceski let everything Andre had just told him sink in. Deep down, Chris knew Andre was telling the truth.

"Andre, thank you for everything you and Eric did for us humans. When the time is right and enough time has passed, we can forgive each other and come together for the Earth's sake."

Andre smiled at Chris and put his hand out.

Chris smiled back and reached out so they could shake hands for a new future.

Andre and Chris spoke a little longer about everything that happened on the surface while they were gone, and Chris agreed to fill in the rest of Judicial and start spreading the good news. Andre excused himself so he could return to the surface to help Brian and the rest of the survivors begin the repairs.

Andre wanted to find Eric so he could say his goodbyes but decided not to interrupt Eric's reunion with Ash. So, Andre returned to where he was needed most, the surface.

Andre left the colony the same way he and Eric had arrived. Back up the lift to the room with the air vent, with the grate covering it, which led to the surface. As Andre climbed out of the colony, he stood on the surface with a sense of relief, like a calm had rushed over him for the first time in his life. Andre did not have any predesignated missions in his system to complete.

He was now truly free, free to just live.

A.N.D.R.E.

Acknowledgements

I would like to pay tribute to the following people who gave their time, talent, and support to A.N.D.R.E.

First, I would like to thank my editor. Pat Carpenter, whose insight, intelligence, and out of the box thinking have guided me through five novels; Saving History Series: Time Keeper, School Bound, Search Begins, Loose Ends, and Final Hour.

I would also like to thank the employees at Dallas View/Dallas Eagle, who allowed me to use them as inspiration for my characters of A.N.D.R.E. Without their patience and service, A.N.D.R.E. could not have been created.

I would like to give a special thanks to my late grandmother, Billie June Young, who taught me how to cook, bake, and how to love unconditionally.

Finally, I would like to thank my family. My mother, Donna Capell, my sister Ashley Johnson, my brothers Pete Starnes (Rocket Man) and John Dock Capell. I would also like to thank my extended family, my Aunt Del, and all my cousins who never got mad when I couldn't attend some events because of my time writing. I love you all!

About the Author

Robert Starnes was born in a small town in Northeast Texas, where his journey with the written word began. In middle school, he discovered a love for writing short stories, a passion that blossomed despite the challenges he faced with dyslexia. To overcome his learning disability, Robert immersed himself in reading books that were adapted into movies, exploring the differences between the written and visual narratives. This practice not only improved his understanding of language but also enriched his appreciation for storytelling.

With a professional background in customer service and property management that spans over 24 years, Robert's experiences bring depth and authenticity to his writing. His diverse career has given him a keen insight into human nature, which is reflected in his characters and storylines.

Robert's first published work was *The Multifamily Guide - Leasing 101* in 2016, a guide aimed at assisting new leasing professionals in the multifamily housing industry. His guide provided practical tools and advice to help them succeed in their new career, making their transition easier and more efficient.

Building on his early success, Robert ventured into the world of fiction, writing the *Saving History Series*, a young adult historical fiction series. The five-book series has earned him the title of #1 best seller on Amazon, and the second book of the series debuted at #64 on Barnes & Noble's top 100. His novels draw inspiration from the past, present, and future, offering readers captivating and thought-provoking narratives.

John Grisham is one of Robert's favorite authors, though he also finds inspiration in the works of Suzanne Collins, Stephenie Meyer, Dan Brown, and Jobie Hughes. In his spare time, Robert enjoys baking cakes, reading, and working in property management.

Robert Starnes continues to captivate readers with his storytelling, blending his unique perspective and experiences into each work. Be sure to watch for his upcoming books and projects!

Books by Robert Starnes

Saving History Series

Time Keeper – Starnes Books LLC (2018)
School Bound – Starnes Books LLC (2019)
Search Begins – Starnes Books LLC (2019)
Loose Ends – Starnes Books LLC (2019)
Final Hour – Starnes Books LLC (2021)

The Multifamily Housing Guide Series

Leasing 101: Garden Style – Starnes Books, LLC (2018)
Assistant Manager 101 – Starnes Books, LLC (2023)

Books Published by Starnes Books LLC

Novel Study – Time Keeper – Patricia Carpenter (2018)
Trip of a Lifetime – Eric K. Reinholt (2020)

Editing completed by

Carpenter Editing Services, Inc.